WITHDRAWN

Barbara Bush
Building a better library

Library Friends
one book at a time.

D0094076

What they're saying about
BLOOD NOTES

"Boor takes a basis in fact and extends it with a vivid imagination and a great sense of humor to give us a suspense novel that entertains and also illuminates some of the issues facing science and medicine today. I highly recommend this book; you will love the personalities as they try to control their destinies (and ours)."

C.J. Peters, M.D., scientist, Chief of the U.S. army unit that battled ebola virus in The Hot Zone, former Chief of Special Pathogens at the CDC, author of Virus Hunter, Director for Biodefense, Galveston

"...a fascinating window into the world of biological research and the human condition...a nightmarish scenario, splicing bird flu and DNA manipulation with human despair. Unseen things are coming to your neighborhood soon. Be afraid. Be very afraid."

James A. Mangum, Author of Dead and Dying Angels and The Vinegaroon Murders (Dos Cruces Trilogy)

"Having spent most of my career with microorganisms that require high-level containment facilities, I found the ring of authenticity in this gripping tale. A combination of Richard Preston's The Hot Zone and Stephen King's The Stand, Blood Notes captures the excitement of basic research, as well as the politics, funding frustrations and drudgery. Importantly, it also exposes the fact that we research scientists are human, with many of the flaws the species bears."

Thomas R. Jerrells, Ph.D., Scientist/Professor of Pathology and Microbiology, Omaha

"Scary, because it's told from the inside. A great concept, full of drama — and what an ending!"

Roger Corman, Filmmaker

"Boor is able to skillfully transport the reader to the daily inner workings of the much-feared and mysterious subjects of viruses and bio-attacks.... The novel's ending exudes a traditional "race against time".... Boor's intention to reach a wide gamut of readers is obvious.... themes of science and the effects of science on man are detailed in a systematic manner and style that generate an energetic novel for both medical and nonmedical world."

The Galveston Daily News

"A compelling read ... a real page turner. Set squarely in the familiar biomedical thriller genre pioneered by authors such as Michael Crichton, Blood Notes paints a chilling scenario. Think mutating Asian bird flu, SARS, ebola, and the flu pandemic of 1918 that killed fifty million people. Truth is scarier than fiction. Let's hope Boor's fiction isn't a prediction of a future truth."

Tim Thompson, Independent Bookseller

"Terrific! ... the bloody detail ... the velocity of the prose ... he's the best of the doctor/poets."

Richard Selzer, M.D., Author and Medical Essayist

"A fascinating page-turner that takes the reader on a journey to the darker side of human nature ... Blood Notes also captures the ambiance and character of the island perfectly."

Kimberly Schuenke, Ph.D, Program Administrator, Western Regional Center of Excellence for Biodefense and Emerging Infectious Diseases Research, Galveston

"A must read for anyone interested in the inner workings of these government-funded virus labs."

Ellen Lively Steele, Former New Mexico State Senator

What a wonderful read! A mystery, tied to science – I was a zoology major and Blood Notes has just enough.... Keeps you wondering, fast paced, and relevant!

Rabbi Jimmy Kessler, Chairman, Community Liason Committee, Galveston National Laboratory

The Blood Notes of Peter Mallow

Paul Boor

SterlingHouse Publisher, Inc.   Pittsburgh, PA

ISBN 1-56315-403-X
   978-1-56315-403-4

Trade Paperback
© Copyright 2007 Paul Boor
All rights reserved
Library of Congress #2007923572

Request for information should be addressed to:
SterlingHouse Publisher, Inc.
7436 Washington Avenue
Pittsburgh, PA 15218
www.sterlinghousepublisher.com

Pero Thrillers
is an imprint of SterlingHouse Publisher, Inc.

SterlingHouse Publisher, Inc. is a company
of the CyntoMedia Corporation

Cover Design: Brandon M. Bittner
Interior Design: N. J. McBeth

This is a work of fiction. Names, characters, incidents, institutions, organizations,
and places, are the product of the author's imagination or are used fictitiously. Any
resemblance to actual events or persons, living or dead is entirely coincidental.

Printed in the United States of America

Acknowledgements

Thanks go way back to editors Colleen Daly and Sal Glynn, and agent Nancy Ellis, for the inside dope on what lay ahead. I especially acknowledge an extraordinary teacher, the late Mrs. Rita Daly, for encouraging me as a young writer. Friends and readers who steered the manuscript from the brink of oblivion include Judy Cook, Marcia Roth, Carolyn Smith, and Charles T. Williams. Special thanks to Judith Smith for positive vibes from the get-go. For inspiration and guidance I am indebted to medical essayist Dr. Richard Selzer and the late, world-renown virologist, Dr. Robert E. Shope, for whom our biosafety lab is named.

Monday, December 8

It's almost funny. Here I am, Peter J. Mallow, M.D., Ph.D., associate professor of virology, a world's expert on viruses, but all this didn't start over a virus. It started with two college kids, one who managed to get himself killed yesterday, and the other, my new student, who went nuts over it.

I woke up this morning anxious to be in my lab at the Medical Research Institute, to get to work on the nasty bird virus that's been my pet project for the past two years. I had some great experiments planned. Then I picked up the newspaper and saw the picture on the front page, a drowning victim being pulled out of the Gulf—the dead kid. It dawned on me that it was my week to be pathologist on-call for University Hospital's Autopsy Service. This kid was my case. I'd be doing his autopsy. I called my research lab and told them to start the experiments without me.

According to the paper, the dead kid was Trey Findley, a 19-year-old UT student from Austin. Motorcycle patrolman Sergeant Juan Martinez was first on the scene, so I gave him a call for the particulars on the case. He told me Findley was driving his red Chevy Z28 along Seawall Boulevard yesterday around 3 p.m. and turned onto Bodekker Road, a beach road where the tidal pools edge up close. The kid was headed to his girlfriend's beach house. Just a lazy Sunday drive down Galveston Island to its desolate eastern tip, on a gray, drizzly, winter day. He probably had his windows shut against the cold, his CD player blasting, nothing on his mind but his girl and what they'd be doing at the beach house.

"The dumb guy flat-out drove off the road," Martinez said. "Surface was a little wet from the rain, but no skid marks. The Chevy crossed the sand into that first tidal pool. Tide was coming in hard."

"He couldn't escape?"

"Water kills the power windows, Doc. Car slowly fills, the kid's history."

"Any witnesses?"

"Eighty-year-old Hispanic male out there fishing. He's the one called 911 from a bait camp. Old man says he heard the kid screaming and punching the hell out of the windows, but that shatterproof glass is way too strong. I seen a shitload of these. They drive into the Gulf, the bay, the bayous, off the causeway, off the piers."

Martinez told me that an EMS truck pulled up just as he shut down his bike at the scene. Like many officers on the Island, Martinez is a trained lifeguard, so he knows the treachery of fast-moving water and the menace a panicked victim poses. He yelled for the EMS fire extinguisher, dove under, smashed in the passenger side window, came up for one more breath, and slipped into the flooded vehicle. Findley was wedged against the back window, unconscious. Martinez maneuvered him to the surface. The paramedics took over, recorded a fleeting heart beat on the sand, and rolled off to the University Trauma Center with full CPR in progress.

When I finished hearing from Sergeant Martinez, I took another look at the picture of Trey Findley on the front of *The Island Daily*. He looked like a typical Texas teen, wearing shorts in December, his legs all pasty and white like two huge maggots floating on the salty gray water. I hopped on my bicycle and headed straight to the autopsy suite at University Hospital. The lousy weather from Sunday hadn't improved much—light rain, cold, the seagulls huddled on the beach.

Our autopsy suite is located on the third floor of the hospital. The autopsy room is old and has no windows, but the fluorescent lighting's good and bright. There's a single stainless steel autopsy table with a hanging scale nearby, a chemical hood, and lab counters cluttered with boxes of scalpel blades and five-gallon jugs of formalin. I pulled on an autopsy gown, mask and shoe covers. Ron Rocker, my autopsy tech for the case, was waiting by the chemical hood. The body lay on the table. Ron had already taken the external photographs.

Ron Rocker's a wiry, pallid little guy, with a chronic, bronchitic cough that sounds like it's coming from deep in a wooden barrel. He's the fastest dissector in the Autopsy Service, despite the breaks he takes to peel off his bloody gloves, step to the chemical hood, and light a fresh unfiltered Pall Mall.

"Did you get good shots of these hands, Ron?"

"Close-ups, dorsal and ventral." The cigarette in his mouth wagged at me as he spoke. "Ain't they something? The guy was right-handed, huh?"

I sketched Findley's hands while dictating into the microphone over the autopsy table.

"The dorsal surfaces of both hands show multiple deep abrasions with large amounts of adherent dried blood. Subcutaneous tissues exposed. Wounds are massive on the right hand, where large fragments of bone protrude."

Ron was right. Findley broke every damn bone he had in that right hand.

I picked up a scalpel and made the Y-shaped incision that runs from each shoulder over the chest, then straight down the middle of the abdomen. I had barely completed the top of my Y when one of the other techs stuck her head in the door. "Doctor Mallow, there's a student out here who needs to speak with you."

My new research student, Jorge Acosta, was shifting from foot to foot outside the autopsy room door. Jorge arrived in my research lab in early November, a month late for the start of his fellowship. Like any curious college student, he'd been bugging me to observe an autopsy.

"Heard you were doing one," he said, beanpole skinny and a bit forlorn. "Can I come in?"

"Sure, with a gown, a mask and shoe covers. It gets bloody in here."

Jorge was born and raised in El Paso. He's a junior at the University of Texas at El Paso, UTEP, where he was awarded a prestigious Fogarty-Hulschbosch Fellowship to spend a year in my lab. El Paso's stuck in the isolated corner of Texas between old Mexico and New Mexico, surrounded by expanses of high desert, and blocked off from the rest of Texas by the Guadalupe Mountains. It's more Mexico than anything else, like a sovereign nation, or a city-state. Families are tight on both sides of the Rio Grande, and the kids grow up rebellious, like modern-day Pancho Villas.

That fit Jorge. He was a freethinker for sure, really bright, and maybe a little too intense, too edgy. A mestizo, his European genes gave him his six feet of height, but his intelligent, broad forehead and the square cheekbones were pure Native American. His skin was pale potter's clay, light amber and barely tanned, odd for someone living under the El Paso sun.

Jorge took off his faded orange UTEP cap and slipped a gown over his big, baggy pants and T-shirt. Ron had him tuck his ratty, jet-black ponytail into a surgical cap.

Ron and I reflected the big flaps of skin away from the Y-incision in preparation for removing all the organs from the body. While we worked, I launched into my standard lecture on the autopsy's role in the history of medicine, its importance for teaching medical students, and its habit of turning up the missed diagnoses and clinical misadventures of our fine local physicians.

My mini-lecture complete, I started to give Jorge the details on Findley's accident, when Ron interrupted.

"I'm getting the breast plate off. Step back."

The whine of Ron's rotary bone saw drowned me out as it worked through the rib cage, rib by rib, spewing bone dust and blood and the smell of burnt bone. Most first-time observers turn green when they see the bone saw at work. Not Jorge. He leaned in closer, dark eyes gleaming, and I caught a glimpse of a peculiar, lopsided smirk through his mask.

Jorge helped Ron lift the breastplate and free the organs for removal. "Incredible! Awesome!" he said as he pulled on the intestine so Ron could snip it free of its mesentery. "You gut them like a deer!"

"We eviscerate," I explained, "then examine and dissect each organ. In these medico-legal cases, though, 90 percent of what we find is on the outside. Entry wounds, exit wounds, and other signs of trauma. Like this kid's hands."

"What's with those hands? Look at the right one."

"He drove his car into the Gulf, Jorge. He was trapped, and pounded the windows until he drowned."

"He drowned? This guy drowned?" Jorge's arms went slack and Findley's intestines plopped back into the body.

Ron stepped to the scale with a lung in his hand. "Hey, help me out, Jorge. Write the organ weights on the blackboard. Right lung, 700 grams." Jorge's smirk was gone. The bloody piece of chalk by the blackboard went untouched.

"*Jesus! Pura Maria!* Mother of God!" Jorge cried, and he bolted for the door. I stripped off my gloves and followed, but Jorge was a fully gowned and a bloody-gloved blur rushing out the main door of the autopsy suite and down the stairs. Then the stairwell went deathly quiet, except for the distant ticking of his heels.

"The first time's always hard," Ron said when I had regloved.

"I'll catch up with him later and make sure he's okay. Let's get this finished."

"Pretty much like those cases last summer. Remember the two college girls who drove off Pier 23?"

My thoughts drifted back to last summer, when my marital problems were coming to a head and I was spending my nights on a cot in my lab. "Oh, yeah. Sweet young things," I said.

"They were out drinking and took the wrong turn," Ron said. "Drove into Chocolate Bayou and never got out of their seatbelts. I've seen several like that out at the M.E.'s facility." Like other experienced autopsy technicians, Ron moonlighted on the weekends, delivering bodies for funeral homes, embalming at night, or doing autopsies with the county medical examiner, the M.E. "In this part of Texas," he said, "lots of people drown in their cars."

Ron took a break by the chemical hood, leisurely sucking on a Pall Mall while I dissected the kid's youthful heart, the pliant great vessels of the chest, the liver and abdominal organs, all routine, all normal. Ron stood directly under the big red sign:

NO SMOKING, DRINKING, EATING
OR APPLYING COSMETICS IN THIS AREA

"Wouldn't Environmental Safety just love to see you now?" I said wryly.

"Don't sweat it, Doc. They never come in here in the middle of a case." Ron gave out one of his husky coughs. "You ever smoke?"

"Sure, in graduate school," I said. "It was seven years of near-starvation, and we were starting a family, so I quit 'em." I gave Ron a look in the eye that said, "You should, too."

Ron lit a fresh one and pulled on new gloves. With the cigarette dangling from his lips, he started on Trey Findley's head. He parted the soggy blond hair from ear to ear, made an elliptical incision to reflect back the scalp, and opened the skull with the bone saw to neatly remove the brain, intact, all before his Pall Mall burned halfway down.

My pager started vibrating. I get lots of pages I ignore, like from Ellen, my almost-ex, bitching about how slow our divorce proceedings are going, or from Ellen's pain-in-the-ass lawyer, or some other woman chasing me down because, for one reason or another, they think I'm in the wrong.

I ungloved, stepped outside the autopsy room, and pulled the pager from my pocket. I didn't recognize the number, but I dialed it.

"This is Doctor Mallow answering a page."

"Peter, it's *Brenn-dah*. I'm finally in my new office. Would you like to get together? I was thinking about lunch."

It was Brenda Danforth, Ph.D., a new faculty member in the Medical Humanities Institute, and my latest squeeze. Brenda's a leggy blonde of the dirty variety, and maybe the smartest, most sensitive woman in the state of Texas, from what I could tell. Her deep, gravelly voice drives me nuts, especially that homey, New England "Brenn-dah" sound.

"No way, Brenda. No way. Afraid not. I'm in the middle of it here, and I need to get to my lab. They'll have data. New data on the virus."

Silence on the other end of the line. I shouldn't have barked at her, but it was turning out to be a bad day. I always do something dumb like that, distancing myself. I hate the way I am about women. Years ago, I thought getting married would fix it, but it didn't. Women. The fact is, at first they find me attractive, and generally they'd agree Pete Mallow's "to die for" in bed, but when they get close, I back away. There's some final point, a final stage I never reach. "True," my soon-to-be ex-wife calls it. "True," like a skilled carpenter builds a house, or an arrow flies to its mark. I'm not "true."

"Maybe later, Brenda. I'll call about lunch. Really. It's a bloody mess in here and I've got to go. Sorry."

I first met Brenda at a faculty sherry-hour get-together before Thanksgiving, and fireworks went off at first glance. I found myself babbling nonsense over a silly glass of bad sherry while she explained her graduate work in Burlington, Vermont, "a stellar humanities training ground," as she put it. I had to take her word on that. I rarely travel at such airy, humanistic altitudes, though I'd like to.

Brenda's perfection, all right, and it was love at first sight, except for one problem—her husband, Tom. She and Tom moved to Galveston last summer, and both had a horrible time adjusting to the tropical heat and the slow, island pace. On top of that, Brenda's been putting herself under a lot of pressure to publish her long overdue dissertation work, those ground-breaking studies she'd completed in Vermont on human suffering, the dynamics of grief, and holistic health.

Tom's a university administrator; he neglects Brenda, and it sounds like a breakup is imminent. That's where I come in. Brenda and I had been meeting at the Motel 6 for a little over two weeks, and each new encounter was hotter and heavier. At yesterday's rendezvous, she nearly tore up my favorite little appendage, my point man, Mr. Gonzo. She taught Mr. Gonzo and me some new tricks, and I'd love to learn more. Lucky for me, the Gonzo's *herpes genitalis* has been in complete remission lately.

When I stepped back into the autopsy room, Ron had the brain ready to examine, the scalp sewn up, the table and sinks rinsed down, and the body washed and ready to bag for the funeral home. I checked the brain. Normal.

"I'm off to my lab, Ron."

"Still working on the same virus, Doc? I heard they had cases in Mexico City."

"Nothing's been verified on that," I said, feeling a chill at how fast news spreads.

"Must be scary working with that bird flu stuff."

"I've got careful, well-trained people working with me, Ron, and right now I need to see what my careful, well-trained people have been doing while you and I were cutting this poor soul." I took one last look at Trey Findley.

Technically, these medico-legal cases are easy. All you need to decide is the "manner of death," which has to be one of four things: homicide, suicide, natural, or accidental. It can be a knotty problem, reconstructing what went on before a death. Did the teenager playing Russian roulette intend to kill himself, or was it an accident? If an old man has a heart attack and drives off Seawall Boulevard, is that natural? Often these cases untangle themselves days later, late at night. Sometimes, it's in the middle of a nightmare.

I stripped off my bloody gear and stepped to the tech's office to dictate my summary. "The manner of death is accidental," I said into the machine. I thought for a moment, then added, "by vehicular immersion." I wrote the same thing on the death certificate and signed the bottom line.

It was mid-afternoon before I finally walked to my laboratory. My lab's in the Medical Research Institute, next to the new prison hospital, across from the sad, worn sandstone of the original medical college, or "Old Red," as it's affectionately known on campus. The rain had cleared and a sea breeze blew balmy, but I wanted to see data and be in the lab with my research team. Often, this transition is difficult, going from the hospital with its violence, blood and death to the intellectual excitement of the basic science lab. I was still seeing Trey Findley's mangled hands, all blood and bone and gristle, as I carded myself through the double security doors and waved to the guards.

My personal laboratory on the fifth floor is a Level 2 on the lab biosafety scale, meaning we can work with killed virus, or the proteins and genes from the virus, but not living virus. Just down the hall is the high-security walk-through to the separate building that houses the Level 4 lab where we store and work with the live stuff, the deadliest critters known to man.

"Hello, Doctor Mah-wo!" my Chinese postdoctoral fellow, Hong Xiao, greeted me with her usual enthusiasm. Dr. Hong Xiao—It's a name I'm honored to see next to mine on the many high-impact articles we've published in scientific journals.

"Hey, Lilly," I said, calling her by her taken name. "I'm here at last."

Lilly has worked in virology as long as I have, more than 10 years, first in Beijing, then in France. Before joining my lab, she was at the *Laboratoire de Génétique de Virus* in Paris, where she learned both French and English. That's why her accent has its peculiar Sino-Gallic twist. It's also in Paris that she took the mellifluous "Lilly." She's a scientist of the highest caliber, excited about the work, and she dresses up the lab with full, feminine curves packed gracefully into sleek, French clothing.

"How did the assays come out, Lilly?"

"Very good. All run okay. I have data together."

We wound our way by the cell culture incubators and lab benches overflowing with test tubes, past the balances and centrifuges, and finally to the protein area. Lilly had her experimental assays laid out next to my other postdoc, Hari Bhalakumarian, who was slumped over onto the lab bench, asleep. Since arriving from India, Hari has cultivated the habit of sleeping in the lab for the better part of the day. Upon waking, he fusses over his experiments until 3 or 4 a.m. These nocturnal habits enable him to stay up all night, chasing American women. I know because I occasionally run into him while I'm chasing American women myself. My research owes a lot to Hari, though. It was through him I got my hands on that first sample of the killer virus, *Bangladesh horrificans*.

Hari attended the finest schools in the Indian Ivy League, which explains his Madras shirts, worn-out loafers, and bleached jeans. He earned a medical degree, trained in internal medicine and cardiology, then transferred to the All-India Institute of Tropical Diseases in Calcutta where my good friend and senior scientist, Praphul Poonawala, was his mentor. Poonawala sent him to the duck farms in Bangladesh, around Dhaka, to collect duck feces, culture duck throats, anything to keep him busy. That's when Hari discovered the virus, sequenced its viral genome and, along with Poonawala, was first to publish on *Bangladesh horrificans* in *The Journal of Infectious Diseases*.

But something happened between Hari and Poonawala. They ended up on the outs. Hari begged me long distance to take him as a postdoc, using his new virus as bait in a series of obsequious e-mails from Calcutta: "Most esteemed professor, I am keen to join your laboratory and assure you the Bangladesh organism will afford you the perfect subject for your research."

It was tempting. *Bangladesh horrificans* would give me a new direction. With one live sample to work with, I'd score another grant, publish a ton of papers, and get promoted to full professor.

Then, in an incredibly ballsy move, Hari filled a small plastic microfuge tube with live *Bangladesh*, wrapped the tube in parafilm, got on an airplane, and showed up in my lab as an unannounced "visiting scientist." When I called Poonawala to explain, he was surprisingly gracious about sharing the virus. He even agreed to fill out paperwork as if the transfer were legit. I suspect Poonawala was happy to be rid of Hari, and he remains my main contact about the outbreak. It's amazing how things fall out. If the public knew, if word ever got out how I came by this virus... but these things happen in science, crazy things, shady, sometimes dangerous things, and nobody outside these laboratory walls ever has a clue.

"Very pretty data, Lilly. These gels are superb."

Lilly's experimental assays, or "gels," floated like paper-thin jellyfish suspended in shallow trays of buffer solution. The fragile, diaphanous membranes shimmered with rows of fine, crisp, sky blue lines—the viral proteins we were after. Science, the way I do it, is all about gels. They define the viral genes. They show us the virus's proteins. That's all you'll hear in my laboratory—gels, genes and proteins.

"But how about the ducks, Lilly? Did you start them?"

"This morning I went to Level 4 by myself. I injected ducks without you, Doctor Mah-wo. Ducks full of virus now. Be sick soon," she chuckled. "Be dead soon!"

Our virus, *Bangladesh horrificans*, is hell on ducks, 100 percent fatal. But our worry is that the virus will "jump" from birds to humans. Viruses have done it before, like the *influenza* virus that killed 25 million people in the great pandemic of 1918. Right now, in Bangladesh, citizens of Dhaka are dying from a puzzling form of pneumonia, and my Indian colleagues suspect that the culprit is *Bangladesh horrificans*. Also, rumor has it that *Bangladesh* virus might have been carried on a commercial aircraft to Mexico.

Lilly and I know a lot about how this virus operates in its natural host, the domestic duck, but defining the virus's genes and tying the genes to the virus's grisly effects is slow, exacting work. I worry that we're running out of time with *Bangladesh*.

A line of assays, some unfinished, caught my eye at Jorge's bench space.

"Are these Jorge's?"

"Jorge was here all day Sunday."

"Look, Lilly." I held one of the pieces of black-and-white X-ray film up to the light to study the rows of viral DNA that Jorge had revealed as dense, black bands. "These are supershift assays on the *PAKG* gene. Here's the gene in this one, where it should come out, and there's the shift of the band. Damn! The *PAKG* gene. He's got it!"

"On his first try?"

"Amazing kid. Stain this other gel for him, would you? I doubt we'll see Jorge today. He saw his first autopsy, and it was pretty rough on him."

Back in November, when he arrived in the lab, I handed Jorge the *PAKG* gene to work on during his fellowship year. My hunch was that the *PAKG* gene makes a viral protein that coats the virus's outer surface, or envelope. That's why I named the gene "*PAKG*," for "package." Theoretically, this viral "package" would act as a protective, biologic armor when the virus attacks its host.

Jorge impressed me during his first few weeks in the lab, but this latest data was astounding. In one weekend, he taught himself to do supershifts, the most complicated assay known to science. Now if only Jorge's unfinished gel, the one Lilly was staining, would show that the *PAKG* protein was localized in the viral envelope. That would be something.

I felt great, back at the lab bench. It was a normal day in research: Lilly was working diligently, gels were cooking, and Hari was snoring. I pulled my personal lab notebook from the shelf to enter a bit of my own recent data. Then I walked to Jorge's area and watched the lines of proteins darken to a lovely blue as Lilly's stain took hold. I was hunched over, squinting at a band that might be *PAKG* when from behind I heard a whispered "Professor Mallow?"

"Jorge! Are you all right?"

"I'm okay now I guess."

"Let's go talk." We walked across the hall to my tiny cube of an office where I have my desk, computer and microscopes. I settled behind my desk. Jorge took the swiveling stool I use at the 'scopes. He started to swivel back and forth. "How far did you get in that bloody gear?" I asked.

"Campus police stopped me in front of the old medical school. They made me go to the surgical clinic and red-bag it all."

"Don't sweat it, Jorge. Everyone reacts differently." I gazed out my office window, past Old Red and over the tops of the undulating palms and the gray slate roofs of the Victorian homes, to the green curve of the Gulf of Mexico. "There's lots of blood."

"It's not the blood, Doctor Mallow. My family has a hunting cabin in *los Guadalupes*. I shoot a buck every fall. It's because that poor guy drowned, just like my little brother."

"Oh, I'm so sorry."

"He was a toddler, 2 years old, the last baby for Momma, *mi hermanito*. This summer, painters were doing our house, painting it white. They took a break and left a half-full, five-gallon bucket open. Somehow… he went in, headfirst. I saw his feet sticking out of the white. And it's all my fault. All my fault!"

"No, that can't be, Jorge."

"Yes! I was supposed to be watching *mi hermanito*. Instead, I was shooting my pistol in the back yard, target practice. It was so loud. Even Momma blames me!"

I stood up and grabbed his shoulders. "So that's why you started your fellowship late."

"Eventually, the medications helped."

"You need more time."

"I thought I was okay, but when I saw the autopsy... and... and what if I flip out when I get into medical school? I *need* medical school, Doctor Mallow. You know my major is physics, string theory and all that. I'll have to leave El Paso if I stay with physics!"

Jorge reminded me of my own teenage years, stuck in a boring Cape Cod village, catering to tourists at our family tavern all summer, suffering through the long, alcoholic winter. How strange. I wanted a medical degree to escape Cape Cod. This kid wanted one to stay at home in El Paso.

Jorge rubbed his eyes with the sleeve of his T-shirt. He had striking eyes, a dark, smoky gray with bright, bluish sclera. He took a deep breath and the rebel thing was back.

"Only one good thing, Doctor Mallow. After *hermanito*, me and our family lawyer hassled the Texas senators to write a law making those greedy paint companies put a warning label on their buckets. We used letters, politics, threats. *CUIDADO!* the label will say. DANGER OF DROWNING!"

"Good for you, Jorge! But right now what you need is to keep busy. Let's go check out your new data."

We walked across the hall, and I held one of Jorge's supershift films to the light.

"These are as pretty as Lilly's. It's looks like *PAKG*, and it's in the envelope. How'd you know how to run these?"

"Logic." Jorge gave a lot of one-word answers like that. A sure sign of a steel-trap mind.

Lilly joined us and we were discussing what assay to run next when I remembered about Brenda and the lunch I'd missed. It was past 4 p.m. I ran across the hall and called the number on my pager from earlier.

"Medical Humanities, Doctor Danforth speaking."

"Hi. It's Peter."

"You never called me back," she said, with an edge.

"I'm sorry, I really am, but it's critical work, Brenda. Research is my first love, remember."

"I'm realizing that, Peter. Listen, you're going through a lot, with your divorce, your work, and I'm thinking it's best to give you some time."

"No! I want to see you."

"And I want to see you," she said sweetly.

"It's just that... well, this virus, its genes, if this thing mutates...."

"I understand and I guess I sympathize. But you know, Peter, holism and holistic health are *my* areas of study. I know how important your work is to you, and to the world, for that matter. But those who have *balance* in life are the most productive, the most creative. You need to learn that, for your own health."

"I will. I mean, I'll try," I said, not holding out much hope I could change. It must've been the right thing to say because I heard a gentle sigh on the other end of the line. "Tell me, Brenda, what kind of underwear do you have on?"

"Hm. I'm wearing a thong, Peter, like yesterday, only fuchsia."

"Please meet me. Is 6:30 good? Motel 6? I'll get our Room 17 and I promise to make up for missing lunch. We can talk. We'll call it a sort of late lunch."

"Would you like the thong on... or off?"

"On. I'll get that with my teeth."

"Yes, Peter, yes. I'm *stah-ving*."

I hung up, took a deep breath, and, in the quiet of my office, reached into my drawer of supplies and pulled out a new lab notebook, its stiff, brown cover crisp and unturned, its quadrille-ruled pages patiently awaiting fresh data. A different kind of tension crept into my belly when I opened the notebook and started writing this note. The drowned kid, the bright but sad, new student in my lab, my private life heating up, all laid out in front of me. Without a thought as to where it might lead, I had added another task to the bloody work I do. This notebook, a non-science notebook. Whenever I find time, I'll write in it.

When I looked up, an e-mail from Calcutta was on my computer screen:

Our DNA sequencing of lung tissue confirms the Dhaka victims are infected with Bangladesh horrificans. We must act quickly, Peter. Few are studying this virus. The death toll may be catastrophic. Millions will succumb. God help us, a vaccine must be found.

Poonawala

Saturday, December 20
(Entry on Lions' Club Party)

Nearly two weeks have flown by. After the Findley autopsy, I filled my days with research, but Brenda was right about "balance," so I've been filling my nights with her. We even had a regular date last Saturday, went to Bayou Bob's, a small country dance hall stuck in the middle of the refineries on the mainland. Bob's is pretty funky, velvet-Elvis on the walls, a faded Pearl beer clock over the stage. The rutted hardwood dance floor was packed with refinery cowboys and cowgirls in their finest Stetsons and Tony Lama boots, and dancin' Pete Mallow showed Dr. Danforth the basic footwork of the Texas two-step.

With the approach of Christmas, the university gets busy with parties, most of which are to be avoided. I allow myself only one Christmas party, and that's the Lions' Club party. The Lions of the Island run the organ donor programs for Galveston County, so their party's a sort of "donor appreciation" event. Those of us who help garner organs are invited, but a good part of the guest list comes from the motorcycle clubs that support the Lions' program by signing on to be organ donors. It's always a great party—the bikers set the tempo, and their leathers, kerchiefs, armbands and chains are the grace notes.

Jorge spent all day yesterday, the day of the big event, running gels. I had trouble convincing him to come out. "It's free food and beer, Jorge," I told him.

"I'd rather catch up on my reading."

I suspected that Jorge was not exactly a frat-boy type party animal. When he wasn't in the lab, working, he was holed up in his three-room apartment near campus. He's got a nice Dodge truck, but never moves it from its parking spot. I figured he could use some "balance" in his life, too.

"Come on, Jorge. Go home, change, and I'll meet you at the restaurant on Pier 19 at 8 p.m. It's not far from your place. I have to finish this gel first, then I'll hop on my bicycle."

"You ride that old bicycle everywhere, don't you, Doctor Mallow?"

"It's a small island, Jorge. Do you have a jacket?" I asked, eyeing his T-shirt's frayed collar.

"I have a warm shirt."

"That'll do. My two sons are coming over to my place tonight, so I'll get them some dinner, then come right to the party."

At dusk, I watched out the lab windows as a fusillade of rain and hail pelted our building. It was the first big storm of the winter, roaring off the mainland. The weather radio forecast a hard freeze by midnight. The temperature plunged to 35 degrees. Then the air cleared and stars shone in the darkening night sky. We were in for the real thing, a Texas blue norther.

My gel turned out to be a useless, crooked mess. When I looked up, it was close to 8:00. I dialed Mr. Kreuger, the retired gentleman who lives in the upstairs apartment of my old Victorian. Whenever my sons Chad and Travis stay over, Mr. Kreuger's my built-in babysitter.

"Your Mrs. dropped them off already," the old man told me.

"I'll grab a bag of burgers on my way home."

"Don't bother. I'm cooking," he said, making me feel like the crappy father I am.

I trashed the gel, locked down the lab, hopped on my old Huffy bike, and swung by the house. As soon as I hit the front steps, I heard the lonesome thrumming of a basketball in the dining room. Thud, thud. My 16-year-old, Chad.

"I have a party to go to. Mr. Kreuger's watching you guys."

"We know." Thud, thud, thud. "I smell somethin' cookin'."

"And no beating on Travis while I'm gone!" I said, father-like, motioning toward the repetitive sounds of a video game hard driven across the hall.

I pulled my tweedy wool jacket out of mothballs, found a clean white shirt, and dug out a Christmassy tie. Within minutes, I was back out in the cold, my jacket affording little protection as I pedaled into the norther. I stashed my bike at the restaurant's front door. My hands were frozen. The Lions' party was cranking up.

Jorge's orange UTEP baseball cap bobbed next to the huge stainless steel pot of gumbo. He wore what he'd had on at the lab, a T-shirt and oversized cargo pants, but he'd thrown on a washed-out flannel serape, his "jacket." He held a red plastic bowl. He seemed flushed. Maybe it was impending frostbite.

"How's the gumbo?"

"I ate a couple of shrimp." He picked up the serving ladle and fished around in the aromatic brown goo. "Never had this before." He dropped three shrimp into his bowl and stirred in a dot of white rice while I warmed my hands near the gas flame under the pot.

"They make gumbo in El Paso?"

"*Caldo, menudo*, but not gumbo." He poked at a shrimp with a plastic spoon. "No seafood out there."

Pier 19 is an old-style fish house, one of the few that haven't modernized to please the tourists or sold out to the chains. It's a string of shacks teetering on a decrepit wooden pier. Murky water laps beneath the floorboards. The norther blowing at 30 knots was sending powerful, icy drafts through the walls. A warped wooden table served as an oyster bar by the north wall, the coldest spot despite the heavy sheets of plastic tacked over the windows.

I led Jorge through a crowd of bikers to the oysters. Restaurant staff was setting out trays of fried food on long tables covered with white paper. With a sweet smile, a teenage waitress speaking Spanish and carrying a tray of beers handed me a bottle of Tecate neatly wrapped in a bar napkin. I immediately fell in love, again.

The Lions had hired a professional shucker, someone with advanced degrees in oyster-opening. The table was covered with lines of plump, opalescent crustaceans. I shouldered in and daubed a big one with horseradish. The 300-pound biker next to me eyed the monster.

I recognized this guy as a regular at the Lions' parties. His bare arms stuck like fence posts out of his sleeveless black-leather vest, which was emblazoned with "Billy Ray" on the front and embroidered with a crimson eagle in flight on back. He sported a ponytail halfway to his waist and a fluffy beard the color of dirty snow. He had combed the beard to a fine point that whipped erratically when he spoke. His upper arm was tattooed with a matched pair of angry eagles. The multicolor birds-of-prey gave the guy a distinct aura of biker authority.

"This one's a regular steak," I said to him, raising my oyster. "Nice and fat."

"Weren't you at last year's party?" the big fellow asked. "I recall some serious drinking and conversatin'. I'm Billy Ray."

"Good to see you again, Billy Ray." I shook the damp paw he extended and introduced him to Jorge. They immediately became embroiled in a discussion of Billy Ray's new Harley, his club, "The Armed Eagles," and the pride Billy Ray took in being a potential organ donor. Jorge seemed to have found an unlikely pal.

We were soon joined by Billy Ray's lady friend, a pale wisp of a blonde, scantily-clad, with classic, sharp cheekbones and sleepy Clara Bow eyes. She had a martini in her hand. I decided to chat the lady up, while secretly admiring the more feminine, but equally wicked, eagle that nested on her milky shoulder.

"Great party, huh?"

"Yeah. Kick-ass," she whistled as she sucked an oyster off its half-shell.

"Not many women like oysters."

"Love 'em."

"You with Billy Ray?"

" 'Bout a year now." She was struggling with a large one, her mouth stuffed. "Since they sprung him from the slammer, he's been our... club... leader."

"Nice fellow, huh?"

"Oh yeah." She swallowed and tossed back the martini she'd brought with her to the table. "He's a kick-ass kinda guy."

I wanted to tell her not to eat oysters and drink hard stuff at the same time. The booze reacts badly with the raw fish in your stomach, or that's what the drunks at my old man's bar always said. But I decided not to spoil her dinner with that tidbit of Cape Cod lore. It was too much fun watching her eat.

With one eye on the blonde, I was doctoring up another oyster when a deep "Merry Christmas, Peter!" came from behind me. My season's greeter was the county medical examiner, Dr. Walter Jawicki, known by all as Dr. J.

"I knew I'd find you here," Dr. J. said, taking my clammy hand in his powerful, spidery grip. Dr. J., in his mid-60s, is a tall, gaunt gentleman with a craggy, Abe Lincoln face. A severe case of Mediterranean anemia keeps him as pale as the oyster he was dabbing with red sauce.

In Galveston County, the position of chief medical examiner is a political job, and the M.E.'s facility is pitifully small and poorly funded. That's why Dr. J. deputizes the university pathologists, like me, to perform autopsies for him. He just countersigns our death certificates.

Dr. J. handles more than 700 forensic cases a year—motor vehicle accidents, boating mishaps, and the murders and suicides that blight our island-city—but despite his grisly line of work, Dr. J. radiates a cosmopolitan air that's out of place on Galveston Island. Always quick with a kind comment, he's the sort of fellow who's never had children, but always remembers to ask how yours are doing.

On this festive evening, Dr. J. was dressed in a dark, well-tailored Italian suit with a bright silk tie the color of capillary blood. The tie I'd selected was more venous, dusky and somber, and already splattered with sauce.

"I must get back to Elena," he said, preparing one last oyster. "I left her in that next room with our hosts." Dr. J.'s wife Elena is a gorgeous, red-headed Venezuelana in her early 30s, about half Dr. J.'s age. Leaving her for long in a room full of male Lions would be a very bad idea.

"Hold on a moment," I said. "Let me introduce you to my new student, Jorge Acosta." I waved Jorge over. "Jorge's in my lab on a Fogarty-Hulschbosch fellowship."

"Terrific! Good to meet you, young man. You'll be working with Peter's viruses, I take it."

"You bet, the recently discovered bird flu, *Bangladesh horrificans*," Jorge replied, launching into an academic discussion of the duck plagues that wipe out the domestic duck farms around Dhaka, Bangladesh, every four or five years. I was impressed by how neatly Jorge summarized the medical facts: how *Bangladesh horrificans* spreads among ducks by aerosol droplets, rapidly enters a GI phase, and settles in the colon, where it causes rectal prolapse.

"Rectal prolapse in a duck?" said Dr. J., wide-eyed.

"The ducks' rear ends turn inside out," Jorge explained, "and they waddle around dragging their rectums behind them. It's not pretty. But that's not the worst of it. After the GI phase comes myocarditis, an inflammation of the heart muscle that kills the ducks in three to six weeks. The heart failure is so severe, the poor birds swell up and pop."

"Hmm…. Popping ducks." The medical examiner slurped another oyster. "But just how does this virus switch from its GI phase to the myocarditis phase?"

"We're calling that 'transdifferentiation,'" Jorge said, clearly on an academic roll. "Doctor Mallow coined the term in his latest paper in *The Journal of Virology*. His hypothesis is that one gene controls the switch."

"I call that gene *SWCH*," I added. "The *SWCH* gene turns on a superfamily of downstream genes that do the dirty work. Jorge's been assigned one of the downstream genes we call the 'package' gene, and he's done an amazing job in only two months."

"Bravo, Jorge!" Dr. J. clapped the grinning Jorge on his bony shoulder. "But that's quite disconcerting. Might this duck flu jump hosts? Tell me, you two experts, will it go global on us?"

I washed down an oyster with a long swallow of beer. I've found that when I talk about viruses to people, they listen. So I try to project calmness, though it's difficult when it comes to *Bangladesh horrificans*.

"It's already jumped, but a bird flu is unpredictable," I said. "This virus is beginning to adapt to humans. It's killing thousands in Dhaka, and a single case was just confirmed in Mexico City. But in humans, the virus attacks the lung, causing pneumonia, and many survive. In ducks, it goes right for the heart, and it's universally fatal."

"Let's hope your virus isn't a fast learner, eh?" Dr. J. said. "Interesting work, gentlemen. I'm off to find Elena now, but if there's anything I can do for you, Jorge, please let me know."

I was searching the room for my dream waitress with the tray of Tecates when I spied Lilly and Ron, the autopsy tech, deep in conversation by the gumbo pot. Lilly elegantly filled a silky, purplish dress that matched her subtly rouged cheeks. Ron wore a dark polyester funeral suit. I wandered over.

"I never misssh this party," Ron was saying, a half-full glass of whiskey in his hand, a half-gone Pall Mall in his mouth. He fumbled with his drink and pulled his pager off his belt. "Damn. Probably a 'first call.'"

"What's that?" Lilly asked.

"Means I have to pick up a body at a scene. First call. I'm the first to move the body and haul it to a morgue." He took a quick slug of his drink and looked at his pager. "It's Felton's Funeral Home. I need to call them."

Ron scurried away to find some quiet, and when he came back, he'd lost the drink and seemed to have steeled himself. "You need to know about this one, Doctor Mallow. It's off the cruise ship docked at Pier 39. It's a middle-aged male, a foreigner. High fever, possibly infectious. Respiratory failure. He's going to the M.E.'s morgue for autopsy. I'm using the infectious body bag, for sure."

"I wonder where he's been?" I said.

"Tomorrow, I will be in lab extra early," Lilly said, already anticipating the work ahead. "I will set up DNA assays before you come in, Doctor Mah-wo."

I searched the faces of the crowd until I found Dr. J., still without his wife Elena, talking with Jorge at a table heaped with fried shrimp and soft-shell crabs. "Dr. J., you're getting an infectious case off one of the cruise ships," I told him. "It sounds suspicious, and I'd like to get samples so Lilly and I to can do viral studies."

"Surely, Peter."

"Be sure to take precautions—cut-resistant gloves, N95 respirators, the full protocol for an unknown infectious agent."

"I appreciate your help setting up my facility for that, Peter. What samples will you need for your studies?" The party notched up a decibel. Jorge listened in close as Dr. J. and I discussed the cruise ship case.

"By the way, thanks for that autopsy you did last week." Dr. J. added. "The drowning on Bodekker Road. I signed off on the death certificate today. 'Findley' was the name. Trey Findley."

Jorge's face went a shade paler. "Do you see many like that, Dr. J?" he asked.

"Seems to me drowning in your car is pretty common along the coast."

"How common?"

"I'm not exactly sure, but stop by the office and my wife Elena, my stats expert, will search our records for some numbers. She can access Matagorda and Brazoria counties, too, with her new computer."

Jorge's eyes brightened. "Sure. We'll create a spreadsheet, maybe run stats with Spotfire or MultiUse. They're hot new programs."

A loudspeaker by the oyster table crackled and the chief Lion began making announcements. "What a year! More corneas, kidneys and hearts than ever before. Over 2000 kilograms of skin and bone collected!"

My vibrating pager went off. It was Brenda's home number. I wrangled free of the crowd and dialed from the public telephone near the entrance. My dysfunctional dive watch read nearly 11 p.m.

"Yeah, I can leave the party. Motel 6 again, baby?"

"No, Peter, I'm at home tonight. He's in Houston."

"Terrific. I'll go by my house and check the kids, then drive over. Make us some drinks, something warming."

I drained my Tecate, probably one too many. The beer gut I've nurtured since my wife left and I became a regular at the local mom-and-pop Mexican restaurants was threatening to push me past 200 pounds, my heaviest since college football days.

The party rumbled to a peak. A drunken biker was doing the backstroke in a half-inch of oyster liquor on the floor. At a table nearby, I spotted Jorge with Dr. J. and Elena, whose olive skin, auburn red hair and dark blue eyes made for a swarthy contrast to her anemic husband. Dr. J. held a colossal shrimp for Elena to snap at. I ran over to tell them I was leaving.

"Say hello to those two boys of yours," Dr. J. said. "And don't worry, we'll give Jorge a ride home in this miserable weather."

"Surely," Elena mumbled, demurely covering her mouthful of shrimp. "Walter and I will keep an eye out for Jorge."

"*Muchas gracias*, Elena," Jorge said. "*Y mucho gusto.*"

To my way of thinking, Elena ordinarily exudes "elegant" and "sexy," but as I watched her speaking softly in Spanish with Jorge, I sensed more. I think it was motherliness.

I made for the door. Outside, a sheet of ice glazed the rickety wooden pier. I eased my bicycle past two drunken bikers cranking their Harleys, then whipped down the pier with the wind at my back. The Harleys revved wildly behind me. The riders howled in drunken harmony.

"Be careful, y'all!" I shouted at them. "No donations tonight, please!"

My hands were frozen to the handgrips by the time I hauled my bike up my half-rotten front steps, through the storm doors, and into the front hallway. I live in a historical home, built in 1886 entirely of Louisiana swamp cypress, a wood you can't buy today. The Victorian gingerbread, the pocket doors, the wainscoting, it's all cypress. During the 1920s, the inside was chopped into small apartments and the once-grand home became a boarding house for seamen. Haunting, drafty and grand, she wears her age well, except for the peeling paint, black mold, and an occasional outbreak of termites.

My almost-ex wife and I bought the old house when we first moved to the Island eight years ago, but Ellen was never much on renovations. She preferred to collect artistic men while browbeating me. I found welcome solitude in knocking out walls and yanking old pipes until the entire boarding house became ours, with the exception of one apartment upstairs in the back. That's where Mr. Kreuger lives, the 77-year-old retiree who's my live-in babysitter. Through the solid cypress walls, Mr. Kreuger's heard it all—the arguments, slammed doors, and lately, the more subtle details of my drawn-out divorce.

Mr. Kreuger is a former merchant marine. He retired from the Wallennius shipping company years back, but he never stopped standing the night watch, 10 p.m. until 4 a.m. When the boys spend the weekend, I keep the door from the back hall to his apartment open, and Mr. Kreuger listens for them while he drinks Scotch and watches wrestling. I eased through his door, my hands tucked into my armpits for warmth, and found him planted in a sagging recliner in front of his TV, well into his night watch.

"Boys go to bed all right?"

"No problem. That little Travis sure knows his wrestling facts." Mr. Kreuger's three small rooms were crammed with a lifetime's accumulation of buoys, nautical maps, foreign flags, and other seafaring memorabilia. A single oil portrait of a dark, Spanish-looking lady hung over his TV. The place smelled of a smoky, nearly-burnt roux. "Made gumbo tonight, Doc. It's a good time of year for gumbo, especially sausage and oyster gumbo. I'd offer you some, but I calculated only enough to feed me and the boys."

"That's okay. I was thinking of going back out, visiting. I'll be back before you turn in, Mr. Kreuger."

The old man smiled. "Have a good visit."

"Ever been married, Mr. Kreuger?"

"Afraid I can't offer any advice on that subject. I always stuck with whores. Much easier that way."

When I stepped back into the hall, Mr. Kreuger called out, "Run your taps tonight, Doc! They're predicting a hard freeze." I walked through the house and cracked the faucets a trickle, then went to check on the boys. Overhead, I heard the doleful honking of Canadian geese riding the north wind to their winter refuge on the far west end of the Island.

Looking into my sons' sleeping faces, I whispered, "Angels. Angels with horns," my mother's saying when she was in a reflective mood, which was rare after my father died and left her with the tavern to run and three boys to raise.

My youngest, 10-year-old Travis, was hidden under the pile of stuffed animals he hauls with him every other weekend. Chad, the teenager, was snoring away, his big feet sticking out from under the covers. As I adjusted Chad's blankets, I felt the cold contours of his electric bass. I pulled it out and leaned it against the wall.

More geese passed over, their honking closer, more blatant.

Damn, I'm a piss-poor father, I thought. *I come home from partying, only to turn around and go back out to get laid. How the hell did those two boys turn out so great? I stay late in the lab, can't cook, and blame it all on my work, my science. In spite of me, they're two good boys, on their way to becoming two good men.*

I went downstairs and made the rounds of empty rooms. When Ellen moved out, she took all the furniture, so I installed a basketball hoop in the dining room. With the 14-foot ceiling, it's nearly regulation height. Nobody else on the block has a private indoor court.

I took my truck to Brenda and Tom's place. A historic Victorian like mine, her house is only six blocks away, but I wasn't going back out in that cold on my bicycle. I have a '86 Datsun pickup for just such occasions. The wind blows through the old truck's rust holes and the engine burns a bit of oil, but she's my baby, my cowboy Cadillac, and she cranked the first time.

Brenda opened the front door before I had a chance to twist her raucous mechanical bell. I stepped into the hallway. It was ice cold. Brenda was wearing tight-fitting purple silk pajamas, a red-plaid flannel shirt and camping-style quilted booties.

"Meeting here is pretty bold, isn't it?" I teased after we'd kissed, my arms still wrapped around her.

"We'll go upstairs to the sitting room. The drinks are there and it's a bit warmer."

· I followed close behind Brenda's silk pajama bottoms, up the ornate staircase. Hung on the walls at each landing were the black-and-white photographs she does as a hobby. Brenda's compositions had superb clarity, focus, and balance. An overcast day in a Nova Scotia fishing village, a tumbling pile of lobster traps, a wrinkled old fisherman with his beat-up pipe. Her pictures reminded me of my New England childhood, except that the shots of Brenda's family suggested an upbringing much classier than my own among the lower life-forms of Cape Cod.

"Why aren't you photographing Galveston?" I asked. "The Island's so unique. The port with its ships, the stone buildings downtown, the people, the palm fronds in the sun."

"The cockroaches."

"Oh, please. There's a tropical feel here, an 'island' feel."

"All I feel on this sand bar is the heat and humidity. That summer was hot as the hinges of hell."

"You wait. The next few months are your payoff for surviving the heat."

"Have your drink, Peter." Two crystal tumblers sat on a black enameled tray, lemon twists floating on a reddish-brown meniscus. "They're Sazeracs."

I took a sip. "You've adapted so well to the local booze, Brenda. Why not the climate?"

"It's ridiculous. This morning I was sweating, tonight I'm freezing my ass off."

She said "ass" so sweetly with her New England accent, it started me thinking about *her* butt, which is like a pair of shapely plums in a cluster, and her walk, which is barely inside the law.

"I'm colder in this old house than I ever was in Vermont," she said, ambling over to the big Lawson heater, its Sheraton-brown finish chipped and rusted, its broken ceramic elements collapsing in blue-yellow flames. I backed her up to the Lawson and cupped my hands over her perfect plums. "That ungodly wind blows right through the walls. Listen to it out there!"

"I'll warm you up," I said, slipping my hands inside her pajama bottoms.

"Jesus Mary and Joseph!" she cried, squirming away. "Your hands are freezing!"

25

We settled on her hard-backed antique couch. I stuck my hands inside my jacket.

"Let's go dancing again, Peter. I enjoyed that. They would never believe *me* doing the two-step, back in Vermont."

I thought about that for a moment, thought about her past. "I know this isn't your first time having someone else, Brenda. So why me?"

"Before, I think I was testing Tom. Maybe I thought we still had a chance. But with you," she laughed, "I just don't think."

I pulled her toward me. "We still haven't figured out why we're doing this."

"As long as nobody gets hurt."

"Someone always gets hurt," I said, man-of-the-world. She giggled.

"Oh, are we fragile tonight, Pee-tah? Do we bruise easily?" She gave me a shove, somewhere between playful and S&M. I was surprised by her strength.

"Quit it, you artsy-fartsy wannabe photographer." I shucked off my jacket and kissed her hard. Her mouth tasted of anise. "You're good for me, you know."

"I suspect you're good for me."

"Tom's gone for the whole night?"

"He stays over when his so-called band is practicing for a so-called gig."

"Face it, Brenda. He's got a woman up there."

"To tell the truth," she sighed, "I couldn't care less." She leaned into me and began kissing me in earnest, her mouth open and warm. "Stay," she gasped. "Stay the night. I can get you out before daylight."

"Not my routine, baby. I'm home by four, when the night watch ends."

"I want us to make another video, Peter. Let's. It makes me so hot. I've already set it up in the bedroom. Lights, camcorder, everything."

The next morning, I dragged into the lab at 10, carrying breakfast. Jorge and Lilly were already at work, early for a Saturday. Lilly was boiling samples of viral protein for more supershifts.

"I brought burritos, you two!" I said. "Burritos 'all the way'—beans, chorizo, eggs, and cheese. And coffee. Eat before you load your gels, Jorge."

"Thanks, Doctor Mallow, but I'm not hungry."

Lilly and Jorge loaded the gels and cranked the voltage to run out the proteins. I sat at the table in our break area, read the newspaper, and ate two burritos, mine and Jorge's. I figured I deserved the extra energy after last night's video production.

Dr. J. called to confirm that the tissue samples from that case off the cruise ship would be delivered late in the day, so we could start our analysis. I asked Jorge to let me know when he finished his repeat supershifts on *PAKG*, so I could check them.

"I was hoping to be knocking out the *PAKG* gene in the damned virus by now," he grumbled. Jorge was right, just a little too eager. "Knocking out," or incapacitating, a gene is a great way to uncover its biologic function. It was the next step, a critical one for us, but tricky.

"You're a long way from knockouts, Jorge."

"Don't forget," Lilly piped up as she fine-adjusted our gel apparatus, "we must bleed ducks in the Level 4 today, Doctor Mah-wo."

"That's right. If everything's ready, let's do it."

Lilly and I packed our sterilized needles, syringes, and other supplies. Under constant video surveillance, we carded ourselves through the double man-lock to the attached building. In the entrance vestibule of the Level 4 lab, we pulled on our sleek, silvery, tear-resistant space suits, fastened the Velcro seals, popped on plastic bubble-helmets, and hooked onto the bright yellow air-supply hoses that dangle down in every room. The hiss of airflow is so loud inside those bulky helmets that communication is strictly by shouts and hand signals. A hot shot administrator once had the suits rigged with walkie-talkies, but the sound's never been right.

The door of the final lock slid shut behind us. We arranged our equipment for processing the duck blood on the single, bare stainless steel table in the procedure room.

"Jorge's doing well with his *PAKG* gene, isn't he?" I said. I got a blank stare from Lilly and I tried again. "Jorge's doing great. Great! Jorge!"

"Oh, yes. Jorge's great! *PAKG* gene!"

Lilly motioned with the tray of syringes to the adjoining Level 4 animal room. We unhooked our air and passed through the lock to the avian area. Once the green light indicated that the room's negative pressure had been established, we reconnected to the air supply and pulled six duck cages off the rack. We were ready to bleed ducks, which is slow, cumbersome work in those bio-protective gloves. It's eerie in a Level 4, too. The comforting lab smells of acrylamide, acetone, and formalin are missing, and there's total silence except for the steady hiss of the air supply, and an occasional "quack" that comes through.

I thought back to when our Level 4 lab was first funded by Washington, and protests from the Island's local bumpkins stalled construction for months. Paranoid letters to the editor filled the *Galveston Island Daily*. The City Council published a self-important statement on the "lack of wisdom in placing this facility on a hurricane coast." Predictions were made that "one errant mosquito would loose a deadly plague." These people! The state-of-the-art safeguards built into a Level 4 were beyond their understanding.

The locals were right about one thing, though. Stored in the nitrogen-filled reference tanks of this biocontainment facility is a collection of bugs that's a bio-terrorist's wet dream. There's yellow fever, leptospirosis, and Ebola, just for starters. There's Russian encephalitis, Omsk hemorrhagic fever, *Shistosoma mansoni*, Marburg virus, and plenty that don't have a name yet. These bugs could wipe out a lot more than the Gulf Coast.

And that's why a Level 4 Biosafety Facility is built the way it is. A Level 4 is like a building inside a building, or a submarine inside a bank vault. The outer building, in fact, resembles a two-story bank, except it's windowless and a cluster of Hepa-filtered exhaust stacks sticks out of its roof. Built into this outer "bank" is a seamless, hollow cube—the "submarine"—made of specially prepared low-shrinkage concrete coated on the inside with a rubberized waterproof material. If the inner cube with its entrance and exit vestibules, procedure rooms, and animal facility were filled with liquid, it would hold every drop.

The safeguards of a Level 4 are absolutely failsafe. Exit autoclaves, air out-takes, and liquid nitrogen lines to the viral freezer tanks are all controlled by computers with foolproof software. Any glitch and the whole building locks down. Even the liquid waste we dump down the drains is boiled for 24 hours in underground cooker tanks before entering the city sewage. There's no way a killer virus can escape a Level 4, unless one of us carries it out, of course.

"Last duck!" Lilly yelled, once I'd found the sixth bird's jugular vein.

We capped and packed our microfuge tubes, secured the needles, double red-bagged the syringes for disposal, and passed back into the Level 4's procedure room to process the blood, kill the virus, and stabilize the proteins and DNA. With the space suit and gloves on, you're scared to death you might drop or break something. A spill of even the minutest amount of viral material kicks in mandatory decontamination, and you're in for one big pain in the ass. Once one of the red "SPILL!" buttons along the walls is hit, the entire facility is sealed, and endless decontamination protocols begin. Every surface has to be washed with bleach, the viral freezer-tanks sealed and their liquid nitrogen feeds shut off, and the entire facility flushed with chlorine gas to kill any living organism still loose inside. Then the biggest pain in the ass begins, the paperwork for the Environmental Safety Office.

Lilly gestured that the samples were ready. We loaded the equipment into the autoclave, walked into the chemical shower room to get blasted from all directions with green sterilant, and removed our dripping suits in the exit vestibule. All we accomplished was to draw two milliliters of blood from three infected and three control ducks, and aliquot the blood into a series of microfuge tubes. Six ducks, 12 milliliters of blood, but it took over three hours. No wonder research moves so slowly and needs so many hands.

Back in the main lab, Lilly set up for viral extraction while I looked over Jorge's supershifts in our break area. "These are beautiful," I said. "You've got it a second time." Jorge took a swig from a green, two-liter bottle of Diet Sprite. He seemed to always carry one. "The *PAKG* protein is clearly localized in the outer membrane of the viral envelope. One more run and…."

"Why must I repeat these assays three times, Doctor Mallow?"

"You don't want to publish your results and then, a year later, find out you were wrong, do you?"

"But in physics, in string theory, a proof is a proof. My work on the theoretical structure of a superstring required only that the theorem be…."

"We're dealing with a virus here, Jorge. Viruses are changeable, unpredictable."

"I want to knock out the *PAKG* gene now!"

"Start your third set of assays, please."

"But I don't have enough sample!" he said. "I'll skip Christmas. To hell with it."

Just then, I saw my chance for a "teaching moment" in science, and I jumped on it. "Jorge, a critical concept in biological experimentation is 'backup'." I pointed to Lilly's samples. "This morning, Lilly and I got plenty of virus from the ducks, enough to spare for your assays."

"Wow. Thanks."

"Back things up, Jorge. Always. Cultures, samples, data, grant proposals, everything."

"Backup. It's a cool idea. Very practical."

"Get your third set started. Lilly and I will finish them for you during Christmas break. When you return, you can knock out *PAKG*. You need a vacation."

"You're right. Billy Ray's looking forward to riding out, too."

"Billy Ray? You're riding out with Billy Ray? El Paso is 14 hours away, Jorge."

"These new Harleys do 140 miles per hour, no sweat. Billy Ray and the guys in the Armed Eagles will love my mom's Christmas tamales."

Late in the day, I was looking for Jorge in the lab to say goodbye for the holidays, when he burst through the door, out of breath.

"Doctor Mallow! I was in the Public Health and Bioinformatics Center, and there's a grant out to study automobile deaths. Why don't we write a proposal for the immersion problem? Remember, Dr. J. said we could access his records."

"Hmm. That would require statistics and complex analysis, Jorge. It's epidemiology."

"Piece of cake. I have plenty of time now that I've dropped work on my superstring theorem."

"Okay, okay. Just don't break your stride with *PAKG*."

"I want to help you with *SWCH* too! That's the coolest gene. *SWCH* modulates the whole superfamily. Understanding *SWCH* will afford new insights into how *Bangladesh horrificans* induces myocarditis in the duck. For the first time, we'll be able to gauge its potential as a human pathogen."

"Go write that down," I told him. "It sounds like a review article we'll be writing a couple of years from now."

I bade Jorge a Merry Christmas, and then stopped by my office to finish this big note on the Lions' party and my crazy new go-getter student. Jorge makes a terrific addition to the lab. With him on board, we're Nobel material.

Wednesday, December 24

Dr. J.'s autopsy tissues from the cruise ship tested positive for *Bangladesh horrificans*. The victim was a Pakistani living in Houston. He'd been in Calcutta on business for a week and probably picked up the virus there. Upon his return to Houston, he booked a vacation cruise to the Grand Caymans. Only a few hours out of port, he became violently ill and the ship turned back for Galveston. His lungs were eaten up by virus. His heart was clean.

I immediately communicated the case in an official report to the CDC, the Centers for Disease Control and Prevention in Atlanta. Then, I got cracking on my *SWCH* assays. I knew all too well what these bird viruses can do. If *Bangladesh* ever got smart and flipped the right genes on, a pandemic could spread between continents in days, killing millions, right here, people I knew, colleagues, people I loved, Brenda, my boys. I didn't want to think about that.

The research institute was quiet. Everyone was on vacation, except me and Lilly. I was free of routine autopsy call until the beginning of February, so there'd be no hospital work interfering with my science, and Chad and Travis were driving with their mother to Arkansas to cram themselves into a trailer for two weeks of holiday festivities with her boyfriend's relatives. I barely managed to pick up a couple of last-minute gifts for the boys before they headed out.

"Really, Peter," Ellen said when I stuck their gifts, still in paper bags, through the window of her boyfriend's Jeep. "Couldn't you have made the effort to wrap them?"

Chad came to my defense from the back seat. "It's a cool shirt, Dad," he said. "Way too cool for Arkansas. Thanks."

I virtually camp out in my lab during the holidays, starting when those damn cranberry ads appear before Thanksgiving. This habit of ignoring the holiday season goes back to my youth on Cape Cod, where the cranberry harvest signals the year's most intense period of drunkenness. Once the locals get their hands on their cranberry money and Christmas bonuses, the bars fill. This boom in business was welcome at my father's tavern, the Salty Dog, a smoky, low-ceilinged dive on the ground floor of our little saltbox overlooking Massachusetts Bay.

During my college years, I'd return for the Christmas holidays, visit a few high school friends and then, bang! I was stuck at the Salty Dog, tending the tacky Formica bar. I poured booze, packed beer coolers and broke up fights until closing time, when I fell into my bed in the small room over the taproom. Believe me, nothing's worse than waking up to "Mommy Kissing Santa Claus" on the jukebox, while your mom types the lunch menu and Dad pours an eye opener.

The busy season ends abruptly after New Year's Day, when the rummies truck off to sober up, or slip into the DTs. Lots of them die, too, in the new year. They die at accident scenes reeking of alcohol, from suicide, and from cirrhosis, like my dad. He had the audacity to die on New Year's Day.

Ten years after my dad, Mom passed away in that first week of January too. Reminiscing at her funeral, my brothers John and Lee and I had to give Mom a lot of credit. She returned to teaching Latin to junior high idiots, kept us at our books, tended bar evenings, and still managed to feed the lunch crowd at the Salty Dog.

Mom was the best at bar food. Clam chowder, corn chowder, fish chowder. Boiled dinner, cod cakes, hash. Just plain, overcooked, New England eating. But Mom had no talent for picking fresh produce. The peppers she chose were bruised and cracked. The fruit she picked harbored dark streaks, off-odors, and other signs of ferment. When she brought home an avocado, you could be sure black spots lurked beneath its knobby skin. We weren't surprised when she went so fast from her cancer. It was like another bad spot, undetected for too long.

None of us wanted the Salty Dog after that. We had it on the market about a month when my brother Lee, who hated it the most, torched the place. He got five to 10 for arson, went up on December 26th, and turned HIV positive in prison before the next turkey went on the table.

Thanksgiving, Christmas, New Year's. The season to be jolly.

So I stick to the lab and leave the celebration to everyone else. It gets a little lonely, but the work's important, and it consumes me, designing these experiments.

Friday, January 2

On New Year's Eve, I gave in to Brenda, and we celebrated by dancing at Bayou Bob's. Brenda's two-step was coming along nicely since we started practicing in the dining room. Bayou Bob put out a big iron pot of jambalaya, black-eyed peas, the whole New Year's deal. Afterwards, Brenda and I sacked out in her antique, four-poster bed, since husband Tom was playing a gig up the coast. I felt surprisingly good for a New Year's morning. No hangover whatsoever as I pulled on my faded old jeans, eager to get to the lab.

"You're going in on New Year's Day?" Brenda asked.

By noon I'd run out a promising gel on *SWCH* and shot off another e-mail to Poonawala. He was nervous about our Gulf Coast case of *Bangladesh*, but I assured him we were hot on the trail of the genes that would eventually lead to a vaccine.

I was looking over Lilly's gels when the lab door opened and in walked Marvin Stepinski, chief of cardiology and one of the few hospital people with access to the high security Medical Research Institute. Marv is in his early 60s. He has frizzy red hair like Clarabelle the Clown's, but streaked with silver. He sports a bushy red mustache that flaps when he talks, and he gives a rock-steady handshake. Marv sticks catheters into people's hearts for a living. If I needed a catheter wound through my coronary arteries, I'd want Marv's hand guiding it. Marv's a solid researcher, too, funded for years by the National Institutes of Health, the NIH, from whence all funding flows. Marv invents devices to blast atherosclerotic plaques. At least a dozen specialized catheters carry his name. He holds a fistful of patents.

"Only you, Mallow," he said, smiling. "I pass by the Ebola lab, the malaria lab, the leptospirosis lab, and they're empty. But you're here on New Year's Day."

"It's as good a day as any, when you're after a nasty virus."

"Got a minute to talk? I need your help." We walked to my little office and Marv set a big fat grant application marked "DRAFT" on the desk.

"I'm sending this proposal to the NIH. Take a look at it for me, would you?"

"Sure."

"It's on my latest catheter, the laser-hyperthermia cath. We heat up the heart muscle with a laser and improve hemodynamic function. It's nifty. It's perfect for cases of myocarditis. Could save a lot of lives." Marv's science is practical, not basic like mine, and in the eight years I've known him, Marv's come up with some pretty weird ideas. "Our preliminary experiments are complete. We did it in rats. Can you examine their hearts? I have the microscopic slides, the stains you like, everything." He leaned back and blew on his mustache so it flapped. "If this pans out, Peter, I'll get money to do a phase 1 clinical trial, and we'll be rolling in dough."

"Bring me the slides. When's your deadline?"

"First of February."

"I just put in a grant application myself, Marv, on my bird virus. It's worrisome. Last word from Calcutta was 6000 deaths. *Bangladesh* infection runs only a 10 to 20 percent mortality, though. Those who die succumb to pneumonia, nothing like in its natural host."

"How's it spreading?"

"Probably by aerosol. The outbreak's been confined to the area between Dhaka and the Bay of Bengal, but we just had a case here."

"No shit."

"I just reported it to the CDC."

Marv stood up to go. "I hope your grant application comes to my study section for review. I'll watch for it. You still have Lilly in the lab?"

"She's a gem. Got a hotshot new student, too."

"The one who went running across campus covered with blood? What's up with him?"

"It was his first autopsy, a case of vehicular immersion."

"Vehicular immersion. You could get money to study that, you know. The chancellor of the university started a grant program, after his wife was killed when she rammed their antique Mercedes into a concrete abutment in the Wal-Mart parking lot."

"I heard about that case. Steering wheel injury, torn aorta."

"Police said the accelerator froze. The chancellor dug up a ton of private money. Poor guy, upset about his wife."

"More likely he was upset about the Mercedes, knowing that little prick."

"These grants are for studies into mechanical defects, but vehicular immersion might fit. I'll bring over the information."

Late in the afternoon, Marv dropped off four large boxes of rat heart slides and a flyer on the chancellor's new grant program.

Sunday, January 4

Yesterday, I spent six hours in my office hunched over a microscope studying *Bangladesh* myocarditis, counting fluorescent green lymphocytes as they invaded the duck's heart muscle. I used the quiet time to listen to old Morphine CDs. I love that pounding bass when I'm on the 'scopes.

Unexpectedly, Jorge was in the middle of my office, swaying to Morphine's music.

"Back early, huh? How was El Paso?"

"Great. Where's Lilly?"

"I made her take two weeks off."

"Did the supershifts come out?"

"Perfect, Jorge."

"The third time!" he shouted. "I'll start on the knockouts."

Mark Sandman groaned in the background:

> "You penetrate my radar
> Drop a bomb in my backyard."

"Hang on a second," I said. I waited until the sax solo faded, then lowered the volume. "You'll be working with live virus now, Jorge, and it must be done under the direct supervision of me or Lilly."

"I can do it on my own, Doctor Mallow. I'll follow the manual and the protocols."

"Not without me or Lilly, you won't! Look, Jorge, I've had undergraduates do this work before, but when you're cutting up genes, knocking them out, it's tedious, and every step must be checked. Funny things happen. Often you don't get the whole DNA sequence, or maybe you get too much."

"But the *PAKG* sequence is straightforward. I already cloned the whole thing."

"In the live virus, it won't be so simple."

Morphine thumped. I wasn't so sure it was a good idea, but I handed Jorge the flyer Marv Stepinski had given me. "Check this out, Jorge. It's the application you mentioned. Vehicular immersions just might fit, and if we write a grant and get some money, you could use it for software, or whatever you needed."

"The data shouldn't be too complex."

"It's a small grant by NIH standards, but you could travel to other medical examiners' offices. Maybe Miami. It sounds like medical examiners see lots of these drownings."

"So we're going to do it?"

I nodded. "I'll worry about the budget, Jorge. But this was your idea, so why don't you write the first draft of the grant."

I quickly outlined the parts of a grant proposal: specific aims, methods, and future directions. I explained to Jorge how even a brief 10-page proposal like this one should start with a hypothesis. Ours would be that "the mortality associated with vehicular immersions could be prevented if more were known about the exact circumstances of the accident."

"It's all yours now," I told him. Morphine started singing "Test-Tube Baby, Shoot 'm Down," and I cranked up the volume. "Do a search on this tonight, Jorge. Get some preliminary data."

"I'll go back to the lab and jump on a computer!"

Jorge stood up and started bobbing. With his hands stuffed deep in his pockets, he made shooting motions at the pictures of viruses that hang on my office walls.

Mark Sandham sang:

> "Shoot a beer drinker down
> Shoot a bartender down...
> Shoot 'em down/Shoot 'em down
> Shoot 'em down/Shoot 'em down."

The bass thumped. The walls shuddered. I went back to the duck hearts under the microscope and counted green lymphocytes.

Jorge worked all night. I stayed until 3 a.m., then staggered home.

Midmorning today, Jorge came into the office with a ream of paper under his arm and a heavy backpack pulling down his shoulder. He had collected data on vehicular immersions from the NIH, the CDC, the National Highway Traffic Safety Authority, anywhere he could find hard facts.

What did we know? In the U.S., 1,582 persons drowned in vehicles over the past two years, or about 800 per year. Most in-vehicle drownings occurred in the coastal counties of Florida, Texas, California, and Louisiana. No surprise there. Vehicle meets coastline. Eighty-five percent of the deaths were salt water drownings. Of the fresh water drownings, half occurred in winter when some idiot went through thin ice while driving across a lake.

"I'll bet these data are an underestimation, Doctor Mallow."

"How many were trying to escape, I wonder?"

"Can't tell. It's mortality data. Forensic details aren't available. If I check the actual reports, I can break down the facts, even get the year and type of vehicle."

"Dr. J. will help, if you write this grant."

Jorge reached into his backpack and plunked down a 50-page document printed in a micro-font that looked like Egyptian hieroglyphics.

"I already wrote the grant."

"A rough draft."

Tuesday, January 6

We polished Jorge's grant proposal. The background section was compelling, and Jorge—boy genius in math and statistics—devised a terrific methods section. Together, we threw some first-class bullshit into the future directions. I taught Jorge the critical grantsmanship phrases, like "Our preliminary data strongly suggest" and "Further studies seem warranted." Jorge ran the final copies and hand-carried the finished proposal down to the research support office for review by a panel of "experts" the chancellor had slapped together.

With the proposal submitted, Jorge and I organized his approach to knocking out the *PAKG* gene of *Bangladesh horrificans*. It was clear the kid had a bottomless reserve of nervous energy, but he hadn't quite shaken his youthful obsession with theoretical physics. For instance, I was at my 'scopes, reviewing our tactics to knock out *PAKG*, when out of the blue, he began pacing and cried out "The Big Bang. Wow! Think of the implications."

"Please pay attention," I said. "If we splice out the DNA sequences perfectly and the other genes cooperate...."

"Don't you see, Doctor Mallow? These sub-microscopic sequences of viral DNA are totally insignificant. The summed energy of all human life amounts to nothing in comparison to the energy of even the tiniest star."

"I'd say that's a matter of perspective, Jorge."

"In universal terms, we barely exist. And when we cease to exist, it won't impact the universe one bit!"

I looked up from the 'scope. "If you wanted to pursue this string-theory thing for a doctorate degree, how long would it take?"

"Six or seven years. My advisory professor in quantum string theory wrote and defended his thesis in only two years, but that's genius. It was his work that established the existence of other dimensions."

"Other dimensions? More than four?"

"There may be up to 11. They're here, but we don't notice. Humans are so biologically limited, we can't cope with more than four."

As if on cue, Lilly—who'd been away since before New Year's—waltzed through the office door. She was struggling with a huge Styrofoam box in her arms. It was as if she, and the box, had arrived from an unseen dimension. I jumped up from my microscope.

"Lilly! You're back, too?" I wrapping an arm around her and gave a squeeze. "What's in the box?"

"Fast growing cells from my friends in Houston. I have them on plenty of dry ice."

"What kind of cells are they?"

"Lymphocytes, but who cares? Fast-duck cells grow really fast, that's all that matters. I will thaw out cells, infect them with *Bangladesh* virus, then harvest proteins and screen for each gene. One by one, I will define viral proteins and genes and solve the puzzle of how Bangladesh changes from GI phase to heart phase. I can't wait to get started!"

We walked across to the lab. Lilly was so wound up, she went over to Hari and gave him a shove to wake him for an impromptu discussion of her new fast-duck cells. In the middle of the excitement, it occurred to me that the boys, Chad and Travis, were to return from Arkansas today and were probably already at the house.

I grabbed the notebook and hopped on the Huffy.

A gentle breeze and the scent of seaweed had replaced the harsh December weather. A spectacular sunset was glowing in the petrochemical haze over the mainland, and the crumbling, pink sandstone of Old Red practically blushed as I pedaled away. Jorge's comments on the universe and the meaningless of life kept replaying in my mind, but the breeze was too mild, the sunset too stunning. Eventually, my thoughts turned to Chad's sorry jump shot, Travis's new skateboard, and an overhand turn I intended to teach Brenda. We needed something new to show them at Bayou Bob's.

Wednesday, January 21

I fired Hari Bhalakumarian on Monday. I had to get rid of his sorry ass for the good of the lab. I made my mind up early, caught him as he strolled in the door at noon, and called him into my office before he could flop over his lab bench for his afternoon nap.

Besides being lazy, Hari's a screw-up. Over the weekend, Lilly was in Houston at the Hermann Analytic Center, learning about a super new spectrophotometer that's scheduled for delivery to our university. Lilly asked Hari to feed her fast-cells. She came back to dead cells. Luckily, she had some cryopreserved, but the loss set her experiments back at least two weeks. All Hari's fault. I decided I'd had enough.

"But kind sir," he argued, "those genetically manipulated cells are in a chronically weakened condition. I was afraid to feed them like normal cells. It's possible they died of natural causes. Perhaps I should have consulted with you or Lilly, but my work has been most excellent otherwise."

He tried flattery. He tried tears and wailing. He threatened to reveal our "lab secrets," which is ridiculous because we don't have any lab secrets. Finally, he resigned himself to change. "I've long dreamt of eventually returning to the clinical arts, the arena of healing. As you know, I am trained in internal medicine and cardiology. Who knows, Doctor Mallow? Who knows?"

Amazingly, within 24 hours, Hari finagled himself another research position as a postdoc in the Coxsackie lab, two labs down from ours. I understand he got a raise and more responsibility as a lab officer for lab security, planning, and enforcement of environmental safety procedures. This morning I saw him—wide awake!—striding down the hall in a fresh white shirt, brand-new loafers with tassels, and a silk tie covered with hand-painted stethoscopes. Good for Hari, but good riddance from our lab's point of view. We'll see him around the building, but only in passing.

Friday, January 23

Jorge's immersion grant was funded. Lilly started Jorge on knockout procedures in the Level 4 after I pulled strings with the biosafety committee to get him certified, but his afternoons and evenings have been spent at the M.E.'s facility collecting immersion data. Dr. J. and Elena are taking a great personal interest in Jorge and his project. He's spent the last two Sundays at their beach house, where Elena cooks him dinner. He's raving about Venezuelan food. He's even put on a pound or two, and started a snappy little goatee.

Jorge devised statistical and combinatorial-probability methods that are mind bending, and he's tested his methods on the vehicular immersion deaths from the past 50 years in Galveston, Jefferson, Brazoria, and Matagorda counties—the Texas coast from Sabine Pass to Matagorda Island. On February 1, he leaves for Florida to collect cases. After Florida, he'll be in Louisiana for the rest of that week. Elena arranged everything. When he's got it all together, he'll use some sort of elegant statistical projection to estimate a national incidence. And the cases he's already collected look similar—victims trapped, a desperate struggle to escape, a grim death—exactly like Trey Findley out on Bodekker Road.

Friday, January 30

Don't ask me how it happened, but Brenda and I are living together. Maybe it was all the dancing. She was dead set on moving out on Tom. She needed "space." She "couldn't breathe" with Tom around.

"This is an awfully big move," I told her, with trepidation, the night she made her decision.

"I can't go on like this, Peter."

"Tom doesn't give a damn, Brenda, believe me. He's got his own thing going. Give it some time."

"No, Peter. I'm telling him about us, and I'm leaving. I could take a place myself, if you'd prefer."

So Brenda told Tom about "us," and I was right, he didn't give a damn. He even helped move her out. The three of us loaded her stuff into the bed of the Datsun at the crack of dawn and hauled it to the carriage house in back of my place. I insisted we stay in the carriage house rather than the main house, because the kids had been coming over nearly every weekend.

"I swear, Peter, your kids want me around more than you do," was Brenda's response to the carriage house idea.

"You know what a fruitcake Ellen is," I said. "She lives in the next block with her dumb boyfriend, and if she found out you were in the main house, she'd make my life miserable."

Besides, I argued, the carriage house was a cozy spot for two lovers like us. Most of the old Victorians in Galveston have one of these little two-story houses sitting on the alley at the back of the main home. Historically, it's where the coachman lived, in two small rooms with a bath over the old stable. Mine's got the basic facilities—a refrigerator for beer, functional commode, and a slightly rusted, claw-footed bathtub. I was using the place as a study. I left the small pine desk and, with Tom's assistance, we wrestled three loads of Brenda's antiques up the narrow stairway. I set up Brenda's futon for our bed.

The snake cage took me by surprise, though. I'd noticed the small snake in its screened cage in Brenda's kitchen before, but I assumed the snake was Tom's pet.

"You keep a snake?"

"Isn't she pretty? It's a corn snake."

"Why?"

"Herpetology 301. I grew up terrified of snakes, so at Vassar, I took herpetology for my mandatory bio course. It's good to de-condition, to balance out your fears with reality."

"Holistic health again."

"Reptiles make okay pets, Peter. Think of her as a living sculpture."

"What does it eat?"

"Live mice. I've been meaning to ask, could you find an occasional mouse at work? One that's to be discarded, and non-infectious? Don't worry. Corn snakes don't grow too large. Not like boas or pythons."

While Brenda settled into this new dimension of our lives, I slipped away to the lab for a couple of hours. On my way home I stopped at Black's Barbecue to pick up a celebration lunch.

Black's is an old-fashioned Texas barbecue joint. Legend is that Mr. Black's grandfather started the business out of a corner grocery store before "The Great Storm," the hurricane that wasted Galveston in 1900 and killed over 6,000 people. When the county courthouse was built across the street during the '20s, the next-generation Black began posting bonds for extra profit. That's why the lopsided sign out front reads:

BLACK'S SMOKE HOUSE
BAIL BONDS

The current Mr. Black, a man the color of blackstrap molasses, continues the family sideline, selling barbecue and posting bail bonds out of the same cash register. Ever since I first crossed the causeway to the Island, Black's has been my favorite barbecue, tender from long, slow cooking, and redolent with carcinogenic compounds achieved by Mr. Black's secret combination of dry-rub seasonings and smoldering pecan wood.

"Oh baby!" Brenda cried when she smelled the brown paper bag I carried up the stairs to our new carriage-house apartment. "We'll need a big nap after this."

"Maybe a short one," I agreed, "once we've recharged our lipids with some good Texas beef." Brenda was beaming. "I got our usual."

We lovingly prepared our sandwiches. Brenda's preference is chopped beef on onion bun, mine is a rib sandwich on homemade jalapeno-bread cut Texas thick. I dissected the meat from the rib bone, then sauced it and laid on sweet onion, jalapeno, pickles and coleslaw.

"Cajun fries, too!" Brenda cried. "Must you go back to the lab, Peter?"

"Jorge and I are going over Dr. J.'s data this afternoon."

"Workaholic."

"It's research, Brenda. It's not a regular job. Next week when I go on autopsy again, that's a real job."

"Publish or perish, I suppose."

"It's more about funding, and I'm lucky there. I came here eight years ago with the big NIH grant on *Huntavirus*," I said, waving a Cajun fry at her, "and I've been funded since."

Those were my early years, hot on the trail of the Mexican *Huntavirus* as an assistant professor at the University of New Mexico. In the shanties of the border *colonias*, I cultured *Hunta* from the stool of a dying infant, and discovered the cause of Mexican Diarrhea Syndrome. Once we got the reptilian carrier, the spotted gecko, under control, the disease was eliminated, and it was time to find another virus and write another grant.

"That was the first time I heard your name," Brenda said, "with all that coverage you got. *Newsweek, Time,* even CNN. All those poor, sweet little babies. So now it's a new virus, and you'll get the bigger NIH grant this summer, right?"

"I'd better. I'm up for tenure and a raise this fall. Next year, full professor."

"Before you're 40. Let's hope. It's different for me, of course. It's not about grants. It's running the groups, the holistic health lectures, and my library project."

"How about publishing your thesis work?" I said, gesturing toward the stack of typed sheets we'd carried to its new resting place on my desk.

"Please don't bring that up."

"Your lectures, your groups—at least it's what you want to be doing."

"You know what I really want to be doing."

"Not this again," I sighed. She smiled. "You want kids. But Tom couldn't."

"There was never a firm diagnosis." She picked up a Cajun fry and stared at it seriously. "One more reason he was getting on my nerves."

"You know how I feel about this, Brenda. I've got two kids, and I'd like to call it quits."

We had demolished our sandwiches. A few fries remained.

"Please stay, Peter," she said, placing her hand tenderly on the inside of my thigh. "We can make some more video."

"We'll do that tonight."

"I'll set it up. We'll be marvelous. By the way, where are you keeping our tapes?"

"At work, stuck in a locked drawer in my office. Every man has a secret drawer."

"Oh, I'm sure you have quite a collection, too. But that's all ancient history, isn't it? Now that we're together, I'm all for you, Peter. And you're for me, right?" She popped the last fry in her mouth. "You certainly haven't had sex with other women."

"No, only my ex."

"What?" She showed me a partially masticated orange fry.

"I mean... it was more like a *duty*, or a habit or something."

"You've been separated a year and you still see her?"

"No, no, not recently. When you and I were first getting together, something might've happened, maybe once or twice."

"I can't believe you're telling me this. You're pitiful, Peter. Have you no moral compass?"

"You know what a nut case she is, Brenda!"

"Sure, Peter. Blame her."

"It won't happen again, okay?"

"Just go to your precious *lab*, will you?"

It was pitch dark when I headed back home, a fitful sea breeze nudging me along. It was one of those tropical January evenings, when the air is a warm coagulum around you. I kicked back under the grinding ceiling fan in the carriage house and told Brenda about Jorge's study.

"It's that common? Getting trapped?"

"It's making sense. Immersion deaths don't occur in a vehicle made before the mid-1960s. Jorge's convinced it's all about power windows. Victims of modern convenience. Jorge and I need to publish this in a top journal, maybe *JAMA, The Journal of the American Medical Association.*"

"I'm so glad you put that hammer under the front seat of my Rover, Peter."

"I do care, you know."

"I'm fine with snakes, heights, blood, pretty much anything. But this vehicular immersion business gives me the willies."

"Everyone who hears about it sticks a hammer in their car. Dr. J. put one in Elena's BMW. A Sharper Image job. German made. It's even got a razor blade built in, to cut yourself out of the seatbelt."

Sunday, February 1

Friday night we fought over the ex again. Saturday we talked it out, made up, and drove over the causeway to Bayou Bob's for a Saturday night dance session. Since we met, I've dragged Brenda to all of my old haunts along the coast, from tiny run-down dives like Bayou Bob's to cavernous halls where professional DJs spin the hottest pop-country tunes for a more urban crowd. Bayou Bob's is still our favorite.

The house band, The Swinging Doors, was on the stage. They're a family affair with mom and pops doing the singing, daughter on drums, and the Gothic teenage son, tattooed and pierced, playing electric bass in a black cape. Bayou Bob's was packed, three deep at the bar. We grabbed our favorite table, the small one next to the jukebox.

I've taught Brenda all the two-step moves I know, from "overhand turns" to "ropes" to "pretzels," but when the floor is packed with stampeding cowboys, as it was that night, it's more like guerrilla warfare. We had had a couple of beers, and danced them off with fast two-steps and polkas when, mercifully, the band struck up a lonesome Texas waltz. "Band's great tonight," we agreed, as I wrapped her up to the fiddle's lament. After a couple of hours and some dizzying triple spins, it was time to switch from Shiner Bock to tequila. I picked up several little shooters at the bar.

"Places like this won't be around forever," I said, setting down the shots, a napkin filled with lime wedges, and a salt shaker.

"Martini bars and Starbucks." Brenda downed a shot and bit a lime. I stared at my second shot. It looked like a hangover waiting to happen. "Come on, Peter. It's the Cotton-Eyed Joe."

It was nearly 2 a.m. by the time we made it back to the carriage house. First, we filled the claw-footed tub and soaked out the smoke, sweat and booze. Then I set a mirror on the floor and Brenda leaned against it while I attacked her with gentle, protracted, oral sex. Finally, she knocked herself out on top, coming with a long line of elegant curses and "Oh baby, oh baby" until Mr. Gonzo gave it up. Brenda's terrific on top. The camcorder caught every move.

Brenda's the one who introduced me to the camcorder, and together we've advanced to the highest level of filthy filmmaking. Sometimes I wonder if she's made videos with other men, then I force myself to stop thinking about that likelihood.

It was a sweet Sunday morning with no kids and Brenda tight against me, all smooth and dry and long shiny legs. We woke up making love, changed positions without a word, and Brenda called out "You dog, you dog, oh, I love you from the back!"

We slept in. At noon, I heard the damned helicopter, its guttural roar rattling the windows as it flew over on its way to the trauma center's landing pad. I sprang out of a warm bed.

"Ah shit! It's Life Flight! There's a case for tomorrow, guaranteed, and I go on call." Brenda, still caught in the afterglow, murmured something unintelligible. "Yep, it's coming from the Gulf, off the oilrigs. The hospital has contracts with the rigs, the prisons... what's next?"

"Maybe the patient will make it, Peter."

"Sure. Cardiac arrest, successful resuscitation. Not with my luck."

"People *do* survive, you know."

"I hate the helicopters. There's no way to tell if they're bringin' 'em in alive or dead. It's not like the EMS trucks."

"What? How can you tell when someone dies in an EMS truck?"

"They turn off their siren. You hear the siren coming up, then total silence. Cardiac standstill. It's rigor mortis time."

Monday, February 2

Autopsy Service had three cases lined up. One was off the rigs, a middle-aged oilman who slumped forward into his chicken-fried steak with an acute MI, a heart attack. There was a second heart attack patient who Marv Stepinksi worked over in the cardiac cath lab. The third case was a gunshot wound to the head, a homicide. I did that one first.

Ron Rocker, the best tech, was out on sick leave, so I got stuck with a trainee, a coltish, sweet college kid who probably didn't get into med school on her first try and figured this job would look good on her second application. That happens a lot.

The homicide victim was shot in a bar in San Leon, a shrimping town up the coast. She looked about the same age as the tech, who languished in the corner of the autopsy room, long-legged and sharp-hipped, with wisps of puffy reddish-blonde hair peeking out from her surgical cap, while I did the preliminary dictation.

"The body is that of a young Hispanic female measuring 165 centimeters in length. External examination reveals a single small gunshot wound to the center of the forehead."

The autopsy was progressing without a hitch until the tech peeled back the scalp, sawed around the skull with the bone saw, and pulled off the skullcap to remove the brain.

"It's like soup in here!" she cried. Blood and pulverized brain oozed onto the table. Just then, my damn pager went off.

"Let me get the sieve under this. I don't want to lose the bullet down the drain."

From the bits of brain we sieved a small caliber bullet, got it properly photographed, and logged in as evidence. Once the tech had secured the bullet in the morgue safe, I ungloved and stepped out to answer that page. Marv Stepinski had been trying to reach me from the Cardiac Cath Unit.

"I need to tell you about this MI patient before you start his autopsy, Peter."

"He must be the one on deck." I shuffled through a pile of paperwork. "Samuel Armstrong?"

"That's him. He's a 55-year-old black male sent down from Jasper with a massive MI. I tried to salvage some myocardium by reaming out his plugged-up right coronary artery. I passed my new rotary-cutting catheter, but when I started reaming out the plaque, the tip of the catheter broke off. It has to be retrieved, Peter, so the catheter company can check it for defects."

I insisted that we start on Marv's patient without a break for lunch. The tech drove me nuts, singing under her breath, "Call Roto-Rooter, that's the name, and away goes trouble down the drain." I discovered Marv's rotary-cutting tip as soon as we opened Mr. Armstrong's chest. The device had chewed right through the artery and caused a massive bleed. I secured the catheter tip in the morgue safe next to the bullet we'd sieved from the woman's brain. The chain of evidence would be unbroken on these two specimens.

"I've got your catheter tip down here," I told Marv, when I had him on the phone again. "The distal two centimeters sheared off and perforated that right coronary. It's the cause of death, I'm afraid, Marv." Silence from the cath lab. "Send a rep from the company down with the paperwork, and we'll release it."

"Thank you, Peter. I'll call them." Dr. Stepinski wanted to get off the line, but I had one more delicate question.

"Your NIH study section just met, didn't it, Marv?"

"Sure, sure, I know what you're asking, Peter. And the news is good. I was out of the room when your grant was discussed, of course, but your buddy Myerwitz from Southwestern was the primary reviewer."

"Myerwitz, the rotavirus man! He's a big wheel."

"That night, we talked in the bar. Myerwitz said the study section loved your proposal, especially the 'transdifferentiation' hypothesis. Should get a great priority score. The epidemic in India, or wherever it was, and that single case you reported gave it real momentum."

Marv had barely hung up and I was already dreaming of hiring two more postdocs, buying a new microscope, pipettors, a gel apparatus, more ducks. But there was one more MI case to do, and any official grant award was months away. I had resigned myself to my last Y-incision of the day, when the door to the autopsy room opened and Dr. J. stuck his head in. "I'm here to pick up January's evidence," he said. "Can you sign it over to me, Peter?"

I ungloved and walked with Dr. J. to the morgue safe, where we completed the forms for the knives, bullets, ice picks and other shrapnel we pathologists had picked out of bodies and stored in the safe in carefully labeled little bags.

"I pulled this one out of that woman this morning," I said. "The homicide in San Leon."

"It's going straight to ballistics. Amazing what a .22 can do."

I locked up the safe. We signed the last of the transfer papers.

"Dr. J., I wanted to thank you for your help with Jorge's immersion project."

"Thank Elena. She's done the work."

"You've both been so good to him, having him out to your place and all. At first, he was a bit of a loner."

"He's about the most distant fellow I know."

Dr. J. packed the evidence in a large brown paper bag and left. I regloved and started the last case. When I finally walked into the lab, well after 4 p.m., I had an uneasy feeling, like something was missing or something had gone wrong. Hard to figure what it was. Residual anxiety from a particularly bloody day, I guess.

Wednesday, February 11

Jorge flew back from Louisiana and cooped himself up in his apartment with his computer for 36 hours straight. The data he merged from the three coastal states was astounding. Jorge had uncovered a totally unknown but highly significant cause of accidental death. The data showed that in modern vehicles, escape was nearly impossible during a vehicular immersion.

We sat in my office and, in one long evening, wrote the first draft of a scientific paper. Jorge worked like one obsessed. He dwelt too much, perhaps, on the horror of it, ways to prevent it, and going after the big automakers. I reminded him that our job was to first provide scientific evidence of the problem's existence, then worry about solving it. Once we had a reasonable draft, Jorge took the paper to Dr. J. for his review.

Today, Jorge and I ran out our gels, squared things away, and hopped in the Datsun for the drive out Seawall Boulevard to the medical examiner's facility on the far west end of the Island. The facility is located in the old Public Health Hospital, an asbestos-filled structure from the 1920s that was shut down in 1970. When Dr. J. was appointed chief medical examiner, the county coughed up enough money to open the abandoned hospital's decrepit morgue, stick in a window air conditioner, and get the water running. For an office, they pulled a used trailer into the hospital garden. Originally intended as temporary quarters, that trailer's been Dr. J.'s office for nearly 30 years.

On Galveston Island, only a week or so during the year might be called "spring," and it arrives in mid-February. The weakened, sporadic northers are supplanted by a southerly flow off the Gulf, there's a brief downpour every morning, and our island turns deep green. It's steamy and tropical, like springtime in Bombay. Jorge and I were dripping with sweat by the time we walked from the crater-riddled hospital parking lot, through a morass of sticky burrs and overgrown oleanders, to the office of the county medical examiner.

Vibrant redbud trees flanked Dr. J.'s narrow, mold-covered trailer. We stepped through the door into a cool, tiny office area where Elena receives visitors, issues reports, and keeps the records. Like the cops, lawyers and media people who enter the M.E.'s trailer every day, we were greeted with Elena's breezy, old-world charm.

"Please come in from this awful heat, gentlemen." She extended her hand to each of us, her ochre-red hair long and radiant, her glossy nails the color of *cafe con leche*. "Summer is here, I fear." She handed us two small cotton towels to wipe the sweat from our faces. "After the morning rain, when the sun bursts through, it is so like Venezuela. Magnificent, in its own way. Please take a seat in Walter's office while I run across to the morgue. He's busy with a case, as always."

Elena led us to a small, windowless office. She pulled out two folding metal chairs with "Felton's Funeral Parlor" painted on the back. Jorge's draft sat atop a narrow desk littered with forensic journals. The wood-paneled walls were covered with Dr. J.'s hunting trophies, including Texas deer of varying size, a Louisiana javelina, a Rocky Mountain sheep, and two more exotic prizes—a sable antelope and an impala buck.

As we waited, I was again struck by how Jorge's Sundays at the Jawicki's beach house had changed him. He'd taken to wearing sporty shirts with a collar, and looked older, even sophisticated, with his dense little beard. Perhaps his travels along the Gulf Coast helped, too.

The trailer door swung open and Dr. J. stomped into the outer office with Elena on his tail.

"I told you before, Walter. Why must you always...?" The flimsy door slammed with a metallic ring. Dr. J. stepped into his office.

"Humph!" Dressed in worn cotton scrubs, he slung himself into his desk chair directly beneath the impala head. "Sorry, gentlemen, I was caught up. Good to see you two." He picked up Jorge's draft. "You've put together a very convincing paper, gentlemen."

"Thanks to your friends in Louisiana and Florida, Dr. J.," Jorge said.

"I'm afraid my only reservation is where you're submitting it. Isn't the *Journal of the American Medical Association* aiming a bit high?"

"*JAMA* will give us tremendous exposure," I said, brightly. "The press, the CDC, even the auto manufacturers will take notice if we publish there."

"Do we really want that? The exposure? And what about this statistical analysis, Jorge? I'm no expert, but it looks like Greek to me. Is it right?"

"Absolutely," Jorge replied. "That Kappa statistic is the most powerful analytic tool, much better than a Schefe test, or Borel's lemma. I ran my analysis by the top guys at Los Alamos, the Division of Experimental Informatics, my father's old division." Jorge gazed up at a large, gray deer head. His voice became soft and far-away. "Poppa was there for 20 years. They gave him a gold watch. He worked until the day he was... committed."

I cleared my throat and took a new tack, one that Jorge, on the ride out, had insisted I pursue. "This is an important paper, Dr. J.," I said, "but there's got to be more we can do."

"These slimy auto manufacturers," Jorge chimed in, "can make a safer vehicle. They need to put their best engineers on it."

The medical examiner squirmed in his seat, a tinge of sarcasm in his voice. "I'm sure this is hot science, gentlemen. Perhaps we should publish in an engineering journal."

"No, we need to go right to the industry with this proof," Jorge said, with his newfound maturity and that old rebel swagger. "The public today is extremely safety-conscious. Wrap-around air bags, advanced crash testing. The CDC is pushing for a 'black box' in cars, like in aircraft. My estimate is that we could save 700 lives each year, Dr. Jawicki."

"You make that point well in your paper, Jorge, but in the real world, 700 deaths is nothing. You boys have been locked in your lab too long. I mean, butting heads with the government? The auto industry?"

This recalcitrance was not typical of Dr. J. It made me think back a few years, to when Dr. J. stepped up to take Golden Petrochemical to task for a rash of malignant brain tumors occurring in the neighborhoods adjacent to Golden's refineries. From his many autopsies, Dr. J. was the first to notice this trend, but the editor of the *Island Daily*, a diehard supporter of the local polluters, eviscerated Dr. J. over the issue on the editorial page. The press almost had Dr. J.'s job, until the national networks caught on. Once the Golden brain tumors were covered on 20/20, the good old boys at the *Island Daily* looked pretty stupid.

"We have to do *something*!" Jorge said, his face reddening. "To do *nothing*, knowing what our data show? How these people struggle? How they're trapped? We've got to do more than publish data in a medical journal. If we don't, it's like we're *responsible* for all those deaths, don't you see?"

"With your experience, Dr. J.," I said, "we thought...."

Dr. J. held up a hand and sighed. "I suppose there's one possibility. Peyton Sweeney, state senator from Laredo. Peyton and I played basketball together at UT. Of course, the Texas legislature is a bunch of fist-fighting good old boys, but I'll give him a call."

"We've got to go to the press, too," Jorge said.

"Not me!" Dr. J. exclaimed. "Talk to them if you want, you two, but leave me out."

"That state senator's a good thought, Dr. Jawicki," I said. "Any other ideas?"

Dr. J. sat back and looked at me. "*You* must know someone, Peter."

I pondered that for a moment. "You're right," I said. "It's been a long time, but I happen to know an epidemiologist at the CDC. We go way back, and I'll be in Atlanta for the Vaccine Institute's meeting this weekend. I could look her up."

"I'll start on the local paper," Jorge volunteered. "I know some of the guys who hang around the bar at the Press Club. I'll get with one of them."

I was surprised by this. The Press Club's a dumpy little corner bar near Jorge's apartment, where drunken journalists argue over beers, and couples smooch in the worn red leather booths in the back room.

"You sure get around on this godforsaken island," Dr. J. said, with a chuckle.

❋ ❋ ❋

The traffic was creeping down Seawall Boulevard. The sea breeze had died, and the same Gulf of Mexico that took 6000 souls on a single, long night in the year 1900 was now as flat as a pond. Surfers in wet suits lay paralyzed on the concrete benches, like stunned seals, gazing at the water's platinum surface. I was thinking about Jorge and what he'd said about his father. Jorge stared at the Gulf, not saying a word.

"So your father was in the Los Alamos lab. Was he there long?"

"He's still in New Mexico, in a government facility for schizophrenics. He'll never get out."

"Sorry to hear that."

"None of the medications worked."

A junker van with a Mexican plate pulled in front of the Datsun and stopped dead. Jorge took his eyes off the water. He had a peculiar, distant look on his face, and a faint smile. "Dr. J.'s setup isn't much, is it?" he said.

"It's amazing," I laughed. "Such a half-assed facility."

"He sure is lucky to have Elena, though."

Wednesday, February 18

Since defending her doctorate in epidemiology at Rutgers, Dr. Laura Sacchi has made her entire career at the CDC in Atlanta. She's a brilliant woman, though she's had her dumb moments, like when she got involved with me 10 years ago.

Laura and I met at a scientific meeting in the most romantic city, San Francisco, at a time when my marriage was less than romantic and heading south. I was standing in line at the hotel store to buy the toothpaste I'd forgotten to pack. She was buying toothpaste, too. She smiled, we joked, and by dawn the next morning, I was seriously considering leaving my wife, abandoning my work in New Mexico, and moving to Atlanta.

Laura and I met dozens of times during the next two years, under the pretext of scientific meetings, invited lectures and consultations. Then I moved to the Island, things changed, and I found myself calling her one downpour-rainy night to tell her we had to put our thing on hold.

"I thought…," she'd said with a drizzle of tears in her voice, "…someday we'd be together, Pete."

"It's not going to work, Laura. This island isn't for you. You need Atlanta, you need the CDC, for your work, for…."

"And you need to work on your marriage."

"I need some time."

I ended up with plenty of time. My wife and I worked on our marriage until it became obvious the work was wasted, and then she left me to go live in the next block with a welder who did sculpture in steel. Now, eight years later, with a divorce in the works and Brenda in the carriage house, I found myself relentlessly rewinding old clips of Laura Sacchi and our blistering love affair.

I knew I was wrong to think of Laura, at least in that way. But I had to contact her. I had to. It was about Jorge's immersion study. It was business. With my heart thrashing in my chest, I dialed Dr. Sacchi's CDC office.

"Hey, Laura, it's Pete Mallow."

"Pete! Damn! I thought I'd never hear from you again," she said, with a single grace note of anger in her voice.

"I need to talk to you about something important."

"Sure, Pete. Fire away."

"It might be better if I explained this in person, Laura. I'll be in Atlanta for the vaccine meetings. Remember those? I fly in Saturday."

Laura volunteered to pick me up at the airport. She'd hardly aged, maybe a few smile-lines here and there, but she was the kind of woman who matures beautifully, without resorting to liposuction or Botox. We drove to a little mid-town bar, our favorite spot from years ago. The bar was unchanged and so was Laura, all professional and button-down in a dark suit. There's something about a woman in a nicely tailored suit, showing a little well-turned leg. A fanatical softball player, Laura had always had perfect legs, and as she hitched herself high on a barstool, they looked as good as ever.

Laura's a high-level government employee, an extraordinary statistician, and a serious federal bureaucrat, but she was never afraid to toss down a few drinks and have a good time. A couple of bourbons later, we were laughing over the foolish past we'd shared. I went on and on about the great science coming out of my lab and how terrific my lab crew was. I didn't bring up Jorge's immersion data, and Laura didn't ask the real reason I'd come to be with her.

We had a leisurely dinner at Miss Katy's Tea Room, where the fried chicken is as good as it gets in the old South. Laura drove around Atlanta, pointed out the changes in the town, and we ended up at Blind Willie's Blue Note, sucking down more bourbon. The dark interstices of Blind Willie's rattled with Delta-style steel guitar and standup bass. Through the Saturday night haze, I felt a longing rekindle from ashes gone cold years before. I couldn't keep my eyes off Laura's dark-tinted, glossy lips as she flashed them from a sullen pout to a broad, willing grin—a grin that ended with the inevitable question.

"Do you have someone now, Pete?"

"No," I lied, bald-faced, the bourbon talking. Then, for once, I thought twice and told her, "Yes, I'm living with someone."

"That's not like you, Pete. Whose idea was that?"

"Hers. My divorce is in the works."

"You never called me, Pete."

"Are you seeing someone?"

"I tried twice."

"I need your help, Laura. It started with an autopsy I did, and my goofy student. The county medical examiner's involved, too."

"So it's business."

"That's what I thought, until I heard your voice." I leaned toward her and lightly kissed some of the gloss off her lips. "Want to dance? For old time's sake?" We slow danced.

It was a night like the old nights, full of laughs, but with a bluesy bass line running through it. I told her about Trey Findley and Bodekker Road. I recited by heart Jorge's data on Gulf Coast immersions, his statistical extrapolation, and the details of the paper we'd submitted to *JAMA*.

"It sounds like a serious public safety issue, Pete. One that's been overlooked." Laura still had her amazing ability to think clearly after a bucket of bourbon. "But you and this student will never convince the auto manufacturers to alter their vehicles."

"How does the CDC do it? I mean, what would be *your* next step, Laura?"

"The Automobile Manufacturers' Safety Board. It's a small group of the industry's top engineers, risk managers, and chief officers. Their highest-level safety honchos. They meet regularly in D.C. to address concerns on safety and keep their asses out of trouble."

"Sounds perfect."

"CDC has a Vehicular Division that takes problems to the industry through this Safety Board. But our division has to be convinced of a serious public-safety issue before it acts."

"How long will it take us to convince your guys?"

"You know how we are at the CDC. We always do our own studies and generate our own data. Once your paper is published in *JAMA*, we'd definitely notice, but we'd want to complete a nationwide study of our own. You're looking at a couple of years before CDC collects the data, then another year to pressure the Safety Board."

"Three years is like ... more than 2,000 vehicular-immersion deaths. Can't we go directly to this board, Laura? Before the CDC gets involved?"

"Unofficially? Sure. But they won't be obligated to do a thing. This board is executive-level, corporate assholes. They're powerful, and they're in it for the bucks."

We were drunk, and it seemed like only yesterday we'd spent a night like this, talking about things important to us. Before I knew what hit me, we had climbed the stairs to Laura's airy fourth floor apartment in midtown, and she was there for me, smooth and warm in the cool Georgia night. I forced myself to think what was important, back on the Island.

"I should go."

"Then go. I insist."

I woke in my hotel room to the vile taste of stale sour mash. It was nearly noon. Laura had left a message to join her at her place for brunch. When I arrived, she had a bottle of Moet & Chandon iced down, like the old Sunday afternoons of our affair. She wore gray, paint-splattered sweatpants and had thrown on a frayed, long-sleeved men's dress shirt. Standing in front of her stove, she rolled up her sleeves and cooked me pasta *alla carbonera*.

"Your mother's recipe," I said, sedated by the aroma of frying bacon.

As I watched Laura drain the pasta, my thoughts turned to Galveston. For sure Brenda realized what a screw-up she was living with, didn't she?

"Will you be hanging around, Pete? It's a Sunday afternoon."

I told myself I was going to make it this time, wasn't I? Do the right thing. Do the right thing. Of course, I've promised myself that many times before, and gone back on it.

"I have meetings today," I said, "and tomorrow. It's been wonderful seeing you again, Laura."

"It has, and I'm happy for you, Pete. Still, I wonder why there was never an 'us,' you know?" The anger I'd heard over the phone a few days earlier crept back into her voice. "We were so perfect together. Why didn't it last?"

"I can't tell you."

"The trouble, Peter Mallow, is that you're fine in your lab, but when it comes to relationships, you lose your train of thought too easily."

My measure had been taken, and it came up short. How could I blame her? She was right about Pete Mallow. Where women were concerned, my life was one long line of piss-poor decisions punctuated by unadulterated screw-ups. Always plenty of foreplay, but never much forethought.

"Laura, this is going nowhere. Look. All I know is that you were once a big part of my life, the biggest part, the best part. But things change."

"Yes, and today you happen to be in Atlanta on a mission, and damn it, Pete Mallow," she laughed, "I'll help you wacko academics on this one. I will. I can't help myself."

After the pasta, I told Laura I was heading back to my hotel room.

"Oh Pete, you're bad, but it's a sweet bad," she said at the door. "I'll miss the old Pete."

I'll admit, it took everything I had to keep from tasting the dark gloss one last time. Instead, I held her tight and she squeezed back, cheek to cheek, my one-time love, a friend for life.

Jorge faxed Laura the entire study as soon as I got back in the lab. That afternoon, Laura called to tell me she'd succeeded in setting up a meeting with the Automobile Manufacturers' Safety Board for the first week of March, right after Galveston's Mardi Gras celebration, which was perfect timing. The Mardi Gras tourist traffic would've made getting off the Island a complete nightmare. After Mardi Gras, Jorge and I would fly to D.C. and meet with the honchos of the auto industry.

Laura cautioned me that the board had scheduled exactly 30 minutes for us to present our case. She wasn't optimistic.

Fat Tuesday, February 24
(Mardi Gras Note)

Progress was roaring ahead in the lab, and Jorge was my golden boy, until Mardi Gras came along. What a fiasco.

They've celebrated Mardi Gras on Galveston Island since before the Civil War, but when the tourism promoters took over a few years back, the party got crazy. Nowadays, it's non-stop parades, bead-frenzy, nudity and insanity for the whole week before Fat Tuesday.

As Mardi Gras builds to a crescendo, everyone at the university takes an unofficial holiday, and the campus shuts down. On the Saturday morning of the big weekend before Fat Tuesday, our lab was the only one at work, I'm sure. Mardi Gras was in the air, parades lumbered through the neighborhoods, traffic backed up on the causeway, Galveston Island hunkered down six inches into the Gulf from the weight of the tourists, and Jorge got antsy.

"I'm downtown this afternoon," he said, knocking back a swig of his Diet Sprite.

"I'll go along," I said.

During Mardi Gras, the Galveston City Council closes the streets of downtown to traffic, creating an "entertainment district." Thus, the taxpayers' public thoroughfares are converted into one big mob scene. As we approached the district, Jorge eyed a herd of Harley-Davidsons lined up at the east gate like horses hitched in front of the swinging doors of an old timey saloon.

"Billy Ray's in there somewhere," Jorge said.

"Along with 50,000 other people."

We paid our way in and pushed through the crowds, startled by the sight of sweaty young coeds exposing their breasts for cheap plastic beads. On one corner, a juggler was doing exceptional work with running chainsaws. A rotund drag queen flanked by his/her entourage of transvestites drifted by in a billow of gossamer boas. Then, the crowd parted for the ultimate statement of frivolity—The Noodle Man—a buff stud, naked, shaven smooth, and entirely pasted over with dried pasta. "Wow," Jorge said.

"This crowd crunch is getting to me," I said. "Let's get inside. The Café Torrifique's always good."

A class act, the Café Torrifique is defined by 16-foot ceilings, poor lighting, cobwebs, soft classical music, and flaky brick walls hung with real oil paintings. The bar at the Torrifique, original to the mid-1800s building, is a broad, mahogany question mark. The soaring back-bar is flanked by intricate pelicans of age-darkened oak. A carved Texas longhorn scowls down at patrons. We were about to grab a spot when Jorge recognized a distinctive leather vest slumped over, further down the question mark.

"Hey, Wayne, how's it goin'?" Jorge said. "You see that noodle guy?"

Wayne lifted his head and focused. "Huh?" Blue-black prison tattoos peppered Wayne's hands, forearms and neck. His club's twin eagles stood colorful and tall on his upper arm. At the edge of his left eye was a single black teardrop. "Hey. It's you. Having a good Mardi Gras, man?" He and Jorge exchanged a slow-mo high five and bumped knuckles.

"Is Billy Ray around?" Jorge asked.

"He's taking a leak. Hey, come on, y'all! Have one on me." Wayne downed the shot that sat in front of him and motioned to the barman with the empty glass. The barman carded Jorge, who produced a slick, undoubtedly faked, Texas driver's license. All UT students had one. The bartender poured a round and brought fresh lime wedges.

Billy Ray stumbled back from the men's room to find two shots of tequila waiting for him. After greeting us, he tossed down both, pitched forward over the bar, glared at Jorge and me and bellowed, "Come on, boys. Drink up!"

"Why don't you sit this one out," I suggested to Jorge.

"No way!" Billy Ray roared, wrapping a beefy arm around each of us. "Jorge's my man! This boy can hang with the best of 'em."

Which is how Jorge and I came to drink shots of tequila at the Café Torrifique.

Billy Ray bought round two, and the barroom etiquette acquired in my youth at The Salty Dog came rushing back. It was my turn to buy. After we downed my purchase, the bartender poured another, on him. My father's words "It's good for business" ran through my head, along with the white bolts of tequila.

The next time my turn came around, all inhibitions had vanished. I kicked it up to Herradura Gold, top shelf. The Gold rolled round, and my mind wandered as Jorge, Wayne, and Billy Ray yakked about Harleys, antique black-powder rifles, and other manly topics. The limes and the salt-shaker were passed. At one point, a less gentle Jorge began to bluster, "Galaxies! Superclusters! Human life is inconsequential!"

"Hey y'all!" Wayne blurted, oblivious to the existential monologue. "Ever try mescal?"

With that, we four tequila drunks were back in the street in search of an illegal bottle of mescal stashed in the saddlebag of Wayne's antique Harley. Luckily for me, I got pressed into a crowd crunch and never sampled the mescal. Unlucky for Jorge, I was alone.

I zigzagged through the entertainment district and, by Brownian motion, found an exit, but not the herd of motorcycles. I weaved toward my neighborhood, where I was intercepted by a passing float topped with Kings in full regalia and Queens with purple-green-and-gold cellophane hair. They were energetically lobbing beads into the air. Captivated by the plastic sparkle, I took a leap, caught my heel on the roots of an old oak, barked my shin on the curb, and whacked my cheek on a parking meter.

Flat on my back in the scrofulous grass, my head abuzz, the odd thought occurred to me that I might have landed on a dog turd. They are exceptionally common in this neighborhood. After checking for signs of excrement, I heard the distinctive click-clack of a skateboard on a sidewalk. Travis. I was home safe.

"Watch me bust this trick, Dad!" Travis said as I stumbled toward him. "First I ollie-up onto the curb." He flipped the board around. "Then the Vertical Indy...." He had it on edge. "And I go to a Vertical Roast Beef."

"Terr-rrific, son! Terr-rrific tr-rrick."

The skateboard lay on the sidewalk, trucks up, wheels spinning. He flipped it over with a kick, jumped on, scowled, and zipped away. I staggered up the front steps and down the hallway to the kitchen. Brenda was standing over the stove, stirring.

"What smells?" I asked.

"You do. You're drunk."

"It's Mardi Gras!"

"I see that by the beads, Peter."

I leaned over a blackened cast-iron Dutch oven with "Wallennius Shipping Ltd.," Mr. Kreuger's previous employer, painted in red on its side. Inadvertently, I burped. When I looked closer, my stomach lurched.

"What's this?"

"A whole grain thing."

Brenda, who stays as thin as a pencil, makes "whole grain things" when she's "cooking healthy."

"You should change those clothes, Peter, and eat something. Oh, my. Your eyes look awful. Is that blood on your cheek?"

I stared into a malodorous pot full of yellowish gruel with gritty-looking specks.

"What's this again?"

"Bulgur and buckwheat groats. You'd better have a bowl, Peter."

Instantly sober, I jogged to the bathroom to vomit large volumes of lime-colored liquid that tasted of salt.

The last person in the world I wanted to hear from the next morning was Sergeant Juan Martinez, the motorcycle patrolman who pulled Trey Findley out of his car on Bodekker Road. My hangover was only a three on a scale of ten, thanks to upchucking the Café Torrifique tequila, and 14 hours in bed. Brenda was mercifully handing me a cup of coffee with gobs of sugar when the phone rang. It was 8 a.m.

"We have a fellow here ... Jorge Acosta? He claims he's a student of yours," Martinez said.

"Is he in trouble?"

"Big time. He used his one call to phone a lawyer in El Paso, but he mentioned your name, so I thought I'd give you a ring, Doctor Mallow."

"I appreciate that, Sergeant. What's this about?"

"Altercation out on 13-mile Road. The Cabana Club." I envisioned a falling-down cantina full of rednecks. "I got called at 3 a.m. for a fistfight, maybe six or seven involved. Your boy was one of 'em."

"Were they bikers?"

"Mostly. Fight broke out over a woman. Bartender claimed a gun was drawn, but no weapon at the scene. Your boy got belligerent, worse than the others. He really your student?"

"He's a brilliant student, Sergeant. What's the charge?"

"Drunk and disorderly, resisting arrest, interference with an officer during discharge of his duty. Without the firearm, the judge might drop the resisting and interference charges. Listen, Doc, I'll go easy on him in front of the judge, but you need to take control of this boy."

A pang of guilt seared my chest as I envisioned Jorge, sitting in a jail cell.

I took the truck downtown. It was my first time inside the city jail, which is on the first floor of the courthouse, one of the more modern buildings in town, circa 1960s. It looked like an egg carton stood on end, but the building had deteriorated rapidly enough to match the rest of the city. Its pale yellow facade was covered with black mold. Inside, the doors, floors, and elevators were polished smooth and worn to their breaking point from the friction of detainees, lawyers, judges, lovers, relatives and friends.

To make bail for the freshly-incarcerated, one enters the courthouse by the side door, the front door being reserved for dressier occasions such as divorces and moving traffic violations. Filthy, beer-soaked Mardi Gras celebrants lined the benches along the walls in the waiting area. The place smelled like what a Depression-era railroad depot must've smelled like. The old man at the desk was straight out of the Great Depression, too.

"I'm here for Jorge Acosta. What's his bail?"

"Acosta... Acosta...." The geezer was running down a long list. "Eight hundred dollars. Cash."

It was early on a Sunday morning. I had twenty bucks in my pocket. No wonder the courthouse was surrounded by bail bond storefronts.

As I turned toward the door, a familiar-looking, wispy blonde on a bench in the corner caught my eye. I loitered for a moment until I confirmed the eagle tattoo on her shoulder. It was the blonde eating oysters and drinking martinis at the Lions' party, Billy Ray's woman. She was leaning forward with her head in her hands.

"How ya doing?" I asked.

"Shitty," she said, glancing up. "Three hundred and 80 bucks worth of shitty, and I'm 200 short. I know you?"

"That Christmas party. We were eating oysters."

"Oh, yeah, the doctor. You got 200 bucks I can borrow?"

"Nope. Sorry."

"This is so shitty, man. A lousy 200 and Billy Ray, Samuel, and Jim Bob are all on the inside. I can't find nobody with no money."

"Did you call someone?"

"Wayne's sweetie, but if she got hold of 200 dollars, it'd go right up her nose."

I walked across the street to Black's Smokehouse and Bail Bonds. The place was shut tight. I circled the building to the alley entrance and found a bell to ring. Mr. Black opened the door a crack. When he saw that I was an unarmed white male, he let me in. He had on pajamas and beat up, backless, red-velvet slippers that made it look like he was wearing a pair of large rats with a bad case of the mange on his feet.

"Need bail, I suppose," he said.

"I need eight hundred." I thought again and said, "Make it an even thousand."

After signing the necessary payback promises, I had the big bucks tucked in an envelope and was on my way back to the jail. I handed $800 to the old guy at the desk. "When's he see the judge?" I asked.

"Acosta... Acosta...." Pops was back at his long list. "Set for tomorrow at 8 a.m. Be a few minutes before he's down." I walked over to the corner and sat down on the bench next to Billy Ray's woman to wait.

"Anybody bring you bail?" I asked.

"No way."

"Here," I said, reaching into my pocket for the last two hundreds.

"Kick-ass!" she exclaimed, and gave me the sweetest smile. "Thanks, Doc."

She paid Pops Billy Ray's bail, and soon a hulking shadow loomed on the other side of the barred gate. Keys clanked and out stepped the hard-riding street-version of Billy Ray, shirtless. His wide open black leather vest was booze-soaked and grimy. His Santa Claus beard was a wild bush with twigs and bits of road debris scattered in it. His shoulders were peeled and burned and re-peeled by the Texas sun, his eyes looked like they'd been etched by a mad cartographer, and he exuded a sour smell somewhere between stale beer and the acrid stench of horse urine. It reminded me of how our street smells after a horse-drawn carriage full of drunken tourists passes by.

"Hey," he said, a stunned look on his face.

"I'm... I'm Mallow." I jumped up from the bench and reached for his hand, which was the color of asphalt. "Jorge's my student."

"Sure. Jorge. Good kid."

"I'm sorry I got separated from you guys. That mescal must've been mean stuff."

"Nah, it was the worm," he said over his shoulder as he slumped out the door with his woman, her arms akimbo, yakking into his face.

I stared at the barred gate for a few minutes. More people who looked like hell came out and were taken away by people who looked like hell, and I thought, hey, I probably look like hell, too. Then I saw Jorge's sleepy face peering through the bars. His cargo pants smelled nasty and something dark was all over the front of them. His UTEP cap was on backward. An irregular, dusky bruise graced his left cheek.

"Jorge, what happened? Jesus! Are you all right? What was this fight about?"

"I don't remember. I'm tired, can I go to sleep?"

I maneuvered him into the Datsun and took him to the house. When I pulled in front, Jorge was out cold against the truck door. Brenda helped me half-drag, half-carry him upstairs. We pulled off his nasty pants and dumped him into Chad's bed. He wasn't responsive, except to mumble something about a "worm."

"What's he talking about?" Brenda asked. She went to the kitchen, opened a large can of chicken broth, pulled some bottles out of the cupboard, and mixed up something to "rehydrate the poor boy." Two hours later, my ace student was sitting up in bed looking chagrined, while Brenda spoon-fed him more of her hot, soy-sauce-colored solution.

"What went down out there?" I asked.

"We got drunk and rode out to the west end of the Island. There was a fight."

"About what?" He went quiet. The soup seemed to do him some good. Color came back into his face. Brenda put an ice pack on his cheek. "Come on, Jorge. You were there, weren't you?"

"Some scumbag was talking trash about Dr. J. and Elena, and how she went with other men. That's all."

Brenda looked up from spooning soup into Jorge. "Enough with the interrogation, Peter," she said. "I'll draw Jorge a hot bath. He needs to steam the toxins out of his pores."

Jorge spent the night. Everyone was up by 6 a.m. on Monday morning, even Chad, who had rolled his sleeping bag out in the dining room. Jorge wasn't too perky, but he assured me that his lawyer, a family friend, was flying in from El Paso. When we arrived at the courtroom of County Judge Jimmy Youngblood, there outside the courtroom door was a tall, dark-suited Hispanic lawyer who greeted Jorge *en español* and quickly reviewed the case for us. Judge Jimmy Youngblood was a personal acquaintance, he said, and they'd already had a brief, pretrial discussion over coffee. He knew the details of the bar fight, even the gun slinging. None of it seemed to faze him.

The courtroom smelled like dirty laundry. We sat in the front row and watched Judge Youngblood dispense with half a dozen drunk-and-disorderly cases. When Jorge's name was called, his man from El Paso jumped up.

"Your honor, I move for a continuance."

"Approach the bench," said the judge, who looked to be 80 and had tobacco stains all over his mustache. "You, too, Sergeant Martinez." The three chatted in hushed tones, then Judge Youngblood banged his gavel and declared, "Case dismissed. A fine of $600 is assessed on the obstruction charge. Pay the cashier on the way out."

I went down the hall to collect the $200 the court owed me on the $800 bail I posted. By the time I returned from the cashier's window, Jorge's lawyer had vanished, Martinez was back in the courtroom approaching the bench again, and Jorge was getting into the elevator.

"So much for the inner workings of the law," I muttered, running to catch up.

Fat Tuesday came at last. Jorge never showed in the lab that morning, but he called to assure me his partying days were over, and he was spending the day at Dr. J.'s beach house. Galveston Island was packed with idiot tourists scrambling for beads, and Fat Tuesday parades chugged down Seawall Boulevard and through the neighborhoods in their fullest, jury-rigged splendor. Brenda and I took the afternoon off, like the rest of the university. I passed by the bank for a packet of money, then to Black's to buy barbecue and pay the bond. Black's was jammed, and I stood in a long, snaking line to pick up a couple of sandwiches. Mr. Black was quite discreet when I paid my bill, which came to just over $1,100, including the barbecue.

Brenda and I settled into the weathered cane chairs on the upstairs porch, and polished off two of Mr. Black's finest. I brought my notebook home from the office, hoping to finish this Mardi Gras entry.

"What's that you're writing?" Brenda asked.

"A sort of general lab notebook. It's not science. What are you working on?"

"Notes for tomorrows lecture on 'Holism and the Grief Response.'"

"That was your dissertation topic, wasn't it?"

Brenda ignored me. I settled back in my chair amid the clatter of the palms and the laugh of the gulls overhead. Horse-drawn carriages loaded with tourists drifted slowly down the street, clipitty clop, clipitty clop. I was dozing off when a deep, resonant thunder breached our lovely seclusion. It was far off, like distant canon, but grew to a ground-shaking rumble as it approached. Brenda looked up from her lecture notes. The low, throaty thunder idled to a stop in front of the house.

"Harleys," I said.

"Why are they stopping here?"

"One of 'em owes me money."

"Oh?"

Over the porch rail, we watched a dozen bikes shut down.

"They're Jorge's friends," I explained under my breath. "The big one is Billy Ray, the leader. I helped with his bail." Billy Ray came up the walk while the others lounged on their bikes, watching the paint peel off my house.

I ran downstairs before Billy Ray could try the doorbell, which doesn't work. "Hey, Doc." His face brightened. "My lady was right about the address."

We stepped into the front parlor, where Brenda, so as not to interfere with shooting baskets, had set up her dining room table, a family heirloom made of cherry.

"Have a seat," I said, pulling out two matching cherry chairs. When Billy Ray sat down, the chair gave a creak and disappeared under him. He looked cleaned up, but still in Mardi Gras mode. I caught a whiff of that tanning chemical smell from his leathers. He leaned his arms on the table, smiled, and shook his head.

"About what happened to Jorge? I'm real sorry."

"It was all my fault, Billy Ray. I don't think he drinks much."

"Hell, it wasn't the booze. I told you that at the jail. It was the worm at the bottom. Him and Wayne split it. That sucker's full of peyote." Billy Ray shifted his weight. "Why I come by, Doc, was so you could get this back to Jorge." He reached into his pocket, pulled out a pistol, and laid it on the table. "It's his piece."

"Jesus," I murmured. My heart began to hammer.

It was a snub-nosed, hard-angled thing, smelling of oil and burnt powder, steely-blue and all business. "BERGMANN" was impressed at an angle across the grip, and along the side of the barrel it said, "Taschen Model."

"It's a Bergmann, six millimeter," Billy Ray said. "I figured you could get it to back him. Might be better that way."

"What went down out there, Billy Ray?"

"I ain't sure. All I know is I had to get Wayne's ass out of there. Wayne just got sprung from Huntsville. He done 10 years for bashing in a man's head with an aluminum baseball bat. Caught this dude in his trailer with his wife. Hell, Wayne ain't even supposed to be *near* a bar. Parole officers don't go for that shit. So once I got the pistol away from Jorge, I slipped it to Wayne. He split, and we got the fight broke up just as Johnny Law showed."

My heart had slowed from its uncontrolled tachycardia. Billy Ray picked up the pistol and plunked it into my hand. I was surprised at how heavy it felt.

"Don't worry, Doc," Billy Ray said, getting up. "I unloaded it. But you have a talk with Jorge. He's a good boy, just a little weird. And here's what I owe you," he said, pulling two grimy hundreds out of his pocket. "My woman really appreciated that. I gotta go."

On the front porch, I reached out to grab Billy Ray's big, rough hand, and he pulled me to him, forearm to forearm.

"Those tattoos," I said. "The other day when I met Wayne, I could tell right away."

"We all got 'em." Billy Ray looked out at his assembly of men. "That's why we're the Armed Eagles. One reason, anyhow."

"Nice tats."

Billy Ray looked me in the eye, our arms still locked together. "Anytime you need some help, for Jorge, for yourself, or anything, just let me know, Doc."

"I appreciate that, Billy Ray."

At dusk, I stuck the Bergmann in a paper bag and rode my bike to Jorge's apartment. It's in an old house like mine, but chopped up by a sleazy landlord. Jorge's apartment, on the second floor, has outside stairs that are partially buried under a sprawling fig tree. Fermenting figs squished underfoot. Jorge took his time coming to the door. He gave me a dazed look, then let me in.

The living room was bare except for a long worktable where he had his shiny high-end Mac computer. Physics, math and molecular biology texts were scattered around, and a couple of notebooks he'd been scribbling in. A poster from a string-theory conference in New Mexico and two neatly typed notes were thumb-tacked above the computer.

The adjoining kitchen was bare; the only signs of life were a ghostly array of Diet Sprite bottles on the kitchen counter, a lab scale, and a large, brown, chemical jar.

"It's your first time in my place, isn't it, Doctor Mallow?"

"This isn't a social call, Jorge." I pulled the gun out of the bag and put it on the table. "Billy Ray left this with me."

"The Bergmann!"

"What the hell are you doing with this thing, Jorge?"

"This is Texas, Doctor Mallow. I have a permit, and I can carry."

"Not in barrooms, you can't."

"Um… you're right. Courthouses, bars, there's still a few places where concealed weapons aren't allowed."

"Take this thing and lock it up, would you, please?"

Jorge hefted the pistol comfortably in his hand and carried it to the bedroom. He rummaged around in there, opening and closing drawers. I took the opportunity to read the notes on the wall above the computer. They were on yellowed, oil-stained three-by-five cards. One was on routine computer maintenance, the other was about the pistol, cleaning instructions, and this:

AMMO: RANGE USE: 6.35MM WAD CUTTERS
HOME USE: 6.30MM MAG HOLLOWPOINTS

Home use? Hollowpoints? That's a dum-dum bullet, I thought. *The one that inflicts a gaping wound.*

As Jorge strode in from the bedroom, it dawned on me how easily he might conceal the Bergmann in his baggy pants pocket. A nasty taste blossomed at the back of my mouth. The wood floor gave off the sour smell of ground-in, rotted figs.

"You do much cooking here, Jorge?"

I stepped into the kitchen. The diet Sprite bottles lining the kitchen counter were empty. The end bottle had a funnel stuck in it. The big brown chemical jar on the counter was labeled "sodium bicarbonate."

Jorge came up behind me and saw me reading the label.

"I drink that stuff to clean out my system, Doctor Mallow."

I opened the refrigerator. Its insides were coated with yellowish mold. I passed by the bathroom and saw serpentine knots of red rubber hosing draped over the shower rod. Stainless clamps, and a half-dozen plastic enema tips lay on the bathtub's edge. *Colonics*, I thought.

"You're a healthy young man," I told him. "All you really need is a decent diet."

What was wrong with this kid? A weird eating disorder? Loose screws in an otherwise exceptional set of cerebral hemispheres?

"I like shrimp the way Elena does them. *Albondigas de Camarones Venezuelanas*," he said, dreamily, and with a South American sound to his Spanish.

"Another thing," I said, suddenly exhausted. "We've got to practice our presentation on the vehicle project. We're off to D.C. next Sunday, remember."

"We can go over it right now. All the data's on the Mac."

"Tomorrow," I told him. "Tomorrow's soon enough. It's been a hectic Mardi Gras."

Tuesday, March 3
(Entry on Trip to D.C.)

For the rest of the week, Jorge jabbered nonstop about our trip to D.C., and how we'd "get those guys." His speech accelerated and saliva pooled at the edges of his mouth. I considered going it alone. I had to remind myself that Jorge was the driving force behind this project. He'd done the legwork, the data analysis, and he was first author on the paper. It was his study.

I felt better about taking Jorge after we'd practiced our formal presentation a few times. When he got himself under control, the kid had a smooth, mature delivery. At moments, I saw a spellbinder of a lecturer, a budding scientist, a future professor. His enthusiasm and child-like excitement also reminded me of a younger Pete Mallow, and that made me proud.

Laura Sacchi had set our appointment with the Automotive Manufacturers' Safety Board for 10 a.m. Monday. We flew in early Sunday afternoon to see a little of the city before they shut it down and left it to the homeless for the night.

The members of the Automotive Safety Board fly every Monday into D.C. to meet at the downtown Hyatt, an upscale setting perfect for the deliberations of high rollers. I slept fitfully that night, despite the Hyatt's efforts to make us feel at home with a fully stocked in-room bar and chocolates on our pillows. I'm not sure Jorge got into his bed at all.

Before our trip, Elena and Dr. J. took Jorge shopping and transformed his look from baggy pants and T-shirt to a necktie, gray slacks, and navy blue blazer with a gold sailing club insignia. Someone taught him to tie a tie, too. The gray silk necktie, fresh white shirt, and shiny new jacket set off Jorge's strong, well-balanced features. My confidence was high, until we stood in the third floor foyer outside the Safety Board's meeting room, waiting.

I've given scientific presentations in places as far-flung as Prague, Calcutta and Tokyo. I was recently interviewed on National Public Radio, CNN, and even the BBC about the Bangladesh epidemic, but as I sipped at a coffee and stared at the greasy cheese croissant in my hand, I experienced irrational fear. It's good to be nervous, I told myself. It's good to be nervous.

It was nearing noon when a heavy-boned trooper of a secretary appeared. "You're Mallow, I take it," she said, with a shriveling, sideways glance at Jorge. "They're ready for you two."

I knew I was out of my element the moment I stepped into the room. Whenever I've been in meeting rooms, from Paris to Shanghai, from Bologna to Bratislava, it's always been about viruses, bio-terrorism, vaccines, or the *Bangladesh* threat. My expertise was needed. In this room, I was unsure how far my expertise would go.

An oval, polished oak table dominated the elegant space. There was the gentle hum of perfect climate control. Gold metallic cards with company names—Ford, Nissan, Mitsubishi, GM—marked six of the eight places at the table. Two places were marked "guest." Each of the six men seated at the table had a thin, leatherette folder opened squarely in front of him, and nowhere a pen or pencil. These men came here to lay down the law and leave. They didn't take notes.

Though differing in size and shape, the members of the Safety Board were cut from the same expensive cloth, tailored in Seville Row or Hong Kong, at boutiques frequented by royalty and captains of commerce like themselves. Well-tanned and clean-shaven, urbane and smooth, they were the corporate plunderers of the modern American landscape. And Jorge Acosta and I were there to tell them they had a problem?

"Mallow, is it?" asked the chairman from the far end of the table. "Professor Mallow?"

"Yes, and my student and colleague, Mr. Acosta."

"Please sit." The chairman, from GM, was the only board member carrying extra weight. "Tell us what's on your mind," he said, dryly. He looked up from his agenda and smiled. A set of doughy rolls undulated under his sparkling white shirt, fresh from the cleaners, extra starch.

I began by summarizing the immersion study. Jorge and I had identical folders in front of us, with copies of charts, graphs, and color photos of the Chevy Z28 with its smashed windows, and the mangled hands of Trey Findley.

"An autopsy performed on a college student made us aware of this problem." I passed the police photos around, and our autopsy hand-shots. When I mentioned the word "trapped," the slightly-built representative from Ford spoke up at my immediate right.

"Thank you for sharing your interesting data, professor, but this was an accidental death, no?" I looked closer at the Ford rep. He had small eyes. The pupils constricted behind his rimless, octagonal glasses. "An unfortunate accident."

The others at the table exchanged glances. Our plan was for Jorge to explain his data at this point, but he looked frozen in place. I passed out one of his graphs.

"According to the historical data Mr. Acosta accumulated, such deaths were a rarity before power windows became standard equipment in the early '60s." The Ford man's left eye began to twitch.

Across the table, the Nissan representative spoke up. "This is most disconcerting, professor." He was the youngest, the most handsome of the board members, and unusually tall for a Japanese guy, easily six-three or six-four. He held the grisly photographs at arm's length. "Are you saying this is a *preventable* form of death?" he asked with a crisp, New England accent.

"That's precisely the point we make in our paper."

The Nissan man pursed his lips, nodded, and began studying the graphs.

The chairman spoke. "Professor, let me assure you, our main concern is safety. Safety is important. Safety adds value. Our stockholders want safety."

I looked around at the nodding heads and shifting eyes. It looked like a skeleton had been pulled out of the automotive industry's closet, and the man doing the pulling was me.

"But accidents do happen," the Ford man interjected. "As a physician, you should know that better than anyone. Where's the vehicular safety issue here?"

"In the majority of our cases," I said, "the victims were trapped in their vehicles. *Entrapment* is the issue."

The chairman, perplexed, addressed the Ford man. "You're the epidemiologist, Jack. What do you think of this?"

"It's a retrospective study based on post-mortem data, and it appears to exhibit a highly emotional bias."

The chairman nodded. "Retrospective studies. Yes, notoriously problematic. You're saying the stats are flawed?"

"I assure you," I interrupted, "our statistical analysis is sound science."

"And you are a trained epidemiologist?" the Ford man asked. He spoke in a flat, professional tone and had a vaguely European accent, maybe Swiss.

"My student, Mr. Acosta, is an expert statistician," I explained, indicating Jorge, who was silently working his foam-flecked mouth.

The Ford man's eyes were two steel beads. "What *is* your speciality, exactly?"

"Emerging viruses, such as *Huntavirus* and the recent outbreak of...."

The Ford man cut me off with a wave of his hand. "Do you intend to publish the results you've so kindly presented to us today?"

"Yes, in the *Journal of the American Medical Association.*"

"Excellent journal. Of course, *JAMA* is not an epidemiology journal per se. I've served on its editorial board for a number of years." With thin, delicate fingers, the Ford man quietly closed his folder. He pushed well back from the ponderous table. He was wearing cowboy boots made of snake, or perhaps it was caiman.

The chairman attempted a smile. "We'll take what you've said under serious consideration, professor, and get back with you soon." He looked at his agenda. "We need to move along to this CDC issue of the 'black box.' Are there more questions for the professor? If not, then...."

Jorge sputtered and rose, wide-eyed, out of his chair. "But... but!"

The Ford man sat silent as light next to me, his eyes closed, his immaculately manicured hands pressed gently together in front of his face, as if in prayer. I searched the monotonously tanned faces one last time, but no eyes met mine. I thanked them, grabbed my bumbling student by the arm, and left the room.

Jorge leaned against the wall just outside their door, trembling and flushed.

"I... I didn't get to say a word!" he said.

"We tried, Jorge. They'll be in touch and...."

"They won't do a damn thing!" He turned and stomped across the foyer.

I decided to hang around, make a cup of tea, and see if the board would break for lunch soon. They filed out less than 10 minutes later, laughing and talking about their golf games, the courses in Bermuda, Antigua, the Bahamas—places where the greens fees surpass a professor's monthly paycheck. The man from Ford broke away from the group and came over. He seemed even slighter of stature when standing.

"Care for a drink?" he asked. "The name's Jon Sokolof, with an 'F,' not a 'V,'" he said pedantically as we shook hands. "You may call me 'Jack.'" His skin was baby-soft but his grasp was tight as a Vise Grip. We rode the elevator down to the glitzy, street-level lounge and took two spots at the bar. He ordered a Skyy martini. I asked for the same, but with a jalapeno, just to be Texan. I was wondering about those boots of his.

"You come to D.C. often, professor?"

"I review grants at the NIH and consult with the World Health Organization on this epidemic in Bangladesh."

"Such a worrisome business going on in the Third World. Whatever interested you in the safety of automobiles?"

"My student, Acosta. It's his project. He wrote a small grant."

"Grants, yes. It's always about money, isn't it, in research?" It was definitely Germanic, the cadence of Sokolof's speech, his choice of words, and those octagonal glasses with their peculiar, yellow tint. "I must tell you, Professor Mallow, the Safety Board has assigned me to you, to your problem. Indeed, I have a background similar to your own, an M.B.B., Cambridge, and the F.R.C.P., Royal College of Physicians and all that. My early work was at the University of Geneva, in the field of bioinformatics."

"How long have you been with industry?"

"Nearly 10 years. I saw the vast financial advantages, and abandoned the developing field of hierarchal clustering. Ironic, really, that my move came just as I was elected to the National Academy of Sciences."

I smiled, but that didn't seem possible. Not this guy, not the National Academy.

"Your student, this Acosta fellow, did he attempt any K-mean clustering or agglomerative nesting in his analysis?"

"I'm not sure."

"It's the best approach to that sort of data. Who else was involved in the study, might I ask?"

"The county medical examiner."

Sokolof gave out a chuckle. "I see. If your student is interested in the potential of clustering techniques, or in generating a statistical 'heat map' of your data, please refer him to my website FORD.org./BIOINFORM/Sokolof. Tell him to be careful about the 'f' in Sokolof."

"I'll do that, Jack."

"Keep in mind, Doctor Mallow, in the eyes of your average man-on-the-street, the perception of safety is more important than safety itself. That's why we have our board in place, to deal with perceived safety issues, whether real or not."

"This is real, Jack. As real as drowning."

"Spare me the melodrama, professor. We're all going to die. Only the time and place will vary." Sokolof looked down the bar. "On a different note," he said, "in your work on these 'emerging' viruses, what grants must you hold?"

"I have one large grant, a federal award. It's ending soon and I have one pending."

"Grants. Sometimes you make it, sometimes you don't. Am I right? How very drab to be competing with one's colleagues for the same pot of money. It makes life a bit... precarious, no?" He fixed me with his rodent's stare, then tossed down his drink.

"Are you...?"

"Stick to your viruses, Mallow. Do not waste your precious time with projects that are not in your area of expertise."

"You are! You're...."

"I simply remind you of certain realities, of the subtle ways one's life may be disrupted in our interconnected world." He said "interconnected" like it was full of k's. I felt a chill, despite the jalapeno. He made a move to go. I rummaged in my jacket and handed him my card.

"I'll hear from you?" I asked.

"Oh, yes. You most certainly will."

He slipped off his stool and dropped my card on the bar without giving it a glance. His wiry frame disappeared into the crowd.

That evening, I took Jorge to a Venezuelan restaurant and told him about my drink with Sokolof. I asked him if he had run a "clustering" analysis on his data.

"That stuff's not very powerful. The Kappa statistic was the way to go with that data set."

"Are you sure about these other tests? This guy, Sokolof...."

"That 'agglomerative nesting'? It's crap. They put up a website, then sell you their software. I'm surprised he didn't mention a 'heat map.' It's all smoke and mirrors, Doctor Mallow. Smoke and mirrors."

Time grew short. We rushed to the airport, only to discover that our flight had been canceled and we were rebooked through Newark on a Delta flight. When we finally settled in the back of the aircraft, Jorge conked out and began talking in his sleep. It was as if the day's frustration and the roaring engines of Delta's 737 set him off.

"No, Momma. I'm sorry! Forgive me!" He tossed violently in his seat, groaning. "*¡NO! ¡Mi hermanito!* All those drownings!"

"Jorge, it's okay."

He calmed down some, then went off on a physics rant. "Microstrings... microstrings." He mumbled something about a "Planck epoch" 25 billion years ago and a cold light filling the universe. "And those men!" he cried out, growing agitated again. "They're evil!"

I jotted down what I could on the back of a cocktail napkin because I knew I'd never remember all that crazy stuff for these notes. I dozed off. When I snapped awake, he was making perfect sense again.

"No way a bogus clustering analysis would be appropriate. That Kappa statistic is iron-clad. All that idiot knows is market share and bottom line."

I drove back from Bush Intercontinental, dropped Jorge off at his apartment, dragged myself up the stairs of the carriage house, and flopped on the futon next to Brenda, waking her from what must've been a light sleep.

"How did it go?"

"Not good. Jorge's a mess."

"I can imagine. Let me get you some soup, Peter. The kids stayed over and Mr. Kreuger cooked for us. There's leftovers." Despite the fact that it was nearly 3 a.m., Brenda trudged into the main house and carried back a hot, steaming bowl of spicy, reddish seafood soup.

"You're sweet. What's in this?"

"It's redfish court bouillon."

I felt better. "One of the board members is supposed to get back to me," I said, lapping up hot soup. "The son-of-a-bitch threatened me. Thinks he's a big shit scientist, the shrimpy little...."

"Relax, baby. You're home." I stretched out on the futon. Brenda threw a cool, silky leg over me and began stroking my back. "Poor Jorge."

Just as I was drifting off, Brenda nudged me.

"Listen, Peter. Travis has a new trick he's excited about. Be sure you see it tomorrow."

Next morning, after very little sleep, I caught Travis before he ran out the door with his brother to the school bus.

"Dad, can you come home before dark? I got a new lip trick, you gotta see it, a vertical nose grab, totally ballistic!"

"I'll try."

"Before dark!" Travis yelled as he dashed out the door.

Back in the lab, it felt good to again turn my attention to *Bangladesh horrificans*. The faint odor of acetone, the feel of the pipette, the shapes of the duck cells under the Nomarski optics of my microscope were familiar and comforting after our futile trip to D.C. Cranking my microscope along, I puzzled over how this nasty virus managed to destroy heart cells when it was lodged far away in the GI tract, in the colon. Lost in a hypothesis, I was startled when Jorge rushed into the office with more news.

"This reporter I know called. His name's Chris. He wants to meet tomorrow, and we buy lunch."

"Fine, just nothing pricey, okay?"

"You look exhausted, Doctor Mallow. Where's Lilly?"

"At the Analytic Center. She's checking out the new spectrophotometer that's due in."

Jorge raced over to the Analytic Center to join Lilly. I was back at my lab bench when Lilly strode into the lab looking smug, with Jorge trailing behind her. "Great news!" she exclaimed. "Brand new spec is here, and it's going to make my life easy. I'll analyze viral proteins, match them to genes, and use the fast-duck cells to figure out which are virulence factors. Perfect!"

"Then we'll verify each factor in the ducks," I agreed. "Terrific, Lilly. Good thinking."

Jorge's eyes were wide.

"What's this new instrument called?" I asked. Lilly looked to Jorge to answer.

"It's a single-microcapillary reverse-phase high-pressure liquid chromatograph," he began. "Directly coupled to the nanoelectrospray ionization source of an ion-trap spectrometer."

Lilly was beaming. "And it's a Finnegan," she added. "The best."

Despite the excitement in the lab over the new Finnegan spec, I still had this big entry on the Washington trip to write and a skateboard trick to see "before dark." I dug in my jacket for the Delta cocktail napkin, found the notebook, and split for home.

Jorge scheduled lunch with Chris, the *Island Daily* reporter, at a soul food place called The Squeeze Inn. Chris had told Jorge, "The City Desk guy says it's good eats."

I drove the Datsun over the broken-up macadam of Martin Luther King Avenue, into the middle of the projects. We rattled to a stop in front of the caved-in community center, where a steady drumming of basketballs came from the center's courts. We strolled past a row of ripped-up telephones, their cords dangling like severed arteries, and turned down a sandy, furrowed alley to the entrance of The Squeeze Inn.

"Is this place safe?" Jorge asked nervously.

"Check the homicide map at Dr. J.'s sometime when you're out there," I said. "This block is one big cluster of red pins." Jorge blanched. "It's safe enough in daylight."

I pulled open the corroded screen door and we stepped into a cool, dark interior the size of a small living room. The place was packed with overweight diners, always a good sign. Chris was waiting. He and Jorge highfived, and we got in the food line.

Chris looked like a typical young reporter, late 20s, blond hair already thinning, slightly paunchy, just a regular guy looking for an angle at a small city newspaper. Mostly these "aces" end up covering the latest wreck on the causeway or the Lassie League scores. He said he was from Atlanta. An expensive cigar protruded from his shirt pocket, just above the egg stains from breakfast.

"Been on this island six months," he grumbled. "Nothing but seafood." He gave his midriff a pat. "Hmmm. I'm smelling fried chicken."

"There's no menu," I explained. "It's cafeteria-style, and 'all you can eat.'"

We loaded our plastic trays with silverware and red-checked cloth napkins. Behind us, eight husky black men in dark suits squeezed through the door and got in line. I recognized one, an embalmer who picks up bodies at the university autopsy morgue. He goes about 350 pounds, and is always in a tailored suit with an immaculate white shirt and tie. This had to be a crew from a black funeral home, stopping for lunch after laying a body to rest in its stone vault at the Mid-Island Cemetery.

"Main dishes today is chicken and oxtails," said the server, a large white porcelain plate in hand. Chris opted for the fried chicken. I chose the oxtails. The server heaped my plate with white rice, and then spooned on oxtails smothered in a sauce the dark, red-brown color of spleen. Jorge asked for a plate of plain rice.

A second server dished out okra, cabbage, butterbeans, and collard greens. At the end of the steam table were rectangles of fresh corn bread, quart-sized glasses of tea, and slices of sweet-potato pie. The three of us crowded around a table that in an ordinary restaurant would seat one. The funeral crew stood with their trays in their hands, waiting for a table to clear.

"Jorge gave me the scoop on your project," Chris began. "It's amazing that you guys are the first to discover this. What do you call it again?"

"Vehicular immersion," Jorge said. "And we intend to solve it."

"Damn, this chicken's good!" Chris said, smacking well-oiled lips. "Crispy, seasoned to the bone, almost as good as Atlanta."

"Can you help us with this, Chris?" Jorge asked.

"Sure. The way I see it, a newspaper's got a responsibility to inform the public, you know?" Jorge, who was working at the edges of his rice, nodded in agreement. "I'd start off with that college guy drowning off of Bodekker Road, human interest stuff, then go into how you guys figured this whole thing out. It would be best if I came out to the university and interviewed you. Might be four or five pieces in it."

"What I really want is to go after the manufacturers," Jorge said. "What a bunch of jerks."

"Industry types," Chris nodded. "They get nasty." He crunched down on a drumstick. "I understand that the chief medical examiner is part of your project."

"We couldn't have done it without him," Jorge said.

"That Jawicki is sure no help to the press, though. It's like pulling teeth to get autopsy results out of him."

I decided to speak up. "Medical examiners have to wait on reports, Chris. The county doesn't give him much to work with, either."

"How about I interview him, too? I'll do you guys first, then write a piece on 'The Trials of a Medical Examiner.'"

"Dr. Jawicki's a busy man, Chris."

"Maybe you could have a word with him."

"I can try, when I happen to see him."

"Can I mention your name, doc?"

"Sure."

"Great." Chris tossed a last cleaned bone on his plate. "I'll call you about the interviews, maybe bring a photographer. With Jawicki, too. I'll fix you guys up with what you want."

The funeral crew was chowing down nearby. I'm sure it's tough work, hauling caskets to the mausoleums or lowering them into the swampy graves of Mid-Island Cemetery. The enormous embalmer acknowledged me with a nod as he dripped oxtail gravy onto his perfectly pressed white shirt, its cuffs dampened with red pepper sauce. All seemed well at The Squeeze Inn.

"I'm actually getting to like this town," said Chris, heaving himself out of his chair to try a helping of the oxtails.

Friday, March 27

It's been more than two weeks since we met with the Safety Board. I called their main number in D.C. every day, left messages for the chairman, and did the same for Sokolof, though I didn't relish the idea of having to deal with him again. Finally, it dawned on me to ask a secretary how I might get in touch with the Nissan rep. "That's Mr. Yamata," she replied brightly. "I'll have him contact you." A couple of minutes later, Yamata himself called.

"Professor Mallow, what can I do for you?...Yes, I'm sure we'll be addressing the problem. Tell you what, I'll ask the board member following that issue to get in touch with you. How's that?"

I made contact. That eased my mind, and I went back to the lab.

Jorge seems less preoccupied with the immersion project, and he's deeper and deeper into his science. Lilly's trained him in the Level 4. She reports that his technique is impeccable, his adherence to safety protocols meticulous. He works alone now on knocking out *PAKG*, and he's eager to do more.

"What about *SWCH*, Doctor Mallow?" he begged me as he emerged this afternoon from the Level 4 facility, smelling of sweat from being enclosed in a space suit. "I've already knocked out my *PAKG* gene."

"*Almost* knocked it out," I corrected him. "Lilly's last genotyping shows you still haven't gotten the whole sequence. It's got to be exact, Jorge."

"In a week we'll have it, and I can move on to *SWCH*."

"First knock out *PAKG*, then we'll see."

"Sure, sure," he said, and he set off for his apartment to shower for the evening.

Laura Sacchi called me at home, late. Brenda and I were at the cherry table, eating leftover Mr. Kreuger meatloaf, when the phone rang. It must've been 11 p.m. on the East Coast. Brenda answered the call. Things had been rosy between Brenda and me, but I could see some of that fade with a late night, female call. Her eyes narrowed and her face hardened when I took the phone from her.

"I wanted to touch base," Laura said, "on your immersion study. Has it been published?"

"We're still waiting to hear."

"I had this odd call yesterday, about immersions, from somebody you know."

"Who?"

"A Japanese fellow named Yamata, from Nissan."

"Oh, yeah?"

"My buddy in our vehicle division tells me Yamata's a real fireball. Degree from MIT, young, bright. His project is the in-vehicle recorder, but he called to ask if I had any national data on immersions. I confess, I haven't had a chance to really look into this on my own."

"What did you tell him?"

"I told him to contact you, and he laughed. Said he already had. It sounds like your little talk made them nervous, Pete. If the press gets wind of this, it could be far worse than the industry's problems with fires or rollovers or gas tanks blowing up. It could turn into a nightmare."

"It's already a nightmare, Laura. I could've guessed they're worried. They sicced their meanest member, this rabid little dog, on me."

"That's not good, Pete. They're planning something."

"Like what?"

"Maybe they'll fabricate data, confuse the issue so the consumer advocates don't pounce on it."

"*JAMA* publishes quickly, and the lay press covers *JAMA* closely. They'd have to act awfully fast."

"These guys do act fast. That's why they haul in huge salaries."

"We've talked a reporter into running a series in the local paper. The medical examiner's contacting a state senator he knows. What else can we do?"

"I don't know, it's just that...."

"Thanks, Laura. I appreciate it. You're sweet. But could you just e-mail me if you hear anything else?"

"No e-mails, Pete. Officially, I'm not involved in this. You remember my home number, right?"

"Sure. I'll call you at home, then."

"Anytime." There was a long silence on the line. "And I hope it works out with your significant other, Pete. I'm sure it will. Best of luck. You deserve good things. Just pay attention to what I told you. Watch your back."

"Great talking with you."

I hung up and Brenda was there. She cut her eyes at me, then away. It looked like what little trust we had between us was now in need of serious repair. It was time to explain everything about Dr. Sacchi to Dr. Danforth.

Saturday, May 9
(The Crawfish Boil)

I decided to throw a party. Imagine that. April had been a good month in the lab, so good that I never found time for an entry in these notes. Lilly and Jorge made real progress on *PAKG* and *SWCH*, and I was sure to get the big NIH grant. Marv told me as much. I was just waiting for the glowing reviews to come in.

And Poonawala's latest e-mail from Calcutta brought good news:

> With the rainy season, cases have diminished. The quarantine of Dhaka has been effective.

We had a breather. The virus had extended its range, even gone intercontinental. It had killed plenty with its attack on the lungs, but it was still a bird flu that hadn't learned to kill human heart cells. With luck, when *Bangladesh horrificans* again threatened southern Asia, we'd have a vaccine.

So I decided to throw a big Friday night party at the house. Mr. Kreuger suggested I boil crawfish. They're in season. Crawfish, crayfish, crawdads, mudbugs, river roaches—whatever they're called, they grow big in the brackish bayous of the Texas-Louisiana Coast, and we eat 'em by the 40-pound sackful, boiled in a huge pot with potatoes and onions, and seasoned with pounds of salt and plenty of cayenne pepper. Mr. Kreuger told me to order four sacks, or 160 pounds, because "a sack of crawfish is mostly shell."

Brenda was less sanguine. After all, we didn't know the meaning of the word "entertain." We were two people keeping their relationship under wraps, even though the whole island knew.

"Are you sure about this party?" she asked.

"Mr. Kreuger says you boil everything in one big pot in the backyard, set up a table under the pecan tree, and stand around eating. How hard can that be?"

"Where's this big pot come from?"

"Wallennius Shipping. The propane burner, too"

I left the lab early Friday to pick up the crawdads on pier 21. The quiescent red-brown creatures warmed up in the bed of the pickup and began to writhe. By the time I set them in the shade of the big pecan in the backyard, the mesh sacks had transformed into four fibrillating, foam-spitting, 40-pound lumps.

Mr. Kreuger set up the pot and burner. I pulled out Mr. Kreuger's long wooden serving-table, also stamped "Wallennius Ltd." in red letters. I took the trouble to hack down the wild vines and noxious weeds, and poison the fire ant mounds for the occasion. I pushed kerosene torches into the ground, and Mr. Kreuger set out cans of mosquito repellent. The tropical evening promised to be mild and sweet.

Mr. Kreuger turned to the boiling process. "Once the salt and hot pepper boils good, add a few potatoes and onions until they soften. Then a tubful of crawfish. Give 'em 10 minutes, pull up the basket, dump the boil onto newspaper. Be sure to add lots of salt and cayenne between batches."

Marv Stepinski showed up first. He and I pulled a couple of longnecks out of the tub of ice. Lilly arrived holding a plate of wontons she'd fried for the party.

Jorge came in fresh from the shower and smelling of citrusy cologne. He carried his bottle of Diet Sprite and four loaves of French bread I'd requested from the corner bakery. I handed him a serrated knife and had him slice the bread. He was wearing a new shirt, a rayon Hawaiian that draped nicely on his broad, lean shoulders. Its muted, purplish orchids went well with his amber skin. Watching him meticulously cut the bread into smooth, even slices, I realized that Jorge had undergone a transformation since his fellowship began. His strong, Native American features and smoky-gray eyes were balanced now against slicked-back, glossy hair and the close-cropped Vandyke. I saw a future professor, a dashing physician-scientist, and I envied Jorge his vigor and youth.

When the boil was right and the potatoes and onions softened, in went the first tub of crawfish. A crowd materialized. I sampled a fresh pile, steaming-hot from the boil.

"How do you eat these things?" Brenda asked.

"Break the tail away from the body, like this, and the meat juts at you. Stick it in your mouth and pinch the tip of the tail. The meat should come right out."

She looked square at me with a crawfish tail dangling between her teeth. I've taught this to a dozen women, I thought, but she is the best, absolutely the best.

"Like thishh?"

"Perfect."

"Hmm! S'good."

"As an optional maneuver, you can 'suck the head.' You've got this left-over 'head' end in your hand, see? Just suck out the thoraco-abdominal contents, like this."

Women always cringe at this part, then they run out to buy a T-shirt emblazoned with a fire-engine red, cartoon crawfish exclaiming, "I SUCK THE HEADS."

"It's quite delicious!" Brenda said, her lips dripping orange-yellow juice.

I started a second batch while Brenda replenished the pitcher of margaritas in the kitchen. Eventually, I knew, someone would start pouring shots of tequila, but Mr. Kreuger's rule was "Stay sober until all the crawfish are boiled."

A heavy cloud cover moved in, obscuring the moon, and the torches cast an eerie, flickering light over the backyard. Dr. J. and Elena arrived fashionably late.

"I didn't know you could cook, Peter," Dr. J. said.

"I can't. I had help for this event." I looked around, but Mr. Kreuger had already retreated to his apartment to stand the night watch.

Elena bit into a peppery-red onion, and asked, "Why didn't you go into... how you say it?... culinary arts, Peter? How is it you went into science?"

"It started at Yale, when I was first introduced to a deadly virus."

"How charming!" Elena laughed.

At Dr. J.'s raised eyebrow, I leaned in close and whispered, "Graduated Summa Cum fuck up, you know." He chuckled. "Truthfully, my advisor, an aquatic parasitologist, put me on the trail of a virus that was killing the Atlantic sea urchin, *Strongylocentrotus droebachiensis*, and...." In telling the sorry story, I downplayed the slacking-off that nearly flunked me out, and skipped directly to the Elihu Yale Prize for Independent Studies that was mine at graduation.

At my side, Marv Stepinski meditatively sipped at a plastic cup of margarita. "Did you hear from the NIH yet, Peter?" he asked.

"Nope. What's the holdup, I wonder?"

"You should have heard a month ago." Marv paused to drain his cup. "You can never tell about grants today. Science has become a giant pain in the ass." There was an awkward silence, broken only by the sound of crawfish bodies cracking. Elena finished the potato she had in her hand and slipped away. Marv droned on. "The funding situation is the worst I've ever seen. The paylines are dismal and...."

I became aware of the pressing need to take a leak, so I set my Tecate down and made for the back door of the house. Brenda was mixing a pitcher of margaritas in the kitchen. She tried to baby-talk me into a kiss, but I dashed past her to the servants' stairway, a set of narrow, spiral stairs in the back hall. There, at the base of the stairway, I saw something I wish I'd never seen. Elena was under the alabaster sconce, her back against the crumbling plaster, face-to-face with Jorge.

"*No, no, guapo!*" she whispered.

"*Elena.*"

They were dangerously close. My eyes met hers. I sidled around them and ran up the stairs to the boys' bathroom. When I came down, they were gone.

Brenda was in the kitchen filling glasses for two of Marv's cardiology fellows. "You look funny, Peter. What's wrong?"

"Tell you later."

When I stepped outside, Elena was standing at the crawfish table with Dr. J. She didn't look up.

I had one more batch of crawfish to boil. I dropped the last of the potatoes and onions in, stared at the murky red-brown broth, and decided that I needed a shot of tequila. Brenda was still in the kitchen, alone now.

"Jeez, Brenda, I just saw Jorge *with* Elena on the back stairs."

"Jorge *with* Elena? You must be mistaken."

"That's what I saw. Should I say something?"

"Well… it's really none of our business."

"I cannot believe this. I'm his sponsor, his mentor!"

"They're of age, Peter."

I poured myself the shot of tequila. At least it was clear, even if nothing else was. Brenda and I stood there in complete silence. Neither of us could think of anything to add to our little segment of *As the World Turns*.

I downed the shot and went to toss in the last batch of crawfish. In the backyard, guests were talking, drinking, picking at crawdads. Children ran like specters through the old house, drawn by the light of a video game. My adolescent bassist Chad was showing off a new rife in his room. It occurred to me that no matter how carefully we plan ahead, things we least expect keep popping up.

Mr. Kreuger's lights were on. He was well into his watch, in front of the TV and pouring himself a Scotch. At least things were on schedule there.

The last of the crawfish awaited their doom. I lifted the tub and carried it to the pot. The damned things were all over each other, clickity-clicking their claws, shearing vital body parts from their comrades, tearing at the lives of others with a random and senseless energy.

In a moment, they'll be cooked.

After the last guest left, Chad helped Brenda and me clear the debris and hose down the backyard. Then Brenda concentrated on the kitchen, while Chad and I bagged the crawfish shells, dragged the sacks to the alley, and tossed them in the back of the Datsun.

"Where you taking this mess, Dad?"

"To the dumpster behind Burger King."

"Is that legal?"

"Mr. Kreuger says everybody does it. Look. I don't want this shell stinking up the alley until Monday's garbage pick-up." I shoved a sack forward in the bed of the truck. Chad frowned. "Let's just say it's a little illegal, Chad."

"A little illegal?"

"We all have a few of these things."

I looked up at Mr. Kreuger's lights again. There was a lot about the old man's odd, solitary life that had been "a little illegal." His life with whores. Stealing from the workplace.

When I came back from heaving the sacks into Burger King's dumpster, Brenda was stretched out on the futon, a glossy sheen on her face. I stood at the sink, washing my hands.

"All that salt. All that hot pepper," she said.

I was using a scrub brush, getting under the nails like a surgeon preparing for surgery.

"Peter, when you were growing up on the Cape, did you have clambakes?"

"Sure."

"Remember how it was? Starting before dawn and collecting the rocks and the driftwood and digging the long pit and building the fire?"

"I always swam out for the seaweed. Damn, that water was cold."

"Once the rocks in the pit were hot, you'd heap seaweed onto the hot stone and layer on the clams, potatoes, onions, corn, more seaweed, and lobsters in the final layer," she said.

"Right. Then cover the pit with a tarp and sand and leave it till dark."

"Remember the smell, Peter? When they pulled back the tarp?" Brenda's eyes were far away and full of sleep. "When we were kids, it was clambakes. For Chad and Travis, it'll be crawfish boils."

Suddenly, I felt very tired.

"Don't you want a little girl, Peter?"

"What?"

"This name, 'Helen.' It's been stuck in my head. 'Helen.' The ancient Greeks said she was the most beautiful woman in the world."

"Another kid?"

"But the name sounds fresh and new."

"I thought we talked about this."

"We did. You know, Peter, after your divorce, we'll...."

Lately, Brenda peppered all of our conversations with that phrase. "After your divorce, we'll move to the main house." "After your divorce, I'll

finish my dissertation." I did it, too. "After the divorce we'll get a dog."
"After the divorce... after the divorce...."

"Brenda, what I really want is to be a full professor before I turn 40. Okay? Okay?" There was no answer. "A girl, you said?"

The faint, sweet smell of crawfish lingered in the bed as we lay listening to the steady whirl of the ceiling fan. I reached for her, we wrapped each other up and she pressed the bones of her face against mine. There was a catch in her voice. "It's just the way I am, and I accept it. I need a man, Peter."

"I'm your man."

"I need a man to myself."

"I'm trying," I said, and I nuzzled down between her breasts to smell the last of her perfume before it dissipated into the night.

Friday, May 29

Lilly finished training Jorge, so she had more time. Her fast-duck cells and the new Finnegan spec helped speed our process of discovery, as she'd predicted. Jorge was hard at work knocking out genes, but he was bringing up the immersion study again. And again. "When will we hear from *JAMA*?" "What's with that stupid Safety Board, Doctor Mallow?"

Personally, I'd all but given up on the Safety Board. I needed to focus in the lab, on *Bangladesh horrificans*, not a game of corporate phone tag.

Chris's first piece came out in the *Galveston Island Daily*, the Sunday edition. He used a file photo of Trey Findley being pulled out of the water off Bodekker Road. He brought a photographer to the lab for shots of Jorge and me. It took hours to get them through security downstairs. For the photo session we put serious, scientific looks on our faces, stacked up some fancy glassware behind us, and piled up our thickest lab notebooks on the lab bench. The week after the article ran, the paper printed letters to the editor from people who'd had relatives die in an immersion, a burst of local reader interest.

In a few days, it'll be the first of June, and the hurricane season officially begins. Weather watching becomes the major pastime, hurricane-tracking charts come out, computer screens swirl with infrared displays of the Atlantic and Caribbean, and everyone's talking "storm." In the lab, we update our official hurricane plan. How will our deadliest bugs be secured? What's on emergency power? Who evacuates first?

All this makes the recent arrivals in town very nervous. Many become stupefied with fear, and I admit that I was scared shitless, too, when I first hit the Island. But that was before I learned about the ultimate, simplified hurricane plan—the biggest bottle of dark rum you can buy, and plenty of mixer. Now, hurricane season is my favorite time of year.

Mr. Kreuger's the one who let me in on the secret one steamy evening during my first hurricane season on the Island. "Sure, we get big storms," he said, "but there's nothing you can do about 'em. Might as well enjoy 'em." We were sitting in the cane chairs on the second floor porch, catching the gulf breeze high above the street. Mr. Kreuger lifted his Johnny Walker, splash of water. "Besides, this old house survived them all, Doc, even the Great Storm of 1900."

"How many hurricanes have you been through in this house, Mr. Kreuger?"

"Six or seven. Carla was the worst. She made landfall on a Sunday, spawned tornados, busted up the downtown, then stalled and blew clear into Tuesday. A Category 4. Three days of misery and six months cleaning up. Water damage was the worst part of that one."

"How much rain are we talkin' about?"

"Fifteen, 20 inches, but the wind's blowin' 120 miles an hour. Water pours in everywhere." I looked out over the porch railing and tried to imagine this balmy, tropical evening turning violent. "You'll see for yourself, Doc, eventually."

Mr. Kreuger's prediction came true my second summer on the Island when a Category 3 hit. My wife took the boys to San Antonio. I had to prepare the lab, so I stayed on the island. Mr. Kreuger and I stuck it out in the old house. The storm blew for 12 hours. Everything the old man described took place. When Ellen returned, we were so exhausted from clearing debris and making temporary repairs that we hardly found the energy to argue. The wail of chain saws, unbearable heat and humidity, a blizzard of mosquitoes, no electricity. But in the evening, when the chain saws quit, everyone pulled the finest steaks from their thawed-out freezers, and the whole neighborhood smelled of grilled meat.

That's when the big bottle of rum comes in handy. It helps during a storm, but it's essential for those dark, sticky evenings afterward.

Monday, June 1

The start of another hurricane season and, like a hurricane herself, Ellen, my soon-to-be ex-wife, made landfall on my front porch. I was fumbling around with a coffee pot in the kitchen when I heard footsteps and the click of her dogs' claws on the wood decking. She was leaning on the rusted-out doorbell that hasn't worked for years. By the time I opened the door, she was going at the brass knocker, her big, slobbery, overheated malamutes pulling her every which-way on their leashes.

She was in a pair of clunky walking shoes and green scrubs. On this island, a baggy scrub suit with a draw-string bottom is the highest of fashion statements. Ellen's had "Texas Department of Corrections" stamped all over it, and it went poorly with her spooky mascara and eye shadow, and the inch-long, curled-under fingernails which, on several occasions during our marriage, had inflicted some very unpleasant stab wounds in my neck.

She peered past me into the house, at the space we'd shared for nearly eight years. I was glad Brenda was still asleep in the carriage house.

"We need to talk," she said, her sleepy eye, the left one, drooping worse than I remembered.

"Talk about what?"

"The boys. And hurricanes. It's June first, you know."

"You'll take them off the Island, won't you?" I stepped out to the porch and closed the door behind me. She opened her mouth as if to say "Yes" but the larger of the two dogs gave a sudden yank and all that came out was a grunt followed by a low curse. "Will you evacuate to Arkansas?" I asked.

"That's none of your business," she snapped, making me acutely aware of the discomfiting fact that I was alone on the front porch with a supremely unpleasant person to whom I was still legally married. "There's a problem. A big problem." I shrugged. "They want to stay on the Island with you. They want to stay in the big house, Peter."

"No, no way. They have to evacuate. I'll tell them that's our hurricane plan."

"You'd better back me on this one, Peter Mallow." Her voice rose as the dogs began tugging her onto the sidewalk. "Don't you undermine me! Don't you undermine my authority!"

I went back to making coffee, glad to be alone in the kitchen at the start of another hurricane season. It occurred to me that, in a way, I look forward to summer on the Island, with its endless sunshine punctuated by downbursts of dense, steamy rain.

I flipped on the NOAA weather radio, listened to the monotonous listing of water temperatures and high-tide times. *"Tropical storm activity is not expected for the next few days."* The Atlantic and Caribbean were quiet. We were cruising into summer.

There's no way to tell how many storms a season will bring, or where they'll come ashore, but I love to track 'em all, to feel my pulse rise when one lumbers into the Gulf, stalls, and gains strength. I tell people at the university, "Just do your work and try not to think of the worst." But I remind them to draw up a hurricane plan, just in case, because an island summer is a changeable season, a treacherous season, a season to be wary.

Friday, July 31

The summer revved up, sunshine blared down, and the humidity was breathtaking. In the cool confines of our lab, the insufferable summer stoked our intellects and, at last, we began to unravel the puzzle of *Bangladesh horrificans*.

Lilly had tracked down more than 30 viral proteins as candidate "virulence factors," thanks to her fast-duck-cell methods. The next step was to figure out which proteins cause transdifferentiation in the living duck. For this, we needed a different approach.

I constructed an anti-sense probe to a short sequence of each protein's DNA. As I explained to Jorge at the outset, "Each anti-sense will block a single protein." Lilly and I loaded experimental groups of ducks with anti-sense probes, followed by a deadly dose of *Bangladesh* virus.

In a blistering month of experiments, we injected duck after duck with an anti-sense probe. By probe number 16, we had nearly wiped out all the ducks in our avian room. Standing knee-deep in dead ducks, Lilly and I became ecstatic at the sight of three lone ducks still waddling and quacking—the group given anti-sense to protein number 16! The cry I heard through her plastic face shield was muffled, but I clearly saw Lilly's giant smile as she pointed at the ducks and mimed their waddle. "The ducks are quacking! Qwack! Qwack!"

Lilly injected a sample of protein 16 into the spiffy new Finnegan spec, and we had the entire genetic sequence. Once again, I was reminded that science advances in fits and starts. With this recent spasm of progress, we huddled in the break area.

"Okay, Team," I began, "here's Lilly's sequence of protein number 16, our new virulence factor." All eyes were on me. "It matches a gene known as '*MORPH*,' a gene that is essential for heart muscle contraction. The only problem is, it doesn't match exactly. It's a few DNA sequences off."

"Precisely, Doctor Mah-wo," said Lilly. "That's why it is a virulence factor. *Bangladesh* virus makes a *MORPH* that doesn't function right. It floods the duck heart with bad *MORPH*, and the heart fails."

"Brilliant, Lilly," I said proudly. "What an insight. Let's call the aberrant, toxic protein *BADMORPH*. Okay, enough discussion. Time to write this up, folks!" I exclaimed, raising both hands high, like a victorious boxer after a quick knockout. "The data's firm, it's novel, it makes sense. We'll send it to the top journal in the field, *The Journal of Virology*. Lilly, you'll be first author."

A shadow passed across Lilly's face. "But are we sure that's how it works in the duck?" she asked wisely. Lilly had anticipated the reviewers' comments to our yet-unwritten paper. "We must infect ducks, Doctor Mah-wo, take hearts, do gels, prove that's what happens in duck."

"If we start those experiments today, we'll be sacking them next week."

"Do we have enough? Must check flock. Must check flock."

Lilly jogged off to the animal breeding colony to check the number of ducklings and see how many eggs were in a "family way." Jorge had been unusually quiet at our meeting. I was afraid he might feel left out.

"Could you take care of the statistical analysis for our paper, Jorge?"

"Sure. Borel's lemma might apply."

As August approached, we were cooking up a paper that would put our lab at the forefront of the field. In the introduction, we planned to stress how "the outbreak of *Bangladesh horrificans* resulted in more than 20,000 deaths during the recent epidemic season in south Asia." We'd propose "hypothetical ways to intervene in the duck's relentless, fatal myocarditis." This paper would be a sure thing.

Hard at work, we barely noticed the dense bands of rain swirling on the computer screens as the first tropical depression of the season slipped past the Lesser Antilles, sucked energy from the hot Caribbean, and took aim at the Texas coast.

Friday, August 7

Last Friday started badly, then things got worse, a lot worse. I woke up with Brenda warm and moist behind me, just beginning to stir. Her hand wandered under the sheet and flopped around until it firmly captured its prey.

"Sorry, can't mess around this morning, baby."

"You can't spare 10 minutes?"

"It's a flare-up. You know the routine. No sex for two weeks until it's blister-free."

She gave out a sound between a sigh and a groan. "It's bad enough you're getting this beer belly," she said, giving me a thump. "How *did* you ever contract this thing, Peter?"

"At least it's not *oral* herpes."

"Hmm."

I couldn't bear to tell Brenda the sordid tale of my *Herpes genitalis*. It went way back, when I had just taken the job on the Island and my marriage was beginning to wash up on the rocks. I had to fly to Chicago for a virus meeting. After a day of boring talks, I rode the elevated train to a North Chicago blues bar where I spied a thin, dark-haired college girl with horn-rimmed glasses. The studious look. I worked my way next to her at the bar and chatted her up with my stories of the great Lightnin' Hopkins' little-known younger brother, Milton, a lesser musician by any standard, who still cranked out classic electric-blues with his aging band in the juke joints along Old Spanish Trail in East Houston, blah blah blah.

I figured she was impressed when she showed me the pink panties under her faded, tattered jeans. Or maybe it was all the rum-and-cokes. In any case, she came back to my third-rate hotel, rode the creaky, museum-quality Otis elevator to my room, and tore me up in a drunken stupor.

I never saw a blister while wandering in the college girl's pink panties, but three weeks later I saw plenty on Mr. Gonzo, and I've seen them sporadically ever since. I've learned, sadly, no matter how much one might know about viruses, it does not afford immunity to your own stupidity. The whole sordid episode was better left untold, especially to Brenda.

So last Friday morning I said goodbye to Brenda, stepped out the door into the sultry breeze, and walked around to unlock my bike. Along the side of the house, the wind died. My shirt moistened. When I turned my bike onto the sidewalk, the raggedy shadow of a mature male grackle cut across its handlebars. His *macho* cry and the flutter of his shiny, blue-black wings had my heart racing as I pedaled, dripping sweat, to the lab.

Black birds are a bad sign.

I saw it right away in my mail slot at work. The address label said it was from *JAMA*, and the big, heavy envelope meant the manuscript was being returned.

"Maybe they want revisions." I pulled open the envelope, quickly read the cover letter. When Jorge saw the letter he was as puzzled as I was. "The reviewers' comments are all good," he said.

"Right. It's the editor who flat-out rejects it. He says they don't have *space* in the journal. What bullshit."

"Is it possible to get them to reconsider, Doctor Mallow? Who makes the final decision?"

"The editor, Steve Leitmann, a guy I know from study sections. I'll call him up about this."

But when I telephoned *JAMA's* editorial office, Leitmann didn't call me back. I tried again and again, so on Monday morning I called his research lab at the University of California. "Maybe tomorrow," is all I got from his lab people. First the damned Safety Board gave me the run around, and now Leitmann. It seemed like the phones weren't working for me anymore.

I finally caught Leitmann late this afternoon, a full week later.

"I see your point," he said, trying to calm me down after I lambasted his schizophrenic rejection letter. "But this was an unusual case. The reviewers were split. One found major flaws in the study design."

"We sent this paper to you because it's exactly the kind of high-impact study *JAMA* likes to publish, Steve."

"I read the paper. I read the whole thing. This one reviewer... to tell the truth, Peter, I didn't want to forward his comments to you. He's from industry and...."

"From industry? Wouldn't be a guy named Sokolof, would it, Steve?"

"I can't tell you that. You know the peer-review system. Besides, one of our editorial board members came out strong, too. He thought the study was emotionally biased, just another retrospective study."

"Oh, come on, Steve. Look how many similar cases we've turned up."

"All I can tell you is what the editorial board told me to do."

"Editorial board? You're the editor in chief, for chrissakes!"

"Just send it to a second-line journal, Peter. It's no big deal. It happens all the time."

"We wanted to publish this quickly, Steve. Auto safety is in the news. The public wants action on vehicular safety problems like this."

"It's a disturbing problem, Peter, I agree. Being trapped, drowned. And your sophisticated data analysis makes your point."

"But you won't reconsider."

"I've discovered that we have these vehicular immersions around San Diego, you know. In fact, after I read your paper, I bought these German-made stainless steel hammers specially made for escaping, for pounding out a window."

"Steve...."

"They've got a razor blade built in, too, for cutting yourself out of your seatbelt. It's not a bad idea, Peter, if you live near the water like we do."

"I just bought one for my girlfriend, Steve. We probably ordered them from the same friggin' catalog."

I got off the phone with Leitmann and called Jorge to my office. He had just finished in the Level 4 and looked exhausted.

"Jorge, Steve Leitmann said the decision was final." Jorge plopped down on the stool and looked gray. "It had one bad review he didn't show us, and someone on their editorial board hated it. Maybe the decision came from higher up. I don't completely understand."

"I do. It was the Safety Board. Those corporate sons of bitches."

"We'll send the paper back out. A different journal this time."

"But it won't be as good as if *JAMA* published it."

"Maybe a forensic journal will be interested. Dr. J. could give you a suggestion. Ask him when you're out there."

"You ask him," Jorge said, his throat tight and his fists clenched. He started for the door. "I haven't been out to their place lately."

That sounded like more bullshit. Jorge's truck was never in front of his apartment. I was getting bullshit from every angle.

After a few moments, I followed Jorge back into the lab. I had been wondering what became of that second article our ace reporter, Chris, had written.

"Last I heard from Chris," Jorge grumbled, "his editor gave him another assignment."

I went to my office and called the newspaper. No Chris. I sweet-talked the receptionist into admitting that Chris was in the building, then I raced home, cranked the Datsun, and drove down there as fast as the piece of junk would go, before they all left for the evening.

The offices of the *Island Daily* are downtown in an 1850s dry goods warehouse, a disintegrating, red-brick building rimmed with turrets and gargoyles. I parked the Datsun in the back of the building among the rusted old wrecks and a solitary brand-new silver Lincoln Continental with plates that read, "BIG ED," evidently the wheels of the big-shot editor of a small-time newspaper.

I walked through the massive front door, under a pair of nasty, horned gargoyles sticking their long, pointy tongues at me. I found Chris's office and walked in. It smelled like a middle-school gymnasium in there. Chris was sitting behind a dented-up wooden desk, fooling with a soggy, cold cigar, his face all scrunched up. He had on a wrinkled, two-day-old shirt with a tie the light-brown color of liver. He looked surprised and put down the cigar.

"Sure, Doctor Mallow, I remember the series of articles we planned," he said, obviously discomfited by this sudden role reversal that had *me* questioning *him*. "I wrote up the second article, did a bang-up job with the statistics, everything you and Jorge gave me."

"What happened?"

"My editor had it in line for another Sunday special, lead article. Then he called me in and told me he wasn't going to run it, he was stopping the series."

"Why?"

"No real reason." Chris picked up the cigar again and began examining it like it was a rare fossil he'd discovered in his ashtray. "Editors don't need a reason. He loved the angle, then he's telling me the piece was too radical. 'Texans aren't interested in car safety,' he says."

"Right."

"Face it, Doctor Mallow." Chris glanced up. "Nobody wants to hear about statistics. Not your average man-on-the-street."

"So he dumped the series."

"Yeah, but he *loved* my idea about Doctor Jawicki." Chris smiled. "Told me to expand it for the Sunday edition, with pictures."

"Did Dr. J. go for that?"

"Thanks to you. Once I mentioned your name, Jawicki had me right out to his facility. He didn't seem to mind the photographer on the second visit, either."

"Has that story run?"

"Uh uh. Not yet." My interviewee was losing interest. He leaned back in his chair, then fumbled in his drawer and pulled out a book of Press Club matches. "It'll be out in Sunday's edition." A surreal smoke ring floated toward me. "My editor wants a few changes, but I'm not at liberty to say what our angle is."

Sunday, August 9

Chris was not at liberty to discuss his "angle" because, at the urging of his editor, he'd cooked up a trashy newspaper article that made the M.E.'s office look like it was run by Bela Lugosi. The article kicked off with "A tour of the facility is like stepping into The Texas Chainsaw Massacre." The purple prose hit Dr. J.'s deteriorating facility, his antiquated methods, and his collection of brains from 30 years of autopsies. The story was the lead local interest article in today's *Island Daily*. The big brother paper in Houston ran it, too. I called Dr. J. the moment I put down the newspaper.

"I'm so sorry about this, Dr. J. I mean, they made you out to be a blood-thirsty ghoul, collecting body parts for the hell of it."

"It's not your fault, Peter."

"But I'm the one who sent that jerk out there!"

"I was a fool. I thought that fellow, Chris, was sincere. I explained the county's funding problems, demonstrated the outdated facilities. Chris came with a photographer, and one kept me talking while the other took the photos, then the video."

"Video?"

"It'll be Channel 13's Special Report tonight. That silly feature they do at the end."

"Oh, no."

Brenda and I watched the ten o'clock news on the boys' TV. They panned around the defunct Public Health Hospital and went into Dr. J.'s broken-down trailer. In the hospital garage where he stores all the brains, the camera went close-up on a damp spot on the cement floor where a brain container had leaked a few drops of formaldehyde. The narrator's voice got deep and serious, like he'd discovered a major environmental threat.

The shots of Dr. J. were worse. At the sight of his angular, anemic face and the wrinkled chicken-skin drooping beneath his chin, Brenda exclaimed, "That's not Dr. J.!" In the final video bite, Dr. J. was citing statistics on the number of decomposed bodies that wash up on the beach each year.

"Is it that bad out there, Peter?"

"This is bullshit. Dr. J.'s a dedicated public servant and the finest of gentlemen. Damn! *JAMA* rejects our paper, then Chris trashes Dr. J. It's nothing but bad news. What's next?"

Tuesday, August 11

Yesterday, after the Channel 13 'Special Report,' I played phone tag with the Automotive Safety Board all day. We had already shut down the lab and it must've been 8 p.m. on the East Coast when I conned a sleepy secretary in D.C. into giving me Sokolof's private office number. It was a New Orleans area code.

This morning, bright and early, I called New Orleans and got Sokolof's personal secretary. I could hear her typing tick tick tick on her computer as she spoke in a dripping, Mid-South drawl. "I do believe he's in. Let me check, honey." There was a pause, about long enough for Jack to tell her to get rid of me. "I'm afraid Mr. Sokolof's not in the office. He'll be out-of-pocket all week, honey." Tick tick.

To my surprise, Sokolof called me two hours later.

"You've been trying to reach me, professor?" he crooned.

"I was wondering…"

"Of course you've been wondering. Rest assured, you will receive no further consideration by our board. Shouldn't you just abandon this whole thing? You are a virologist, after all. You've been misled by your emotional student, Professor Mallow… what was his name?"

"Acosta."

"Yes, Jorge Acosta. It's his misguided venture. Face it. Incidentally, how has your manuscript faired?"

"It was rejected by *JAMA*."

"Some manuscripts were never meant to see the light of day."

I began to curse under my breath. He begged off, claiming it was "necessary to take another call," and I held a dead phone, cursing to myself. I paced in my office for a few minutes and decided to call Yamata again. The Nissan man himself came on the line, smooth and confident.

"Yes, of course I remember, Doctor Mallow. Quite alarming data, really." I placed Yamata's accent more precisely now. It was pure Boston Brahmin, old Louisberg Square.

"It's been nearly six months, Mr. Yamata."

"Our board considers an inordinately high number of safety concerns, Doctor Mallow. I spoke with Dr. Sokolof, and he mentioned an analysis he was pursuing."

"I'm sure Dr. Sokolof is already overburdened. Might you shepherd this along yourself, to some degree?"

"I suppose I could devote a bit of time to it."

"Wouldn't you agree, Mr. Yamata, if only one life were saved, that one life would be worth the effort?"

He paused for a moment. "That exact thought crossed my mind when I first heard your presentation. But these issues are complex. And it's not my area."

"Perhaps you could make it your area. Informally, of course?"

"Informally? Yes, I suppose I could."

Tuesday, August 25

Brenda was messing around by the calendar this morning before she rushed off to lecture. I got a closer look after she left. She'd been marking down her body temperature for all of August. That could mean only one thing. We needed to talk. And I needed to check my supply of condoms.

In the lab, our paper on *MORPH* and *BADMORPH* had gone winging off to the *Journal of Virology*. To celebrate, I took Lilly and Jorge out for a Mexican lunch. Ever since *JAMA* rejected his vehicular immersion paper, Jorge had been deathly quiet, literally locking himself up in the Level 4. He'd become an expert at knocking out genes, but he'd lost a few of the pounds he'd gained earlier. Our lab celebration at *Los Pericos* felt more like a funeral.

I sucked down too many margaritas before the plates arrived, and after lunch, I took a nap in the library. I woke up with the taste of lime juice and *salsa verde* at the back of my mouth, my sinuses wrecked from the ozone in the August air. I grabbed my bike and rode home to wait for Brenda. The Galveston sun was bearing down. Moribund from the heat, I turned the window unit on high and lay on the floor under the ceiling fan.

"Hey," I barked as soon as she walked in. "What's with the temperature chart? Looking to get pregnant?"

"Just keeping track."

"When a woman's charting her temperature, she's looking to get pregnant. You're still on the pill, right?"

"No, Peter. I stopped them."

"What? What the hell?" I sat up and tried my best to glare. "Please start the pill again, Brenda. We've discussed this. You know I don't want more kids, I've said it over and over. Not now. Too much is happening. There's Chad and Travis. You're into the boys, they're around, and they *adore* you. Maybe someday, I don't know. But not now."

So it went all night, a clash of biologic agendas in the warm, tropical darkness. I made a mental note to stop by the pharmacy first thing in the morning.

Wednesday, August 26

Brenda woke up early, sat at the desk, and wrote furiously. I rolled over on the futon and stared at her knees. I had not a clue that this would be a second really bad day.

"What are you writing?"

"The wrap-up for my Grief and Grieving course. It's at 9."

Brenda had been asked by her department chairwoman to share her expertise on the grief response with medical students. Two lectures quickly turned into a whole course with group sessions, patient interviews, and more of Brenda's intriguing lectures.

"I'm sorry about last night, baby."

"It's all right."

"It's just that...."

"I know." I lumbered toward the edge of the futon and thought about kissing her. "Stay in bed, Peter," she said. "I need to finish this and get ready for the library meeting."

"Your new library's coming along, huh?"

She leaned back in her chair. "It'll be the finest medical humanities library west of the Mississippi. That second shipment of historic books is finally on its way from Vienna."

I lay in bed watching Brenda grimace over her notes. She had given my little pine desk a workout since we moved into the carriage house, even managed a sputtering start to her dissertation thesis. The desk was so incredibly overburdened, one of its legs looked like it was bowing out, warped and weird, like a desk in a Salvador Dali painting. As I watched, the distorted leg broke clean in two, the desk tilted over, and Brenda's papers dumped onto the floor.

Brenda started screaming, "Oh, God! Termites!" She leapt up as the desk leg expelled thousands of tiny white xylophagous bodies to writhe in the slats of sunlight streaming through the old cypress shutters. "How disgusting!"

The desk had been turned into a labyrinth of winding catacombs. Kilograms of worker insects spilled out in a pile of splintered wood and soggy, fetid, sawdust.

"It even smells disgusting!"

"They must've come right through the floorboards. This place is loaded!"

And that's how my second really bad day began. With stinking termites.

I calmed Brenda down, swept the mess into a garbage bag, and promised to call a termite service. In the lab, I was haunted by visions of a dark, subterranean kingdom devouring Victorian structures across the island. I went to my office to call the exterminator. That's when I saw the brown envelope sticking out of my mail slot.

I tore at the envelope and pulled out the sheaves of blurry copies that I knew were the reviews of my NIH application. I scanned down to the bottom line, the priority score, and gasped.

"How did *this* happen?" The bottom of the summary read "unscored."

I skimmed the sheets. "It's got to be a mistake. These reviews are too good."

I picked up the phone and dialed cardiology. I needed to talk to Marv. I made them pull him out of a procedure.

"I *was* sure, Peter!" Marv said. "You should've gotten a great score, definitely in the funded range. Myerwitz told me at the bar. Look, take your time, read the reviews over carefully, and fax me a copy. I have to get back to my patient."

I took the reviews to the library and read and re-read them in the cool hum of the powerful, university air conditioning. They were the weirdest reviews I'd ever seen. Marv walked into my office at 6:30 p.m. and I poured him a coffee. His big frame was wrapped in a blood-spattered white coat, straight from passing catheters and salvaging hearts in his cath lab.

"You're right, Peter. Something's screwy. You get glowing comments like *'proposed experiments will elucidate mechanisms highly relevant to the recent outbreak in Asia.'* Then comes the bullshit."

"How is that possible?"

"Peter, those bullshit comments were added *after* the scientific review. Someone fudged the score."

"How do you know?"

"Myerwitz, over the phone this afternoon. He's sure negative criticisms were slipped in at the council level."

"No one can change the score of a study section."

"Administrators can. They prioritize, skip grants, mess with the pay line. No telling why something like that should happen."

"I'm beginning to think I know why."

"Peter, in science, every investigator will have an unfunded period. It's bound to happen, and the most important thing is to maintain your focus in the lab. You'll need to find some small grants, maybe try the Carnes Foundation."

"That's nickel-and-dime, Marv."

"You've got to keep people in your lab or you'll lose your lab space, Peter. It happens, my friend."

"I can't lose Lilly," I muttered.

"Get small-grant money, then write a new NIH grant. There's no sense in even trying with this thing. It's dead in the water with a score like that."

"What about *Bangladesh*, Marv? The epidemic? It's a bird flu poised for the next season, and if it should mutate just right, people will die."

"Listen, I'll help in any way I can. I could even pick up Lilly's salary for a month or two. Let me know."

Marv walked out of my office and I was left alone to stare at the pile of dark, smeary copies that spelled out my future.

Laura Sacchi called me at home. It was late in the evening, well past 10. Brenda answered the phone. "It's your friend Dr. Sacchi from the CDC."

"Pete?..." Laura hesitated, as if she'd been stopped by Brenda's voice.

"It's fine, Laura. Good to hear from you."

"How are *you* doing?"

"Not so good. I've run into a funding hiatus, lost my NIH grant. I'll be downsizing. In fact, the Mallow lab may disappear."

"What happened to your vehicular-immersion paper?"

"*JAMA* rejected it." Silence on the line. She'd warned me, hadn't she? "We've sent it to a forensics journal."

"I've been working on this thing myself, Pete. Ever hear of a researcher named Zoltan Szabo? He was an epidemiologist, a pioneer in toxic exposures. He published hundreds of papers during the '50s and '60s on what we'd now call 'environmental health.'"

"So?"

"Pete, this guy Szabo wrote two papers that are *exactly* like yours."

"He described vehicular immersions?"

"Same data. In 1966. I'll send you copies of the two papers from the *American Journal of Mortal Statistics*. It's a discontinued journal. But listen to this. In his second paper, Szabo advanced a hypothesis about this 'new' cause of death. Do you know when power windows came in?"

"Sixties."

"Good guess. The first automatic transmission was actually a stock item in the 1939 Buick. During the '50s, a few upper-end models had automatic, push-button transmissions and auto windows. Not until the '60s did auto-locks come in and power windows become standard equipment in American cars, even in a few low-budget models."

"His studies were ignored, like mine."

"Szabo was at NYU. I checked, and two older faculty members remember a crazy Hungarian, brilliant, outspoken, even loud when he was into the vodka. And here's the amazing part, Pete. The Congressional Record cites three separate times Szabo brought the immersion problem to the attention of the U.S. Congress. He also filed one of the earliest consumer class-action lawsuits, against Ford Motor Company. It was unsuccessful."

"So Szabo knew, and he tried to publicize it, but nothing ever came of it."

"In mid-career, he quietly disappeared from science and never published again. He's not on NYU's faculty list after 1968. Do you know what this means, Pete? The auto industry has known for years. Think what consumer advocate lawyers could do with this. Disregard for scientific evidence? The tremendous loss of life? Maybe even a cover up?"

"Sounds like 40 years' worth of lawsuits waiting to happen."

"Retract that paper, Pete. Let the CDC handle this. For your own good."

"You talk like they'll hire a hit man, Laura. Aren't you overreacting a bit?"

"What about that student who wrote the paper with you, Pete? He wants to go to medical school, or was it graduate school?"

"Hang on. They can't influence something like that. Admissions?"

"These bastards can do what they want. They could mess with *your* future, too, Pete."

"Shit. You may be right. I've been getting an awful lot of bad news lately...."

As I recounted for Laura the details on Steve Leitmann and our *JAMA* paper, and the trashing my grant took in review, I ticked off in my mind the plans I had for the fall—our big paper under review at *The Journal of Virology*, the decision on my tenure and promotion, small-grant proposals I'd be sending off. All my plans had suddenly developed hairline cracks, thanks to the downtown Hyatt and Sokolof, with an "F," not a "V."

"Laura, I appreciate your concern," I said, shakily, "but with Jorge, if I back down now...."

Friday, August 28

Since June, two small storms have been named by the National Weather Service. The first one fizzled and the other turned and hit the Yucatan. The third big one of the season was just named Eduardo, but it's still a tropical storm.

I've been staring dumbly at my computer screen, watching swirling red and violet bands of bad weather hover near Florida. Looks like Eduardo slipped over Cuba, jagged north, and stalled. Good for us, bad for Florida. A stalled storm can take a week or more before it commits to a course onto land. I already purchased the big bottle of rum and plenty of mixers, so there's little else to do.

In fact, it seems there's little I can do about anything.

Saturday, August 29

As of 6 a.m. this morning, tropical storm Eduardo edged away from Florida and waffled. This gave the storm the chance to draw strength from the Gulf's overheated, canicular waters, and Eduardo was quickly upgraded to a Category 2 hurricane. The university went under a hurricane watch, or code-orange alert, and now the lab computers stay permanently on the weather radar and the NOAA radio station is full-blast everywhere.

Jorge, oblivious to the weather, was bugging Lilly all morning to help him with his knockout viruses. He seemed to have a problem with the tail end of one DNA sequence. Lilly was preparing buffers in the main lab.

I pushed aside the paperwork on my desk, stood by the window, and watched students and clinic patients amble across the quadrangle in front of Old Red. It was gorgeous Galveston weather, hot and humid, a steady southerly flow whipping the palm fronds, but none of that provided a clue about Eduardo. On the Island, the weather can be perfect right up until a storm hits.

I watched as a glistening stretch limo pulled up at the main entrance to the building, right below my office window. The driver, in a gray uniform, hopped out, jogged around to the rear door, and, incredibly, Jack Sokolof climbed out into the fulgent mid-day sun. He was dressed in a lightweight, tan suit that went perfectly with his splendid snake boots.

I ran to the lab to find Jorge. He had to be in on this, and I knew Sokolof would take a while to get past security. Lilly's finished buffers were lined up in a neat row on the bench.

"He's in the Level 4, titrating virus," she said.

"Get him out of there immediately and to my office."

The second Lilly dashed out of the lab, a tanned, smiling Jack Sokolof entered. He didn't even have a security escort.

"Sorry to drop in on you so unexpectedly, professor Mallow," he said. "Could we go to your office? We need to talk."

I grabbed my desk chair, hoping the stool would put him at a disadvantage. He looked more muscular than I remembered. His personal trainer must have been driving him hard lately.

"I've come today to help you, Professor Mallow. Certainly you're beginning to realize what a huge mistake you've made. Shall we reiterate? First, your paper was refused by *JAMA*."

"We've submitted it elsewhere."

"And now your grants are in trouble, correct? I warned you, professor, how precarious these issues can be, how fickle the funding mechanisms of modern science." He paused. "Honestly, I've come to help you today. I have a proposal."

"A proposal?"

"Corporate funding. I have influence with several exploratory drug firms and the tobacco industry. These concerns provide substantial, high-dollar support to basic scientists exactly like you, Doctor Mallow."

"I've always been an independent scientist, Jack."

"What I am offering has no strings attached. Virtually unlimited funding for your newest virus. Forget this tiresome automotive business, professor. It's sapping your energy."

"No strings attached?"

"None, except you forget your little paper and stop playing Ralph Nader." The faintest smile crossed Sokolof's face. "Get back to your science, professor. I'll have the applications on your desk later today. The review process is minimal, and the turn-around time is fast."

Sokolof leaned back, pulled up his elegantly trousered leg, and showed off his snake-skin boot. I stood up, looked out the window, and thought about my future, downsizing, losing Lilly, giving up the work on *Bangladesh*.

"You can be fully funded within a few weeks."

I thought about Lilly's paycheck, cut off at the end of October. No more students. No more postdocs. In a couple of months' time, no money for equipment, no lab supplies, a research career winding down.

Then, in my mind's eye, I saw the outline of a sleazy academic, heaving a bag of stinking crawfish shell into Burger King's dumpster under cover of darkness. I saw a 16-year-old, questioning everything, being told that some things are only "a little illegal." I turned back to Sokolof.

"No, Jack. No thanks."

"Of course, you may reconsider. Take your time."

"No."

"You haven't any idea how deep our influences run, Mallow. No idea whatsoever." I dropped back into my chair, my mouth clenched tight. Without warning, Jorge rushed through the door, sweaty and flushed. "Ah! Mr. Acosta," Jack said, without missing a beat. "We were just discussing your work." He stood up and gave Jorge a tight, lingering handshake. "I trust your family is well? Your mom? So sad about your father."

"Don't I know you from somewhere?"

"No, and I was just about to leave. Professor Mallow," he said, turning to me, "please take under consideration the matters we have discussed. Remember, it would be a few weeks, well before your present funding lapses." He made a small bow toward Jorge. "Best of luck with your medical school applications." Jack fixed me with one last stare and walked out the door.

Jorge made a grumbling sound in his throat. "That was *him*! And I didn't get to say *anything*."

"It doesn't matter. I didn't either."

I stood by the window and watched Jack stride out the front door of the building and climb into the cool of his air-conditioned limo. His fine linen suit was buffeted by the Gulf breeze. His rough-scaled boots were shining in the late-August sun. He looked like he owned the whole damn university.

Friday, September 4
(Storm Entry)

Hurricane Eduardo luffed in a circle over the Gulf, built strength, and set a westerly course toward Texas. The hurricane "watch" was upgraded to a "warning." We put our experiments on hold and prepared to kill the last of the ducks, secure the lab, and execute our hurricane plan.

"Where are y'all headed for the storm?" I asked as we began working through our list. Not surprisingly, Lilly had the best plan.

"To Houston, on helicopter," she explained. "Chinese embassy make arrangements for their helicopter to come to hospital heli-pad. I'll catch a ride with my Chinese friends."

"What about you, Jorge? Heading off to El Paso?"

"I'm staying," he said, his eyes gleaming.

"No one stays, Jorge."

"When do they declare martial law?"

"It's a code-red situation, Jorge. You have to evacuate. It's in our plan."

"What about you, Dr. Mah-wo?" Lilly asked.

"I'm the code-red person, the last one to leave, so I'll stay here on the island. I've stayed in the old house for hurricanes before, Lilly. Besides, it might take a week to open the damned causeway."

"No, Doctor Mah-wo! I'll arrange embassy helicopter for you. The trauma center's heli-pad is very convenient, and for heaven's sake, Eduardo is a Category 4!"

"Quit worrying, Lilly."

"You are going on helicopter tonight, but right now we have six ducks to kill. I'm almost ready."

By "almost ready," Lilly meant that she had sterilized the surgical tools, arranged the specimen containers, neatly labeled several rackfuls of microfuge tubes, and was now testing the guillotine's sharpness by slicing several Meyer lemons cleanly in two.

Who should stop us, just as Lilly and I were heading out, our arms laden with gear, but Hari Bhalakumarian, now a member of the Coxsackie lab, swaggering down the hall with a clipboard in his hand.

"Professor Mallow. Lilly. I trust that your laboratory's emergency preparations are progressing according to plan. As you're surely aware, I now represent our floor on the University Emergency Preparedness Committee. I'll be checking for proper containment of all hazardous and radioactive materials, before my own evacuation, of course."

Hari was in and out of the labs like a high school hall monitor. He obviously had taken well to being given a modicum of authority, and I had to admit, he was more alert than I remembered him. Perhaps that's where I went wrong with Hari. I was a bad boss for him because I didn't push or demand much. It's not my lab style. I figure each researcher, at any level, will rise to their highest potential solely because the work is so fascinating. Science should be its own best reward. Pushing people doesn't work, at least in my lab.

Lilly and I made short work of the ducks in the Level 4, less than three hours, done by noon. Then she and Jorge covered the heavy equipment with plastic, packed delicate items in plastic bins from Wal-Mart, and battened down the computers, freezers and centrifuges.

I was in my office securing the microscopes when the phone rang. It was Dr. J. He was doing an autopsy, of all crazy things, and he needed help.

"It's complicated, Peter. I'm in a spot," he said. "There's a lawyer in this family...."

"Uh oh."

"... and he wants to autopsy his grandfather, a Houston City Councilor who died after heart surgery. Unfortunately, Granddad was buried in our county eight months ago."

"And they dug him up."

"The family's thinking Denton Cooley didn't put in the heart valves they were charged for. My techs have left the island, but by court order, I need to release this body today."

I left the hurricane preparations to Lilly and Jorge and drove out Seawall Boulevard in the magnificent noon-day sunshine. It's weird how a killer storm can be a few hundred miles away, and it's gorgeous on the island. Must've been like that for the 1900 storm, taking the citizenry by surprise. One sure sign, though—the Gulf was pounding the seawall with rolling lines of long-breaking, eight-foot waves, and the surfers were all over it.

When I opened the door, Dr. J. had already made the Y-shaped incision and exposed the abdominal contents. Dr. J.'s morgue is stiflingly small, with walls of decrepit, flaking brick, and poor, yellowish lighting. Bodies in his facility are stashed in old-fashioned pull-out drawers, un-refrigerated. Dr. J. operates mostly with hand tools. It's like something out of the 19th century.

"Phew. Must've been a poor job of embalming," I said.

I quickly pulled on an apron, skimmed the hospital charts, and gloved up.

"Ready for the storm, Peter? Have the boys already left?"

"They should be long gone by now, with their mother. I need to finish in the lab, then board up my house." I began helping Dr. J. eviscerate. "I'll stay on the island. I have before."

The heart was well-preserved by the embalming, but the abdominal contents were in an advanced state of decomposition. I excised and dissected the heart while Dr. J. continued with the routine procedures of slicing the decaying liver and piecing together rotten bowel. Waves of nausea washed over me. I tried moving to a far table, but it didn't help.

"Sorry, Peter. With only this old window unit and that oscillating fan... Here, let me turn the fan toward you."

"Nothing unusual in the heart," I told him, fighting to keep from gagging. "Prosthetic valves are okay, suture lines intact."

"Looks like we've stymied another gold-digging expedition, Peter. Go ahead out, but would you wait in the trailer a moment? I'd like to talk. I'll be right over."

I sat in Elena's office chair, surrounded by the looming, white shapes of the plastic sheets that covered the desk, the office equipment, and the plastic bins filled with records. A few streaks of late afternoon light filtered obliquely through the boarded-up trailer windows. The office was airless. When Dr. J., pale and bent, slipped through the trailer door, he looked like a ghost, and the stench of his bloody scrubs seemed to confirm the impression. He sat on Elena's plastic-wrapped desk, his face as gloomy as the darkening sky outside.

"I wanted you to know, Peter, I plan to retire this year."

"Uh, good for you!" I said, at a loss for words.

"The time is right. Elena and I will return to Venezuela, her homeland. Perhaps I'll continue forensic work there, part time. I wasn't planning this, but the changed atmosphere in the office, the fiscal pressures, and the recent bad press.... It's the best decision, Peter, especially now, with the investigation by the Environmental Protection Agency over Channel 13's 'formalin spill.' The paperwork promises to be insurmountable."

"I wish we'd never dragged you into all that."

"No, Peter, don't blame yourself. There are personal reasons for my decision as well. Elena and I have been going through a trying time in our relationship. She has tremendous mood swings, you know."

"I would never guess."

"She's tortured by her problems, a variety of things, but we've agreed it's best to take her away from here. With time, things will heal."

"It's a good idea to retire. You have your health, Dr. J."

"This chronic anemia saps my strength so. I'm not a young man, Peter. I need sleep. And Elena has needs."

His saying this reminded me of three summers ago, when I covered the M.E.'s office so Dr. J. could be hospitalized. Something about the prostate. I know too well what that might entail. The urinary problems. The impotence. I was trying to think of a positive comment.

"Count yourself lucky, Dr. J. You'll be away from our local politics."

"Oh, speaking of that, I meant to tell you I heard from Peyton Sweeney, the state senator. Peyton's bringing your immersion problem to this fall's legislative session. He's planning a regular crusade. He's a good man. He'll carry the ball for you, Peter."

"Maybe, Dr. J.... Maybe. I need to go," I said abruptly. "Sorry to hear you're leaving, but I'm sure you and Elena will make the best of it."

In the shadowy room, Dr. J.'s ghostly, forlorn smile looked more like a rictus. I was glad to step out the trailer door. The sickening-sweet smell of decay clung to my skin. A black cover of clouds had moved in, but at least it was fresh air.

By 6 p.m., we had wrapped the centrifuges in plastic, moved computers to interior rooms, boxed up lab notebooks and backup data, and locked down the radioactive isotopes. Lilly completed our lab's check list and handed it to Hari. All that was left was to secure the Level 4.

I told Jorge to get out of Dodge. The weather radio had nothing but bad news.

"Sustained winds of 140 miles per hour have been measured by NOAA reconnaissance aircraft."

Lilly and I suited up and passed into the Level 4. We ran through the viral security protocols, connected the viral tanks to the emergency liquid nitrogen, double-checked everything, and wrote it all up for Environmental Safety. Finished at last, we surveyed the unfamiliar shapes of the plastic-covered equipment in the main lab's eerie silence. Out the lab windows, black clouds raced through the sky like time-lapse photography.

"Please come with me, Doctor Mah-wo. Embassy helicopter is waiting at heli-pad."

I hugged her. "Take care, Lilly. Be safe," I said, choking up.

"I be back soon."

I shut the lights and locked the lab and was on my way to close up my office when I thought, *Bangladesh*! A ripple of anguish ran through me as I realized our stocks of *Bangladesh horrificans*, a living virus impossible to replace, were stored in a single viral freezer-tank in the Level 4. Backup! I needed backup!

I returned to the Level 4, pulled on a space suit, slipped through the locks to the infectious storage area, and extracted two stock vials of *Bangladesh*. Out through the chemical shower and sterile-lock, I spirited the two vials back to the main lab and stashed them in the bottom of an old freezer, definitely not authorized for viral storage. And to hell with Environmental Safety.

As I was locking the lab door behind me, Jorge came jogging down the hall. "You're supposed to be gone," I said.

Big blue veins were pulsing in his neck. "Billy Ray wants me to hang with The Eagles. They're throwin' a monster hurricane party in the Old Jack Tar Motel."

"No way. Uh uh," I said. The Old Jack Tar, the oldest motel on the Island, should've been shut down years ago. It's the kind of dump where they rent rooms by the hour. "Okay, listen. Do you want to stay in the big house with me?"

"Sure. Thanks," he said, swaying back and forth, his hands stuffed deep into his pants. "And for after the storm, Doctor Mallow, I brought the Bergmann along!" he exclaimed, and he slipped the pistol out of his pocket. With the Bergmann professionally grasped in both hands, he sighted down the hall as if picking off imaginary looters.

"Jorge! You're packing iron on campus?"

"When they declare martial law, Doctor Mallow, we'll need it."

"It's not loaded, is it?"

"Of course it is."

"Well, unload it. And when you get to the house, you're putting it away."

I raced home. Brenda had already closed the storm shutters. All shut up, the old Victorian looked angrily down at me as I biked up the sidewalk.

"Peter! Peter!" Brenda ran down the front steps to me. "Come. The boys are still here! In Mr. Kreuger's. They didn't evacuate with Ellen!"

Mr. Kreuger was in his easy chair, Scotch in hand, the NOAA radio blaring next to him. Chad and Travis were at the north window, watching a gusty east wind torture the pecan tree in the backyard.

"What the hell?" I scowled. "You two are supposed to be off-island."

"I thought it would be okay," Chad said, nonchalantly, without looking away from the window.

"Well, it's not okay." I grabbed him by the arm and Brenda and I hustled them both to Ellen's place, one block over. But Ellen's was boarded shut, no boyfriend's Jeep on the street, and the whole street looked abandoned.

"What the hell? They left you two?"

"I lied, Dad," Chad confessed. "I told Mom you wanted us to stay in the big house."

I was speechless.

"I'll load the boys in the Rover," Brenda said, "and I'll evacuate with them."

"No. No. It's too late. This storm is coming tonight. You can't get caught on the road. They should have gone yesterday with Ellen. But thanks to you, Chad...."

"Peter, it's okay," Brenda said. "Let's board up and make the best of it."

"You two guys get inside the house and stay there!" I was boiling. "Don't budge! We'll talk about this later, Chad."

Brenda and I had positioned the ladder to nail down the first shutter, when Jorge came up the sidewalk. I took him inside, confiscated the Bergmann, and stashed it in its spot at the bottom of a kitchen drawer, under the dishtowels. His box of ammo went in with the silverware.

"Give us a hand with the shutters, would you?" I asked.

"Ah, it's not much of a storm," he told me, with a long face. "I think I'd rather see if the Press Club is open." He sauntered off.

As darkness fell, the sky turned the color of red brick, a sign noted by Isaac Cline, Galveston's meteorologist at the time of the 1900 storm. I nailed two-by-fours across each shutter while Brenda held the flashlight and steadied the ladder against a gusty, shifting east wind, another bad sign.

When we'd finished battening down, Brenda stepped off the top of the ladder onto the rail of the second-story porch, and began working her way up the side of the house like a rock climber, using the porch poles and gingerbread for handholds, until she clung near the peak of the south gable. She'd been complaining about a rusted rain gutter banging against the side of the house, and she aimed to pull it down.

"Jesus, baby. Don't you need a rope or something?" I'd forgotten about her mountaineering experience in the Grand Tetons with husband Tom.

"There's plenty of handholds up here, Peter," she shouted. "The adrenaline helps, too."

She worked the gutter loose and threw it with a crash into the front yard. Once she was safely down, we found everyone inside getting into bed. Jorge had returned and sacked out on the floor in the boys' room. Brenda and I staggered to our carriage-house apartment to listen to the weather radio. I cracked open my big bottle of dark, Bermuda rum, poured some into two glasses and squeezed the juice out of a grapefruit. I drizzled the pale pink juice into the booze.

"We're long overdue for a big storm," Brenda said. "Everyone says so."

"People always say that, Brenda, but these big storms can swerve at the last minute, reverse course, anything. Maybe it'll make landfall in Corpus, or Mexico."

"We're way overdue." Brenda's eyes were at half-mast.

"We'll know soon enough. In the summer of 1915," I said, softly, "there were two big hurricanes in one week." I got up to make more drinks. This time I used ginger beer for the mixer.

> "The present track of Eduardo will bring the storm along the upper Texas coast during the early morning hours. Landfall is predicted for Galveston Island."

Brenda climbed into bed. I tossed back the last of my drink and stepped into the backyard. The changeable east wind had calmed. A pale, hump-backed moon ducked in and out among black, anvil-shaped clouds. To the north, lightning spasmodically scored the sky.

I crawled into bed next to Brenda and closed my eyes, but all I could see was that peculiar red brick color of the sky at sunset. Rain began to drum on the slate roof.

I dreamed of Jorge. He was with Dr. J. They were taking target practice, with pistols, walking together in a misty, heavily wooded bottomland, swaggering, smiling, shooting at small birds, at fleeing wolves. Abruptly, they paced off in opposite directions, turned, and took aim at each other under an eerie, brick-red sky.

Hurricanes come in peaks and valleys, and the first big peak woke us at 2 a.m. with a blast against the east wall. The carriage house shuddered and Brenda and I jumped from bed. The shutters rattled and bowed into the wood-frame windows, scattering chips of old paint onto the floor.

"Let's get into the main house with the others, baby."

"Will my snake be all right?"

"It's high enough here. But put on your tennis shoes. You don't want to step on anything in the backyard."

"Like what?"

"Like real snakes. Wild snakes, not pets. Mr. Kreuger says the storm surge forces them out all over the Island."

At the first lull in the wind, we waded through a foot and a half of water in the backyard. Bits of debris flew by like bullets, writhing balls of fire ants bobbed in the dingy water, and the neighbor's wooden slat fence was folding in and out like an accordion. At the back stairs, I swooped my hand into the water. Salt. The briny taste of the bay meant tidal flooding had begun.

Mr. Kreuger sat at Brenda's cherry table with a glass of Johnny Walker Black Label, neat.

"Getting a little wet in my place, Doc. Your boys are still up there, listening to the wind."

In Mr. Kreuger's apartment, the boys were with Jorge at a north window that had had its storm shutter torn off. There was a continuous thumping sound, and when the wind peaked, the house creaked like a wooden ship at sea. Water was coming in around the windows on the east side. I mopped up the floor and threw down towels, but the water kept coming. Out the window, the neighbors' asphalt shingles peeled off in long, tumbling sheets.

"Is our roof doing that, Dad?" Travis asked.

"Ours is the old slates, son, and it went through the Great Storm, don't forget."

"We're cool," Chad added. My thoughts turned to the Medical Research Institute and its roof. Would the building hold? Would my lab be trashed? Roofs came in all sizes and strengths.

"You two aren't even supposed to be here!" I said, raising my voice above the storm. "Come on, boys. Let's get downstairs."

We waited for daybreak. The NOAA radio blared its prediction that the Island now lay east of Eduardo's powerful center, and we were doomed to the "wet" side of the storm, the side with the heaviest rain, the highest winds, and the deepest storm surge.

The electricity died. With the storm and the shutters closed tight, the dawn would never come. We lit oil lamps in the dining room. Jorge ventured upstairs to watch the storm at Mr. Kreuger's window, but came racing back.

"That big tree is falling over!"

I went with Jorge to see for myself. The towering pecan leaned at a nasty angle against the carriage house, breaking into its south wall and caving its roof. Our lovers' hide-away was crushed. The wind raised an octave, like a woman screaming in the night. Roof slates and palm fronds tumbled through the air. We stood in an inch of water. I motioned to Jorge, and we ran downstairs to huddle with the others in the central hall and listen to Travis reel off facts he'd memorized about The Great Storm of 1900.

"People's heads were chopped off by flying slates!... Horses were impaled on stakes in mid-gallop!... Snakes hung in knots from the trees!... Bodies bobbed in the bay for weeks, but when they took 'em out to sea on barges, the bodies washed up and rotted on the beach!"

"Enough with the history lesson, please!" Brenda cried.

We pulled a mattress under the central staircase and sat there all night near a single, dull lamp. Brenda, raised a good Episcopalian, led us all in prayer. She did a good job of it, getting us to join hands in a circle, even Jorge, to ask that "Our Heavenly Father watch over us in this perilous time."

Jorge ran through the house, reporting on the latest leaks. I paced the dark hallway in the insufferable dampness and heat, listening to the house groan, the wind scream, and NOAA's final, frenzied report, before its antenna blew away:

"Tornadoes have been sighted at 30th and 33rd Streets! For God's sake, take cover!"

"Are we gonna be okay, Daddy?"

"Yes, son. It can't last much longer."

"Jorge! Would you please stop that incessant rocking?"

Only Mr. Kreuger slept, thanks to his friend, Johnnie Walker.

When dawn finally broke, it brought an ominous silence. The sudden, total quiet could mean only one thing—the storm's eye was passing directly over the island. We all rushed onto the front porch, where we heard the cry of birds, every species of bird, trapped in the hurricane's eye. Circling overhead in the uncanny light were clouds of laughing gulls, tiny V-tailed swallows, and mammoth brown pelicans with wings outstretched like pterodactyls in a prehistoric sky.

As we watched, the wind moaned from the other direction, and I pushed everyone back through the door as Eduardo roared to life again.

There were four more hours of hurricane, and when it died we stood with our neighbors in the windless street, stunned, speechless, and surrounded by devastation. The only sound was the cheep of baby birds as they floated, still in their nests, down the street's gutters.

I walked to the university but was stopped by security at the edge of campus. I could see the roof of the Institute. It looked okay. Brenda and I went with the boys on foot to the Gulf, where mounds of oceanic detritus marked where Eduardo's tidal surge had breached Seawall Boulevard. The roof of *Los Pericos* Mexican restaurant had been torn away by a tornado and dropped two blocks inland onto the roofless bowling alley, astraddle lanes two through 12.

In the fading light of day, citizens gathered on the boulevard to marvel at the flat, green Gulf. The mood was solemn. The sea's surface gave off a pale fluorescence. Few spoke.

"All accounted for?"

"Boil the water."

"Ice is on the way."

Outside the Old Jack Tar Motel, we found Billy Ray bare-chested and his blonde lady, in a skimpy bikini, sipping on a pint of Jack Daniels. Every window in the Jack Tar had been blown out. A falling oak had smashed its roof and cleanly cut the manager's Cadillac in two.

"We're fine, Doc," Billy Ray said. "Bikes are inside. They'll dry out."

"Kick-ass storm," his girlfriend added, tipping back the Jack.

Brenda and I surveyed the old house. Windows out, the roof over the east gable splintered, massive interior water damage. The carriage house roof was creased down the center by the pecan tree, but Brenda's snake survived.

I was asking myself whether I had any two-cycle oil for the chain saw when my thoughts were shattered by the crack of a gunshot.

"What the...?" I muttered. "In the backyard?"

Pow! Pow! Two more gunshots. Brenda and I peered out the carriage house door. It was Jorge, taking aim at something high up in the fig tree. I froze.

Brenda walked calmly toward him. "Give me the gun, Jorge."

"What's he shooting at?" I asked.

"Snakes," Brenda said as she took the pistol. "Poor, defenseless, snakes."

Saturday, September 5

The moment hurricane Eduardo left the Island, the weather breathed a sigh of relief. Today felt like a warm, autumn day, and it looked like autumn, too, since Eduardo blew every last leaf out of the trees. The causeway was closed, but the island streets were passable enough for a squall line of zigzagging motorcycles to roar up to the house. Jorge climbed onto the back of Wayne's smoking '32 Harley, and the Harley smoked off.

The boys' room had stayed miraculously dry, so it temporarily became home to Mr. Kreuger as well. Brenda and I moved our digs to the upstairs parlor of the main house. We un-boarded the south windows to catch the breeze, repaired the screens, evicted the soaked furniture, and threw down a mattress spared by Eduardo. In the tepid darkness, we lay between two oil lamps, the breeze swirling around us, the tropical moisture smooth and slick on our skins. It was strange to think that only the night before, we shook with terror and uncertainty. Now, in the moonlight, we made slow, methodical love that was full of purpose.

"I'll miss the carriage house, Peter."

"It's perfect here."

The southerly breeze buckled the screen inward with a snap and Brenda edged firmly against my back, murmuring something I didn't catch. Outside, the island night deepened and filled with the rustle of palm fronds and the peep of tree frogs. I was wide awake.

"This weather's perfect, too, isn't it, sweetheart?"

"Hmm, yes. And Mr. Gonzo's so much nicer without the condoms."

Sunday, September 6

The third day after Eduardo, the causeway is still shut down, and the neighborhood is filled with the smell of grilling steaks. Everyone's been on the street, sharing their ice, reviewing their losses, surveying how life has changed. It feels like we've been through an epidemic, but the unseen, infectious organism circulating among us has failed to invade our flesh, our organs, our tissues. Instead, I'm afraid it's subtly damaged something deeper, perhaps our souls, where it will form a dense, choking cicatrix—a scar that, with time, will mature and surround everything that's normal and good.

Tuesday, September 8

The university locked down for five days. The Medical Research Institute was shut tight, until university security recoded my badge for the building and I was finally able get into the lab. The new Prison Hospital's brick facade had peeled like a bad sunburn, but the Research Institute took little damage, thanks to its solid-brick construction and heavy tile roof. I opened the lab to find everything already unpacked and in order, and Lilly at her lab bench with her head in her hands, weeping.

"You're here!" she cried. "Oh! Doctor Mah-wo!" Her face was blotchy and full of strain. She threw out her arms and slumped against me.

"Lilly, what's wrong?"

"Viruses all dead!" My heart started to race. "Level 4 viral freezer-tanks, emergency generator, liquid nitrogen backup, all go down. Viruses thawed out and died!"

"Impossible. Those systems are foolproof. They've got to be shut down one by one."

"Backup systems not work! All researchers have to replace viruses, but it's not possible to replace the *Bangladesh*. It's not possible!"

I grabbed her shoulders and looked her in her red and puffy eyes. "Calm down, Lilly. There are ways of replacing *Bangladesh*. Trust me. I'll come up with a vial of virus."

"You sure?"

"I'm positive." Icy sweat covered the back of my neck. Had Sokolof returned? During a hurricane, when the Island was evacuated, the causeway closed? "Lilly, you haven't seen anyone strange around the building, have you?"

"No one."

"How did you get back so quickly?"

"Embassy helicopter, yesterday."

"And your badge?"

"Recoded by Chinese friends at university security," she said, smiling at last. "For immediate re-entry."

"I'm so glad you're safe." We embraced. "And you've already unpacked everything."

"All equipment working perfect. You sure about another vial of *Bangladesh?*"

Lilly started a new gel and I went to my office to plug everything in, boot the computer, and recalibrate the microscopes.

Everyone gets a little crazy after a big storm. Life is a jumble of martial law, National Guardsmen, and ice lines. Friends and neighbors stand on the sidewalk arguing, and kids can't find a thing to do without electricity. The death rate goes sky high from the homicides and suicides. Half the men past 50 suffer a heart attack, though I expected Mr. Kreuger would be spared, since he kept himself so well fortified with Scotch.

My office looked a total mess. At first, I thought it was the hurricane craziness. The piles of papers on my desk were in the wrong places, as if they'd been shuffled. My can of pencils had toppled over, and—what was this?—the bottom desk drawer, my "secret" drawer, was open! I felt a single, hard thump beneath my sternum, a peak of adrenaline in my blood. I pulled the secret drawer open. Totally empty! Years of photos, videos, letters—an intimate history, gone missing.

I sat and listened to my own harsh breathing, trying to think of what to do next. Stupidly, I felt compelled to lock up an empty drawer. I found the key in its usual spot under my Nikon microscope, locked the drawer, returned the key, and started for the door. I hated to do it, but I had to tell Brenda.

Stepping out of the office, I found myself face to face with Jorge. He wore the same T-shirt and baggy jeans he'd had on four days ago. His breath reeked of alcohol and his clothes smelled like the beach. Damp patches of sand were stuck in his hair.

"Me and the guys rode all the way to Surfside. We've been camping out."

"How's your apartment?"

"Lots of windows out. My landlord nailed up plastic sheets. The Mac with all my string theory work got trashed."

"Is it salvageable?"

"Probably not. The *Bangladesh* and *PAKG* data is here, so I'm cool."

"You look like you need some rest, Jorge."

"Nah, what I need is a shower. I thought I could get one in the hospital somewhere."

"Get a shower and we'll get cracking in the lab."

"How about tomorrow? I'm driving out to Dr. J.'s. They're back now and I want to help with their hurricane repairs on the beach house."

I left the lab and raced home with my bad news about the videos. At home, Brenda had bad news of her own. Her pet project, the humanities library, had been inundated by the tidal surge, and hundreds of valuable books had been soaked.

"Stupid administrators," she said, with tears welling at the outer corners of her eyes. "What a horrendous lack of foresight! All those beautiful old volumes, one-of-a-kind editions from Vienna, Munich, Bologna, destroyed by salt water because those idiots went with the low bid and put the new library on the ground floor."

I wrapped my arms around her and pulled her to me. "At least the house came through okay. Once they open the causeway and the insurance adjustors come, we'll fix things." I kissed the residual tears from her cheeks, hating what I had to say next. "I've got bad news of my own, baby. Even worse. Our sexy videos got ripped off."

"What?"

"Somebody found the key and took everything. Tapes, letters, everything."

Right in the hallway, Brenda plopped on the floor and leaned against the wall. "Oh, Peter, no. All that… of *me*? All that… of *us*?"

"I can't explain it."

"Oh, God, why did we do that? Why?"

She covered her eyes and sobbed. I could see tears flow down the sides of her face, first in rivulets, and then her cheeks were awash. I couldn't come up with words, so I held her, shaking like she was, and I started to choke up, too. When her sobbing slowed, I pulled the handkerchief from my back pocket and dabbed at her sweet, smooth cheeks. They stayed pretty damp. Then I blotted my own eyes and gave her the handkerchief to blow her nose. We hadn't said a word. It's times like that I'm glad I have a clean handkerchief in my pocket.

"Nothing will come of it," I said, hardly believing it myself. "It was probably some pervert stealing stuff out of offices, Brenda."

"Let's hope so."

"We need to go on." I told her to try to relax—not likely, though, with the hurricane stress, her library, and now this. "I'm going to take my aggressions out on the pecan tree," I said.

I pulled out the ladder, climbed onto the carriage house roof, fired up the chainsaw, and mounted an assault on the busted tree. It was hot work, jockeying the saw in the heat of the afternoon. I was drenched by the time dusk covered the Island with a darkness it only knows after a hurricane. The main electrical trunks to the university and some city facilities were back on, but most of the residential areas were still blacked out, except for the yellowish light of oil lamps and candles.

Brenda used some of our precious ice to make drinks. She drew me a bath—luckily, our water's heated by gas. I lowered myself into the near-scalding tub by candlelight. Brenda handed me a sweating glass of rum and tonic. I eased back and let the icy glass sooth my raw hands.

"Do you really think it was some weirdo, Peter? How did he know about your drawer?"

"I guess it was an obvious spot. It must've happened during the hurricane preparations. Besides, I was at Dr. J.'s for most of the day."

"I can tell what you're thinking, Peter. This whole business—your grant, Dr. J.'s premature retirement, even our videos getting ripped off—it goes back to those people in D.C., to that guy from Ford."

"Sokolof."

"You have to realize, Peter Mallow, that when bad things happen, it's natural to find someone to blame."

"I'm not making this up, Brenda. He threatened me, then he hijacked our *JAMA* submission, bought off the newspaper, screwed my grant, and he just keeps on coming."

"But your secret drawer? Our tapes?" The water in the tub was getting cold. I felt a sudden chill. "What would he want with them?"

"I'm afraid to think."

Wednesday, September 9

At first, I figured Jorge was coming in late. Lilly and I were quietly cranking out gels, until Jorge burst into the lab, out of breath and flushed.

"Doctor Mallow, I need to talk to you. I need to! Please! In your office!" I herded him out. His eyes were darting every which way. "Did you hear about Dr. J? They're *leaving*." I felt my heart convulse. "*Elena's* leaving for *Venezuela*!"

"Yes, I heard that."

"I was there, visiting with Elena. Dr. J. came home from work and we all talked and… they told me. She *wants* to go, *needs* to go, she said."

"I'm sorry, Jorge, but maybe this is best."

"It's because of all that bad press. Dr. J. even said so. 'Political pressures,' he said. It's those auto executives in D.C. He was sure, like you. You're sure, too, aren't you?"

"It's going to work out for the best, Jorge. Just give it some time." I was thinking as fast as I could of all the clichés and platitudes I'd ever heard for times like these. "You've got your whole life ahead of you, Jorge. Time will heal everything. Elena will keep in touch."

I walked Jorge to my office where we sat for over an hour, saying the same things over and over. Lilly came in, took one look at Jorge, and guided him back to the lab to discuss his knockouts, to change the subject. Then I was back in the office with him for another hour. That's the way it went late into the night, back and forth between Lilly and me.

Friday, September 11

It's now seven days after the storm, and the causeway finally opened to traffic. I was working late, it must've been after 10 p.m. when I heard the scuffle of loafers, somehow familiar, in the hall. Out the lab door, there was nothing. Then, peering out my office window, I saw him, and I knew. It was Hari Bhalakumarian. I watched him slide into the driver's side of a brand-new Mustang GT, a metallic, candy-apple red. It looked fully loaded. It was Hari, bought off by Sokolof. I was sure.

Just before Eduardo hit, Hari had been running around the building like a maniac. He could have rifled through my office and emptied my drawer while I was off helping Dr. J. with that stinking autopsy, or any time, really. Nobody would have noticed, and he probably had keys to all the labs because he was on that hurricane monitoring committee. He had plenty of time to sabotage the Level 4. He was smart enough, and he knew enough about the fail-safe systems. Hari had joined Sokolof's team.

But there's not a thing I can do, except ignore the traitor. I can't very well file a complaint with the Scientific Misconduct Committee. What would I tell them? That my postdoc, the one I fired, ripped off my personal porn collection?

Luckily, thanks to my backup plan, Hari's attempt to kill the *Bangladesh* virus failed. I feel sorry for all the scientists who lost everything, though. All those bugs—like Ebola, Marburg, and that still unnamed Argentine encephalitis virus—bugs so rare it'll take weeks, even months, to replace them. But we can forge ahead with our work on *Bangladesh*. I admit, Lilly sure looked at me funny when I pulled out my backup tubes of the virus.

Monday, September 14

This is a date I won't forget. It was the worst, most shocking news of my life. When Dad and Mom died, that was bad, as bad as my brother Lee dying of AIDS in prison, but at least everyone was prepared for all that bad news. I should've expected bad news, barely two weeks after the hurricane. Still, this came as a complete surprise.

It started off with nothing special, yesterday, a comment in a little box on the bottom of the front page of the *Island Daily*.

> The body of an unidentified Hispanic woman estimated to be in her early 30s was discovered on Matagorda Island's west beach. The Matagorda County Medical Examiner's office is seeking dental records for definitive....

The devastating blow came today. Lilly had been in the Level 4 all morning. Jorge was busy at his lab bench when Brenda threw open the main door to the lab and motioned me into the hall. I was perplexed as to how she'd talked the security guards into letting her by. Probably, they had a look at her face, and that was enough.

"It was *Elena*," she whispered. "Her BMW was found on the beach road, Peter."

"Elena? Oh, God, not Elena. It couldn't be."

"The news is all across campus. Nobody knows exactly what happened."

"Are you sure?"

"The police released the name. The identification was conclusive."

"I can't believe this. Who?... How could this happen?"

"Is Jorge in the lab, Peter?"

"I'll have to tell him. I've got to be the one."

"Stay with him, Peter. Be sure to keep him near."

I stepped back into the lab. Jorge was standing at the lab bench preparing to run an assay, meticulously pipetting tiny aliquots of viral protein onto the gel, the most delicate step, critical for the outcome of the data. The last thing in the world I wanted was to give Jorge more bad news. I stood next to him and waited until he'd finished the row of tubes. There was something funny about the way he was moving, all jerky and mechanical.

"Jorge, I'm afraid we need to talk about something. Some bad news."

"I know all about it," he said, dead still, staring ahead at nothing.

"You heard?"

His hand gave up the finest of tremors, barely perceptible as he set down the pipette, and for a second I thought he was about to break down and cry.

"She talked about this. She was always talking about one thing or another."

Jorge went back to his gel, gently lifted the fragile membrane, and carried it in its dish down the bench for the next step. I walked along behind him.

"I know you feel awful. I'm so sorry, Jorge. Do you know how it happened?"

As he loaded the gel into the electrophoretic apparatus and cranked the voltage, I realized what was strange about him. Turning the dials, his arms moved in tiny increments, with incredible precision, at sharp angles. He was moving like a robot.

"I know there was a lot between you, Jorge. You were close to Elena, and Dr. J., too."

"Not anymore. Not him."

"You were upset they were leaving."

"I won't talk about it. I won't. I need to get into the Level 4. There's work to do."

He turned his head at me in a sudden, precise movement, but his face showed something that wasn't precise, wasn't even human. It was something ugly, something in his eyes. I thought he might've been crying, but his eyes were as dull and dry as dust. They were shot full of red, and capillaries had burst on his cheeks. This wasn't lack of sleep, or gloom. It was far beyond that. His face changed color, from an off-gray to a darker hue. He balled his fists and I thought he was going to take a swing at me.

"Jorge, I want to help with this," I said, stepping back. He jerked his head away, picked up an empty test tube rack, and stared blankly at it. "You can talk to me, Jorge. Anytime. If you need me, I'm here."

"Sure, Doctor Mallow. In your lab, until they screw you out of that. Nobody gives one good goddamn, and you know it," he said, laughing, actually letting out a Jekyll-turning-into-Hyde peal of laughter.

"Jorge, please."

"And what's the big deal about another drowning or two, anyway, huh?" he said, sullen again. "Another drowning or two. Nobody cares one goddamn bit about them. Either of them."

I backed away slowly. It was no sense messing with him. He needed time, plenty of it.

Once I was alone in my office, I called the Matagorda County Medical Examiner. Most of the medical examiners in the adjacent counties are graduates of our medical school, and all have been trained by Dr. J. at one time or another. The Matagorda medical examiner, a fellow named Sinha, was no exception.

"I feel ghastly for Dr. J.," Sinha told me. "The case is clear, though. I'm ruling it a suicide. A note was found in the car, and the east end of Matagorda island is infamous for its rip tides. Warning signs are posted quite thoroughly on the beach. Anyone wading into that surf has got to be suicidal. The body was swept so far out, it washed in a mile and a half down the beach.... No, no, there were no signs of trauma whatsoever. The sharks never got to it. The crabs barely started their work. You're close to Dr. J?"

"Quite close."

"Such a shame. She must've been a smart one, clever enough to cross the county line to get out of her husband's jurisdiction. She was a beauty, that's for sure."

"Yes, she was a wonderful, warm person."

"And two months pregnant. Really sad about that. It's like two deaths, you know? Two drownings, in fact."

❉ ❉ ❉

Later, at home, I told Brenda, "I just don't get the way Jorge's acting. It's like nothing happened." We were dressing to go out to Dr. J.'s beach house for a couple of hours in the evening for a remembrance gathering arranged by Dr. J.'s two brothers who'd come down from Houston to help. I dug an outdated suit, a dark one, out of the closet. Brenda looked great in her little black dress.

"Something's wrong with Jorge, Peter," she said. "Seriously wrong. Sometimes a person stalls in one of the stages of grief, and it can be disastrous. Most bog down in the denial stage."

"That's not Jorge. He seems rational, and he knows the facts."

"Others get stuck in the anger stage of grief. 'Why's this happening to me?' they ask over and over. They blame others, or themselves. Anger, confusion, revenge build and build, unless one is able to let it all out and get on with life."

Brenda's so good at these things. After all, she's an expert, and she's right, I've got to stay close to Jorge to help him through this. It's been a tumultuous year in the lab, we've survived a hurricane, and now we've got to get through a different sort of storm.

"Why did she do it *now*?" I asked. "You think she just found out now that she was pregnant?"

"She was in the worst possible situation, Peter. Pregnant? By Jorge? Her life must've been so out of balance."

I thought we didn't have any tears left, Brenda and I. But it turns out we had plenty, with some left for Dr. J., at the beach house.

Friday, September 25

It's been almost two weeks, and things are back to normal in the laboratory, or at least they give the illusion of normal. Lilly, my scientific Rock of Gibraltar, has been steadily defining proteins that might be virulence factors, and Jorge's banging away at the *PAKG* gene, ignoring any references I make to his grief, or real life.

Without funding, without that NIH grant, the future of my lab is bleak. No matter how I juggle the numbers, we're running out of funds, and fast. Everyone in the lab senses the sinking ship, but Jorge's taken it the hardest, which doesn't make sense. His fellowship doesn't end until January. It's Lilly who's going to go.

"What will happen to our research?" Jorge keeps asking me. "Lilly's work with the ducks? My *PAKG* knockouts?"

"Dr. Stepinski offered to cover Lilly's salary for a month or two, but after that, I'm out of funds. That's the way it is in science, Jorge."

Jorge was cutting his eyes around like a cornered animal. His breathing sounded like he was starting an asthma attack. "But... but... I was hoping to come back after the fellowship, next summer. Your lab won't even be here!"

"I'll carry on as best I can." I tried to sound upbeat, but I wasn't convincing anyone, least of all myself. "I'm going to try for some small, local grants."

Local grants, I thought, and local review boards and local politics, so easily tampered with.

"It all started with my vehicular immersion study, didn't it, Doctor Mallow?"

"Look, I wish that project had turned out better."

"They really screwed us," he said, scowling.

"You're probably right, Jorge."

"Those shits."

"Let's do our science, man!" I said, clapping him on the back.

Jorge's doing his science all right. Serious science. For him everything is "virus virus virus" and "*PAKG PAKG PAKG*." He's up to his eighth try at knocking out the virus's *PAKG* gene. Jorge now knows more than I do about targeting promoters, exons, operons, and introns. He's an ace at chopping and splicing bits and pieces of genetic material, an expert engineer of the virus's genome.

But Lilly's worried about Jorge. Late last evening, while Jorge was still in the Level 4, she came to me complaining. "So *many* knockouts, Doctor Mah-wo," she said. "He make new knockouts before we understand the ones he has! Now Jorge is fooling with DNA for a heart receptor. I don't get it."

"Heart receptor? He's supposed to be analyzing the operon of his latest knockout, the KO-008."

"No, Doctor Mah-wo. Jorge splicing some sort of new genomic material into 008 tonight. I can't keep up!"

Friday, October 2

Jorge secluded himself in the Level 4. I waited a couple of days, then sat him down at the break table, went over his data, and had a serious discussion. "Lilly and I both think you're moving too fast," I told him.

"I'm careful. I know what I'm doing."

"Sure, sure, but there are big problems," I said. "Look at this one, your *PAKG*-KO-008 knockout? You deleted DNA sequences from base number 355 to 421." He nodded. "And now its infectivity ratio is sky high! The packaging function's drastically changed, Jorge. We need to understand *why* your *PAKG*-KO-008 virus is so much more infectious."

"Maybe I'm impinging on the promoter region of the gene. Or maybe an exon, or an intron." Jorge's enthusiasm appeared to be flagging. "I should define its promoter, I suppose," he said, dreamily. With a jerk, he stood up to go. He was moving like a robot again. "Maybe I'll splice in a new one. I don't know. It must be super-expressing some aberrant protein."

"It's worrisome, Jorge."

Then, another bit of bad fortune struck—the autopsy schedule came out, and I was given a horrendous load of autopsy time. It looked like three times my normal number of weeks. I would be on call for practically the rest of the year. I ran to the autopsy service to protest.

"You made some mistake on this schedule," I told the secretary.

I was informed that word had come down from the chairman, and the word was, "Mallow lost his grant, therefore Mallow gets more autopsy time." I knew about this sort of redistribution of the work load, but since I had always had a big grant, I never felt the brunt of the policy before.

When I checked it with the chairman's office, I was also told, "By the way, Doctor Mallow, your discretionary funds have run out," meaning any books, travel, etc. would be at my own expense.

The chairman giveth, and the chairman taketh away.

Friday, October 9

More than ever, I need to be in the lab. Instead, I've been stuck on the autopsy service doing post-hurricane heart attacks. On Wednesday, I had two MIs nearly wrapped up when an especially nasty AIDS case came in, a 26-year-old woman, long-time IV drug abuser, who picked up the HIV virus in Hawaii doing "ice," the Hawaiian Islanders' version of home-cooked amphetamines. The last of the woman's brief and unfortunate life was spent in a hospice trading infections with other dying patients.

Ron Rocker was back at work. It seemed like months since he'd gone on leave. Despite his chronic cough, Ron and I quickly dispatched the two MIs, took a short break, then switched to the infectious autopsy room to dismantle the "ice" lady.

"Get much damage from the hurricane, Ron?"

"Totaled our double-wide. Don't have no insurance, and.... " Ron was stopped by a coughing fit. He pulled off gloves and mask and stood over the autopsy sink. I focused on slicing the patient's lungs, which were as solid as a hunk of liver and riddled with tuberculosis.

"Haven't seen you take a smoke break all day, Ron."

"I quit...." He spat a bright red string of blood into the sink and tied on a fresh mask.

"Good for you! What made you decide?"

"Lung cancer."

The long, stainless knife I'd been using clanged on the autopsy table. Our eyes met over our masks. "Shit. That's why you were on leave, wasn't it?"

"Small cell CA, Doc. A bad one. They took out half a lung, blasted me with radiation."

"You getting chemo?"

"Made it through two rounds. Tumor shrunk some. I'm stage 4. More chemo might buy time, but I feel pretty good, so the hell with it."

"Anything I can do, Ron, let me know. Are you eating?"

"Yeah, steroids done wonders for my appetite."

"Then I'm buying you lunch one of these days. You name the time and place."

Night had fallen. The lab was shut down and deathly quiet. I went to the office and played Townes van Zandt. "Too late to wish I'd been stronger," he sang. He's another poor bastard who died on New Year's Day. I tried to sit at the 'scope but ended up staring at the ugly heaps of slides, unopened mail and works-in-progress on my desk.

In three weeks, my lab would downsize. What a euphemism. Downsize. It was over, thanks to a series of downhill events that began with a bad encounter with very bad men. It could be worse. Like Ron. In the background, Townes sang, "flying shoes, flying shoes, I'll be tying on my flying shoes." I guess Townes was singing about dying. That's worse.

I flipped idly through a stack of unopened mail, then decided to go home and call it a day.

Wednesday, October 14

"Cutbacks, Peter. Cutbacks. The entire academic landscape has changed."

Those were his exact words. "Academic landscape." I was asking myself, "Why?" Why was I called to the office of my burly, red-faced chairman to hear about academic landscapes? I studied the blank, watery blue eyes set deep into his enormous, graying head. It occurred to me that in the eight years since he'd hired me, I'd hardly spoken with the man.

"What's this about?"

He shook his big, chairman head. "I'm afraid I can't renew your contract, Peter. You'll have the rest of the academic year to look around, to make a decision about a move. It's too bad. You're a solid researcher, with an excellent funding record. Until now."

"But you supported me. You put me up for tenure."

"I've already notified the tenure committee. Non-renewal of your contract stops their deliberations, naturally, since you'll be leaving."

"But my work! We're at a critical point with *Bangladesh*!"

"At the associate professor level, a move to another university might be the best thing for you, Peter. Houses can be sold and families moved. We do it all the time in academia. Try to see it from my perspective. You lost your funding, and I have investigators who need lab space."

"I see. I don't have tenure, so...." The reality of the situation settled in. "But why now?"

"Things change. There was pressure from higher up, too."

"Pressure?"

"From administration. The chancellor's office. They have something... unsavory." He held the word harshly in his mouth, a cruel edge to him now. "I haven't seen it, Peter, but they say it's bad."

I was in the middle of the next autopsy, a stillborn infant with multiple congenital anomalies. "I can't believe this," I muttered to myself. When I cracked open the baby's diminutive skull and revealed its tiny, malformed brain, all I could think of was my chairman's big fat head. Then I wondered if the "unsavory" material he'd mentioned was a certain collection of sexy videos featuring a couple of amateur faculty performers. And I wondered how many times the chancellor had rewound them.

"How about that lunch when we finish?" Ron said, when the stillborn's autopsy was nearly complete. "Maybe a beer or two?"

"I could use about 10."

"The M&M's got the coldest beer in town."

So that's how Ron Rocker and I came to spend the afternoon at the M&M Bar and Grill, easing the pain of his terminal illness and the termination of my employment at the University of Texas.

The M&M Bar and Grill is located in the dreary, dimly-lit part of downtown still untouched by Fuddrucker or Ruby Tuesday. It's run by an old geezer who goes by "Moose." The bar is open only for lunch, when it does a brisk business in the po'boys prepared by Mrs. Moose in her spotless kitchen in the back. Mr. Moose's poorly-lit barroom is decorated with dusty deer antlers, cobwebs, a ceramic rattlesnake in striking position on the back bar, and—not surprisingly—a gigantic, moth-eaten moose head.

Ron and I took two bar stools in a mélange of longshoremen, mechanics, and bankers in dark pin stripes. We plunked ourselves down, leaned over the cigarette-scarred bar, and stared past the rattlesnake for a moment at the reflection of two unlikely pals in the bluish mirror of the back bar.

"What'll it be, Moose?" Moose asked us. At the M&M, everyone's "Moose."

"Corona for me," I said. Ron asked for a Bud Light.

Ignoring our orders, Moose pulled two Lone Star beers and two beat-up mugs out of a big ice pile under the bar. Moose never installed refrigeration or air conditioning at the M&M. As Ron pointed out, the beers are the coldest in town, but once the ice melts, it's closing time.

Moose set the beers in front of us. It was my first in months, and its icy bite felt good. I hadn't lost my taste for it, even if it was a Lone Star.

"What are your docs saying, Ron?" I asked.

"They're talking chemo again, but I'm not listening."

We ordered po'boys that came dripping with chili, cheese and jalapeños. Ron dug into his, thanks to the steroids, but my sandwich rapidly lost its appeal.

"Not hungry, Doc?"

"I lost my grant, Ron. Basically, they're kicking me out."

"You're their golden boy, as long as you bring in the bucks, huh?"

"I need to find another university."

Ron and I spent the afternoon guzzling Lone Stars, lamenting poor Dr. J.'s horrendous personal loss, and roasting every asshole administrator at the university. The M&M emptied. Moose settled on his stool under the moose head, smoking and listening to us bitch. The ice pile at the M&M must've been a big one because Moose opened about 20 beers. Then we said good-bye, staggered out, and Moose locked the door behind us.

Ron climbed into his windowless Dodge van and sped away while I stumbled around in the dark, looking for my bike. In the gutter, I found its severed chain coiled like some dark metallic serpent.

"Some fucker stole my bike!"

I walked home to the rude electronic blast of a video game. Travis sat six inches from the screen, working the controller hard. Chad's bass rattled the windows, and I silently cursed the day that the electricity came on after the hurricane.

"You smell like an ashtray," Brenda said, when I lurched into the kitchen. "Where have you been?"

"At the M&M, getting drunk. I got fired, and it seemed like a good idea at the time."

Friday, October 16

No autopsies for the rest of the week, but I couldn't muster any momentum in the lab. I sat in my office, immobilized, reading Poonawala's e-mails from Calcutta:

> With the approach of the hot season, sporadic cases again appear. A quarantine of Dhaka is imminent, but do you think the virus has established itself on other continents? May heaven forbid it.

Bangladesh was back on its dangerous biologic track. And I had no funding. What if the virus adapted, became even more virulent? Poonawala was counting on me:

> You must find a biologic weakness in this virus, Peter.

Lilly took charge of Jorge, who was in the Level 4 day and night. When Lilly came to report on Jorge's progress on knocking out the *PAKG* gene, I couldn't focus.

"Jorge disrupted the *PAKG* different ways, 12 times, Doctor Mah-wo, and he's found an adhesive domain in the *PAKG* protein. I confirmed it by Southern assay."

"That's great, Lilly."

"Doctor Mah-wo? Did you hear me?"

An adhesive domain? Who cared? Our big paper on *MORPH* languished under review at the *Journal of Virology*. I'd already missed that small grant deadline Marv insisted on, and all I could do was sit at the computer, pose as a scientist, take up space, and exchange air. I stared out my window into the blackness sweeping across campus from the gulf, until Jorge jarred me out of my funk.

"I have an idea, Doctor Mallow."

"Maybe tomorrow, Jorge."

"It's about the vehicular immersion study. We need to withdraw that paper from the *Compendium of Forensic Sciences*. It isn't going to make a difference anyway, not in that journal. What we need is another chance at those guys in D.C., the Auto Safety Board. I have a plan. First, we trick them into a meeting, tell them anything, tell them we have new data."

"What will we say when we get there?" There was an awkward silence. "No, Jorge. I'll try Yamata again. He's the only reasonable person on the board, but unless something changes, another meeting would be useless."

"Call Yamata, then. Tell him we need to talk."

I didn't want to talk to anyone, which is a problem when you're looking for a new position. My job hunt was stalled. I looked into San Diego and Boston, excellent universities that sounded interested in Mallow, research virologist, but in my present state, I couldn't follow through.

There were decisions to make about jobs and small grants. And Brenda—what about her? In a few months, I'd be at another university. Brenda loved her work here; she'd adapted to the island, the university. Would she follow me? I didn't have the guts to ask. And what about Sokolof? Was he already behind the scenes in San Diego and Boston, messing with my chances there?

"Peter, you're an absolute mess," Brenda cried when I walked in the front door well past midnight. The air conditioner gave out a continuous grinding sound; it was nearing the end of October and a norther still hadn't blown through. "What is it? What's wrong?"

"First it was my grant, then my job, and now my worthless bike."

"You'll get a grant. You'll find a position. It'll turn out okay. It will."

I plopped onto the bottom stair of the staircase. I felt as if somebody was sitting on my chest. "You can't relate to this, Brenda. It's my life's work!"

"I believe in you, Peter. Doesn't that count for something?" She tried to hold my face in her hands but I pulled away. "Tell me honestly, Peter, you're not so low that you might hurt yourself, are you?"

"I already *have* hurt myself."

"Let's start small, Peter. This weekend, we'll buy you a new bicycle."

Wednesday, October 21

Walking home late from autopsy service again, I stopped to pick up cheese-burgers for the boys at the corner store that's run by an old Vietnamese guy. Brenda and I like the egg rolls he rolls up for 50 cents apiece. The sweet and sour packets are a nickel extra. I was putting my faith in a 50 cent egg roll to lift my spirits.

I stood on a corner six blocks from home, holding the bag of food and waiting to cross 25th Street, when up roared an old jeep, open air, driven by someone who looked an awful lot like Ellen. She was in green scrubs. When she pulled to the curb, I made the definitive identification from her vampy mascara and the lazy eye.

"What happened to your bike?"

"Stolen."

She offered me a ride home, so there I was, sitting next to my almost-ex, together for the first time in months without a lawyer present. I knew she would start something. She had it started as soon as we pulled away from the curb.

"You really screwed up our hurricane plan."

"You left."

"You'll never change. You're so sorry. You don't care about those boys."

This is how it went—the taunting, the arguing. In the old days, it was a prelim to lovemaking. I'd come home from the lab and Chad would be bundled up in his baby blanket in a plastic basket on top of the clothes drier. The motion and warmth helped his colic. After the argument, after that first contact, Ellen would twist the drier's knob, set it for another 45 minutes, and we'd head for bed.

"Say something, Peter. We need to talk."

This time, I decided, I wouldn't argue back. Why had I made such a big deal out of nothing for so long? She really wasn't a bad person, my almost gonna-be. She'd probably balance her life out better than me, if I only let her.

"I agree," I said.

"Agree to what?"

"Everything your lawyer wants. Everything she has in it right now."

"Peter, you're so distant lately."

"Ellen, we're getting divorced."

She stopped the Jeep with a jerk at the light two blocks from the house. In the shifting urban shadows, with a warm bag of burgers and egg rolls on my lap, I watched the catch-light in her good eye turn from red to green. She put the Jeep in gear and we rumbled toward home.

"However she has it written?"

"It's just a piece of paper. You decide."

Saturday, October 24

Nearly the end of the week, and no cases pending for an autopsy. Finally, a break. Then, a prison suicide came down from Huntsville. A hanging.

Ron and I made short work of the case. We confirmed the furrow in the neck, matched its ugly purple contour to the ligature, and documented the signs of asphyxia—the burst capillaries in the eyes, on the surface of the lungs, along the linings of the heart.

"Where in hell," Ron asked, "does an inmate find a nice piece of nylon rope like that?"

"They buy anything they want inside, Ron. Drugs, weapons, why not rope? Look, the furrow fits the ligature, and no sign of foul play. You finish, I'll dictate, and we'll get us a beer."

"It just don't seem right, so many prisoners killing themselves."

"It's too easy," I said, snapping off my gloves. "They do it with sheets, shoelaces, with pieces of rope or wire they get in exchange for sex. They probably hold friggin' tutorials on it."

I scuttled toward the dictation area where I caught a glimpse of Dr. J. crouched by the morgue safe in the tech's room, collecting evidence. I hadn't seen him since Elena's funeral. A new tech, a quiet, older woman, stood next to him, dutifully logging out each item as Dr. J. called its number and placed it into a brown grocery bag on the floor. I backtracked and stepped in.

"It's been a while, Dr. J.," I said, taking the bony hand he offered from his crouched position. "Are you making it okay?" He gave a weak, ambivalent nod, and slowly straightened. The lines in his face had deepened into shadowy fissures.

"Good as can be expected."

"Anything you need, Dr. J., just let me and Brenda know."

"You've been so kind. Incidentally, Peter, I heard from Peyton Sweeney, my friend from Laredo. About your immersion project. He planned to take it to the legislature this January, but apparently some corporate people changed his mind." Dr. J. again bent into the safe.

"I'm not surprised," I said. "I wonder what he drives. A pickup? A Ford F-350 diesel, maybe?"

Dr. J. looked at me askance with an ice pick in his hand. "I don't have any idea, Peter." He called out the number on the ice pick and went back to logging out the last of his evidence.

"You've been around the law a long time, haven't you, Dr. J?"

"Too long."

"I've got a hypothetic question for you. Suppose a manufacturer knows of a big defect but ignores it, conceals it. Would that escalate the cost of a settlement?"

"A cover-up is criminal, Peter. Somebody goes to jail." Dr. J. stood up and hefted the bag of evidence. "You're talking about the immersion problem, aren't you?"

"It's just a hypothesis."

"Proving a cover-up is difficult in court, Peter."

"Especially after 40 or 50 years."

❉ ❉ ❉

It was well past the lunch hour and the M&M was desolate. The last few bottle necks poked out of a dwindling ice pile.

"Just fixin' to close," Moose said. "But I'm glad y'all stopped by."

Moose dug into the ice and pulled out a mug that was broken in half. He studied its jagged glass edges with his rheumy, ancient gaze, and, without blinking, stuck the mug back into the ice. Then he set two cold bottles of Corona on the bar in front of us.

"You boys can drink straight from the bottle this evenin'," he said. Ron and I settled onto our stools like the regulars we'd become.

"Hangings are easy autopsies," Ron said. I heard the whistling sound that kicks off his coughing fits. "Must be horrible to choke to death."

"They don't choke. They tighten their ligature enough to cut off the venous blood flow, and that's it."

"Brain dead."

"No need to dangle, either. I've autopsied prisoners who simply got down on their knees and leaned forward into their ligature."

"It takes some planning, don't you think?"

"More than just picking up a gun."

"Do you think they practice?"

"They probably tie a few nooses, until they come up with one that suits 'em."

I thought about that for a moment.

Ron said, "It's sad, Doc. This very minute people are fixing to do themselves in, while me and you are fighting to stay alive." A paroxysm of coughing finally shook him, and his lips turned blue. Moose, a freshly lit cigarette dangling from his mouth, was quietly sweeping the floor. I waited for Ron to tuck his bloody handkerchief back into his pocket.

"So how's the job hunt going?"

"They're opening a new Level 4 lab in Boston. Next week, I'll take a trip and have a look."

"Moving your wife and kids will be hard."

"Actually, I'm divorced. Papers are signed. It's final in six weeks. Our two boys will stay on the Island with her, I suppose."

"I went through that. Then I got re-married."

"I have a girlfriend. A significant other."

"So how's that going, Doc? Taking her with you?"

"I don't know. I don't know anything. I'm confused."

"That's not true. Men always know. They say women always know, but that's bullshit. Men know, too."

"I know I love her."

"There ya go. Don't forget to tell her."

With a thud, Moose set down the last two beers.

"On me, boys. I'm fixin' to close after this one."

That night was dark and moonless. I slept deeply, but my sleep was filled with a repeating, crystal clear nightmare. Someone had locked me inside our morgue's walk-in cooler. I was surrounded by corpses hung on hooks. Gray bits of flesh lay scattered on the floor and dried, blackened blood was flung on the walls. Organs soaking in open buckets exuded the acrid stench of formalin. The buckets began to spring leaks. My eyes were scorched, my throat excoriated.

Too many weeks on autopsy.

Before first light, a cool north wind blew across the sheets and carried one last dream. It was a dream about ligatures, and the feel of the cord as you lean into a noose of your own design.

"Peter! Peter! Are you all right?"

Brenda was shaking me awake. I mumbled something about the dream and rolled away.

"I'm calling in sick for both of us, Peter. We need to spend today in bed. Right here, the whole day. I'll make soup."

"Brenda, did you ever just... want to be held?"

"Come here. Hold me, Peter."

Friday, October 30

The official downsizing of my laboratory was today. Jorge and I were at the break table waiting for Lilly to arrive so I could make a little speech. I was feeling pretty nostalgic about this, our last official day.

Lilly staggered into the lab dragging a big red plastic bio-hazard bag full of dead ducks. "Yesterday's experiment," she gasped. "I've got tons of samples to run on the Finnegan."

"You can't start a new experiment, Lilly. You need to find another job."

"But work with *Bangladesh* must go on!"

I leaned back in my chair and stared at the stack of papers piled on the break table. We were so close to solving *Bangladesh*. So close.

"I'm terrible at this, but I wanted to say... how great it's been working with you both. It's the best lab group ever. I've always kept my lab small, three or four people at most, but that's because I believe ideas come from everyone in the lab, from the most experienced researcher to the lowliest guy who's making up buffers and washing glassware."

"Ideas are what science runs on, and the ideas that you two have come up with—the *MORPH* and *BADMORPH*, Lilly's fast-duck cells and the Finnegan spec—all just terrific, innovative stuff. And never any hidden agendas lying beneath the surface. You're tops, you two."

"Incidentally, Doctor Mah-wo," Lilly interrupted, "I've applied for a McKinney Fellowship, and my Chinese friends on the McKinney board are very optimistic."

"Jorge," I continued, "you've started down the road of science with your work on *PKG*. You've got a great mind. You're young, but keep after it, man. I see great things in your future." I gave Jorge a quick hug. He looked shocked and maybe a little pissed off.

"It's too bad we're done for, but I'm afraid this is how it is in research. I hope some other lab will pick up where we're leaving off, test our theory of transdifferentiation and solve *Bangladesh* before it's too late. If this sucker hits, we'd better be ready. My only regret is that our lab won't be part of it. And…. Sorry," I said, choking up, "Give me a second. You two have… been phenomenal. I'll be in my office if you need me."

We shook hands all around. Lilly started extracting duck tissues, Jorge headed to the Level 4, and I sat in my office, pretending to type a manuscript.

It was over, but it wasn't. We'd downsized, but I still had Lilly for two months more, thanks to Marv, and she was trying for a fellowship. Dare I dream of a laboratory resurrection? Could I pull it off in the face of Sokolof's meddling?

I needed to get back to the bloody work of discovery.

Later, I was alone in the lab running a new gel, when the security desk called. Someone named "William Raymond Postlewaite" wanted to see me. In the background, I heard, "Billy Ray! Tell 'em it's Billy Ray!" Twenty minutes later, the big biker swaggered in, surrounded by four guards.

"Man, I was down there for an hour. What's with the security?"

"In this building, Billy Ray, we've got the most dangerous bugs known to man. Viruses, prions. We've got hepatitis A through E. The stuff stashed here makes smallpox look like a mild case of acne."

Billy Ray shook his head and asked, "Is Jorge around?"

"He's in the biosafety facility with his virus."

"Can we go talk? Somethin's been bothering me." He was staring at the laminar-flow hood where Lilly had stacks of purplish, fast-cell flasks under a big, red label, BIOHAZARDOUS MATERIAL. "Maybe we can ride down by the water?"

In my youth, whenever I broke free of the drudgery of The Salty Dog, I'd spend a summer afternoon roaring along the beach roads of old Cape Cod on my brother's 500cc BSA Clipper. Since then, I haven't straddled anything faster than an old Huffy. The ride along Seawall Boulevard on Billy Ray's Harley V-Rod was smooth and solid. We coasted to a stop in a grove of date palms just off the boulevard. It was a cloudless October day, the palms clattered in a brisk south breeze, and we were minutes from a blazing Texas sunset.

"I'm worried about the kid, Doc. What's this bullshit going on in Washington?"

"Jorge told you all that?"

"He don't talk about nothing else. He won't hardly ride no more, Doc." Billy Ray leaned against a towering palm and gazed out at the Gulf. "Sounds like these guys screwed you, Doc. And Jorge says they're goin' to screw him for medical school, too." Billy Ray turned and glared at me. "Can they do that?"

"I'm not sure."

"You mean you don't know?" The muscles in his arms flexed and the twin eagles fluttered.

"All I know, Billy Ray, is that the best thing would be to forget this damned project."

"Jorge says 700 guys'll die next year because of these assholes, and you say forget it? This one dude, the big shot who's screwing with you and Jorge, he needs to get his ass kicked!"

"I wish it were that simple."

"He may be a big shit in Washington, but he ain't nothin' down here. I'm not talking about no high-priced lawyer types, Doc. I'm talking about me and the Armed Eagles."

"It's complicated, Billy Ray."

"Nah, it's not. We just take him for a ride."

"A ride?"

"At night. Blindfolded. A little roughin' up, not much. This dude's gonna have one major change of heart, Doc. You'll see. Just tell me where he's at."

"Look, Billy Ray. Violence is no answer."

"I ain't talking violent.... Well, maybe just a little."

"You haven't mentioned this to Jorge, have you?"

"No, that's why I'm talkin' to you. So where's this dude at?"

"I appreciate your wanting to help, Billy Ray, but half the time this bastard's on an airplane. He lives in New Orleans. He's in Washington, and Houston."

"We'll ride to where he's at, or you figure a way to get him down here, Doc. Just give me the word. And don't worry. I done this shit before, and I'm handling this personally. Me and my biggest and meanest."

"No way. It won't work."

"You got a pen on you, Doc? I'll give you my cell number."

To appease him, I rummaged in my pockets and found a pencil stub. Billy Ray took a package of Zig-Zag papers out of his pocket and pulled off a single leaf. He laid it against the woody scales of the palm tree and wrote down his number. I folded the cigarette paper and slipped it into my wallet.

"Thanks, Billy Ray, but there's no way...."

"As soon as you know when and where, Doc, call my cell. Twenty-four seven. We're ready to ride."

Thursday, November 5

At the start of the week I was back on the autopsy service, but I had to fly to Chicago to chair a Monday plenary session at the meeting of the Society of Intracellular Parasitism, so I conned a colleague into covering the service, flew into O'Hare Sunday night, and spent a day listening to scientists rehash the antiquated theories they've been talking about for years.

I closed my session and was walking through a poster area when I saw Steve Leitmann, the editor of *JAMA*. He was standing in front of his poster board, dressed in designer jeans and a bright yellow, Hawaiian shirt, rocking on his heels, his head down. The poster area was all but abandoned. Steve looked bummed out, like he was disappointed at the turnout.

When I asked him how things were going, he said, "Pete, I need to apologize about refusing your paper. I should've stood up to those people. I don't know how it happened."

"I do."

"Well, I'm sorry. It's hit home now, Pete. Your study. Me. Personally. My nephew, my favorite nephew. He's in oil exploration in Alaska. He went through the ice in his pickup."

"He drowned?"

"No, not drowned. He was crossing a stream only four, five feet deep, and was trapped in his truck. He tried to pound his way out, just like the victims in your paper. He had breathing room, but just inches." I felt an involuntary shiver go through me. "In the icy water, he died of exposure within minutes."

"I'm sorry, Steve."

"It was wrong, letting them tell me what to do. Have you published your paper yet?"

"We sent it to the *Compendium of Forensic Sciences*."

"Withdraw it and publish with me, in *JAMA*. I'll put it in a spring issue, write an editorial, and demand action from the industry. The editorial board won't like it, but I'm the editor, right?"

"I'm going to send you a couple of older papers, Steve. There's an interesting history to this problem. Let me buy you a drink, and I'll tell you about it."

I swung by the university on my way back from the airport. It was nearly midnight, but the lights in the main lab were on. Jorge was at the lab bench with a line of complicated gels laid out in front of him. He barely reacted when I tapped him on the back.

"I have good news for a change, Jorge. I saw Steve Leitmann, and he's going to publish your article in *JAMA* after all."

"It doesn't matter, Doctor Mallow. Nothing will come of it. They'll find some other way to get at us. Have you asked them about another meeting?"

"Another meeting would be useless."

"You know what? I'll go up there myself."

"They won't meet with you alone, Jorge."

"We'll see about that. We'll see."

I walked down the hall and photocopied Zoltan Szabo's old papers to mail to Steve Leitmann. I wondered if maybe Jorge was right. Maybe we should confront them one more time. I also wondered, sealing the big brown envelope, if I was sealing my own doom.

Friday, November 6

Half past four on a Friday at the M&M. We had labored over two easy autopsies that should have gone quicker. Ron was losing his edge at the autopsy table.

Moose rummaged in the ice pile. The ceiling fans groaned and beat a cloud of lustrous dust into the warm autumn air. The shabby, skeletonized moose looked down at us, its plastic eyes cataracted by time.

"Sorry, boys, but y'all are working on the last two beers."

"Only so much time," Ron was saying. "Only so much, for each of us."

Moose slipped off his stool and picked up Ron's empty plate. "You got around that po'boy all right," he said.

"I'm eating for two, Moose. Me and the tumor." The cough reappeared with a rattling, lethal sound. Ron slipped a handkerchief out of his pocket and put it to his mouth. "How long you been doing autopsies, Doc?"

"Ten, almost 11 years."

"I've been around dead people my whole life. Started embalming right outta high school. Couple of years later I had the autopsy job. I used to be immune to it, but since I been sick, things bother me. I think about dying. I think about all who've died on this Earth since time began."

"The human species, huh?"

"You and I, we're just the tip of it, Doc," he said, grabbing my arm for emphasis. "It's like one big compost heap, and we're the top layer, the living layer."

"Close to closing time, gents."

Two customers, a barman, and a moose head, like a scene from prehistory. I had tuned out of the conversation and was listening for the long, slow turn of Ron's dying Earth.

"Let's make a deal, Doc." Ron still had a hold on my arm. "We'll make a pact, me and you. There's only so much time, so let's live it up to the last gasp. No regrets. No crybaby shit."

I raised my mug. "Deal! No crybaby shit."

Ron took a sip of his beer and said he was ready to leave. We sat for a moment in silence and scooted our stools back. I glanced out the window at the spot on the sidewalk where I'd locked my new bike.

"Ah, shit," I gasped. "Not again."

We walked out and stood over the crumpled chain, the second I'd seen in less than a month.

"Fucking brand new Huffy."

"Remember our pact, Doc," Ron said. "No crying over it. Have to go on living."

"A deal's a deal, Ron. I just didn't figure we'd test it out so soon."

"You can afford another bike," he said with a smile. I put my arm around his shrunken, bony shoulders and held him for a second. The lights inside the M&M flicked out.

"See you, Ron. Only two more days on call."

"I'm not coming in tomorrow, Doc. There's things I need to get done."

"A will."

"We only been married a year. She don't have a dime."

Ron coughed the cough again, or the cough coughed him. I looked toward the university, then said goodnight and hiked to the lab.

Lilly was about to leave for the evening. All the buffers were prepared for the next day, so I decided to set up a new gel on *SWCH*. Something funny was in the air. I caught Lilly before she walked out the door.

"Is that liposomes I smell?"

"Jorge's making them again."

"What size?"

"Small. Two microns. I don't understand, Doctor Mah-wo. Sounds risky to me. You go ask Jorge. He still in the Level 4."

The sweet, oily smell of fresh liposomes hung thick in the lab. The last time I smelled liposomes was during that project for the army, four years ago.

I fastened down the Velcro of my space suit in the fluorescent glare of the Level 4's entrance vestibule. Through the hazy, prion-proof glass, I could see Jorge at the work bench inside. He was portioning out aliquots of an orange liquid into small tubes. He set down his pipette when I came in and yelled at him through my face shield.

"Doing knockouts?"

"Working on 014. I'm adding liposomes." He pointed to his pipette.

"They're small, Jorge. Too small. They'll make the virus even more dangerous to handle. They can go down into the lungs, deep." He gave me a blank look. "Why are you using them?"

"They stabilize the virus. Don't worry, *PAKG* is knocked out. I'll extract the liposomes later," he said matter-of-factly, and he went back to pipetting. As long as he extracted the liposomes, he'd be okay. He was a smart kid. He knew better than to put himself in harm's way.

I watched his hand, steady as stone, layer liposomes onto his knockout stocks. He'd come a long way in the lab since he'd started this fellowship. "Be careful," I yelled. He nodded.

I unsuited in the exit-vestibule and headed to the main lab to set up my new gel.

Monday, November 9

Over the weekend, Brenda talked me into driving to the mainland for a Saturday night at Bayou Bob's. "Attitude adjustment," she called it. She drove the Rover while I stared out at the black water of the bayous and the blur of used car lots, taquerias, and refinery flares, splitter towers and blow-down drums that look like an explosion waiting to happen. Brenda asked me about my job interviews, but I didn't feel like talking, so we drove in silence.

Bayou Bob's was empty. The band never showed. We were stuck with the jukebox. We tried to find a two-step but all that came up was polka after polka.

"You don't lead like you used to, Peter," Brenda told me.

We settled at a table next to the darkened bandstand. I tried another sip of piss-warm Corona. The jukebox jammed on another polka, its chorus repeating to a monotonous triple beat, "*Una mas cerveza, por favor, Senorita. Una mas cerveza, por favor...*"

Brenda groaned and said, "This is driving me nuts."

She walked over to the jukebox and began pushing buttons. No response. She gave it a shove and "*Una mas cerveza*" warbled once and quit. She put another buck into the slot and waited, leaning over the pink and blue lights. I heard her gently curse, and she walked back across the silent dance floor.

"Let's go," she said. "You drive."

I pointed the Rover down the bayou road, concentrated on the dark pavement ahead, and mulled over all that had gone so wrong, so fast. It was time to do something about all this, just do something.

"Why don't you just *do something* about this, Peter?"

"You're reading my mind, aren't you?" I accelerated onto the four-lane and the Rover began the long, gradual climb up the causeway.

"It's like your dancing, Peter. Take control! Get some friggin' back-bone! It's this auto exec in D.C., right? Confront him. Go after him."

"I can't even find the guy, Brenda."

Brenda's face went violet in the pale highway light. "One more stupid excuse and I'm going to push you out of this car!"

I hit the auto-lock button.

"You've dwelled on this for too damn long," she continued.

The Rover crested the top of the causeway and was picking up speed on the down slope.

"Quit being so damned cerebral and *kick some ass for once in your life, would you please?*"

By the time we reached the other side of the causeway and the highway flattened out, Brenda had convinced me that Sokolof could be beaten, that he had some unknown vulnerability, an attackable fault. A "psychological weak spot" is how she put it.

"What do you know about this creep?"

"Jorge searched the details on him," I said. "Born in Austria, moved when he was 9 to a small town outside Mobile, Alabama. He's been Ford's chief risk officer for ten years. Lives in New Orleans with his third wife, all of them fashion models. No kids. And that election to the National Academy? That was pure bullshit. Years ago he published a few papers on set theory, and that's it."

"Find his weakness, Peter. Every man has one."

I smiled for the first time that evening. Lots of people were eager to get Sokolof. Jorge's biker buddies, Steve Leitmann, Zoltan Szabo, posthumously. And now, even gentle humanist, Dr. Brenda Danforth.

Until this moment, Sokolof had seemed untouchable, almost superhuman. How could such a wimpy little shit screw up my life so badly?

I tried to imagine Sokolof as a young boy. A foreigner, a brainiac, a twerpy kid, the one the bullies shoved around in the school yard at recess. The dweeb who grows up vengeful, makes a bunch of money, and starts collecting trophy wives.

I daydreamed of whispered threats in a darkened, elementary-school cloakroom, of pounding Sokolof's face in at the back of the school bus. But I'm no bully. In high school, when I lifted weights and played linebacker, I could've threatened Sokolof, but the years locked in the lab had left me a soft, amorphous, slightly overweight scientist, far from an imposing physical presence.

My thoughts ran wild all day Sunday. Then, overnight, they blossomed into a plan. Conceived in the schoolyard fantasy, born from a lack of options, and maturing into something as concrete as any specific aims I'd ever conjured, my plan had solidified when I walked into my office this morning. Aim number one of my plan was to get another meeting with the Automotive Safety Board. Jorge was right. Nothing would ever happen without another meeting.

First, I called Steve Leitmann at *JAMA*. He'd received the copies of Szabo's work that I'd mailed, and he assured me he was behind me. My next call was to Yamata, the Nissan man.

"Are you familiar with the publications of a scientist named Szabo, Mr. Yamata?"

"Yes… I've read Szabo's papers." The confident, Boston accent had a catch of hesitation in it.

"Give me your honest opinion of his work."

"Very disconcerting. After Szabo's studies, several lawsuits were filed against Ford Motor Company, you know."

"I'm aware of that."

"Are you also aware, Professor Mallow, that the preponderance of vehicles involved in immersions were Fords?" Yamata had been doing some digging.

"But nothing came of those lawsuits," I told him.

"No."

"Nothing, except that Szabo ended his research career shortly after he filed the suits."

"Indeed," Yamata continued, more quietly now, "Dr. Szabo ended his *life* within a year of the dispute. Committed suicide." I tightened my grip on the phone and eased myself into my desk chair. "He put a bullet through his head in his apartment in the Bronx. There had been a short period of therapy for severe depression, quite common among high-strung academics whose careers are failing."

"My God. Szabo sues Ford, his career mysteriously ends, and then he kills himself? How convenient for Ford."

"What are you suggesting, professor?"

"Keep in mind, Mr. Yamata, that none of this has anything to do with *your* company."

Yamata chuckled. "I'm fully aware of that. Nissan Industries was hardly a presence in this country at the time, and our early models were without power windows."

There was a long silence. Yamata cleared his throat. "What are you asking from me, professor?"

"Think back to the data we showed you and remember that lives hang in the balance. That's all I ask."

"There's hardly anything I can do."

"I'm going to ask your chairman for one more interview. You could influence that, couldn't you?" There was another long pause.

"I can't guarantee anything, you understand."

"I'd also ask that you speak with a friend of mine named Steve Leitmann."

"I'll expect his call."

Wednesday, November 11

Yesterday, I called the chairman of the Automotive Safety Board. The receptionist put me through to his voice mail, and I left a lengthy message emphasizing how badly we wanted a second meeting with his board, and how he'd be getting a call from a scientific editor "deeply committed to this issue." I promised him "additional data." I made notes on my little speech so I could leave the same message for as many days as it would take to get a response.

This morning, I looked at my notes, preparing to repeat my message to the chairman's voice mail, when Jack Sokolof called. He could barely control the anger boiling in his voice.

"You have gone behind my back. Not smart, professor."

"Jack, I'm willing to talk."

"Our board will not be meeting on this issue."

"Look, Jack. My student's an idealist, but I'm not. If you back off, I'll retract the paper. Give it some thought."

"You are in no position to bargain, professor."

"I have damaging evidence, Jack." I paused to let it sink in. "Up till now, you've been ahead of the game, but if I get this into the right hands, it won't matter what you do to me. Cover-up, fraud, corporate malfeasance...."

He exploded. "*You* have the nerve to threaten *me?*"

"It's not goin' away, Jack."

With the next breath, he was back to his icy, Germanic self. "Do you think I've exhausted all my options? I understand you are looking at a new position. San Diego, and such a fine institute in Boston. Sounds perfect, if you get an offer."

"Jack...."

"You must understand how deeply my influences run, Mallow. And remember, there are *others* to think of. Your boys, for instance... so much life ahead of them. Is college in their future? I'm sure they'll be applying to some fine schools, with those genes of yours."

"Why you...."

"And your 'girlfriend?' Is that what I should call her? Such a nice person. I would surely hate to see anything happen to *her*."

"Bastard!" Covered with cold sweat, I slammed the phone down. Jack was right, there were others to think of. So far, my plan had accomplished nothing except to piss Jack off.

I took two deep breaths and walked to the lab. Jorge was hunched over a gel. A tremor rattled my hands like an aftershock.

"You look awful, Doctor Mallow. Are you sick?"

"No, no. I'm fine." I needed to get a grip on myself. My resolve had vanished. With Sokolof's words ringing in my head, all I felt was cold, unadulterated terror.

"Did you ever hear from the safety group?" Jorge asked. "Yamata? That Ford guy?"

"Let's just wait, Jorge. I doubt anything will come of it," I said, hoping now that nothing would.

Sunday, November 15

Last Friday morning, two days after I heard from Sokolof, the big call came from the secretary for the Automotive Safety Board. Jorge and I were given an appointment for Monday morning at 8:30 sharp. They'd allotted us 15 minutes of their precious time. "You'll be the board's first order of business," the secretary said.

Sokolof had been wrong. So wrong. I wasn't surprised when he called.

"We must talk again, professor."

"Talk, then."

"Not over the phone. This weekend we will meet, face-to-face, to discuss the 'evidence' you intend to present Monday. I will contact you with details of our private meeting."

I walked over to the lab to tell Jorge that we were flying to Washington again.

"Jorge's gone," Lilly told me. "He loaded his gels and went home."

I locked the office and hiked to Jorge's apartment. A damp, November wind was shifting around, like me, deciding what to do. I climbed Jorge's sagging, outside steps, and he let me right in. It was two months since the hurricane, but his windows were still covered with plastic sheets. Jorge sat at his work table. I noticed the faint odor of liposomes on his clothing.

I whacked him on the shoulder. "We did it, man! We're on our way to D.C. and another round with the Safety Board." Jorge's eyes got wide and he put that tight, confident smirk on his face. "We leave Sunday night."

"Kind of short notice. How'd you do it?"

"A lot of phone calls and professorial charm. We'll need to go over our presentation, Jorge."

He had pushed aside his defunct Apple, its screen growing brown mold on the inside. On the table, he had five or six of our cheap, blue-plastic mechanical lab timers lined up and ticking. A precision stopwatch was running alongside the lab timers. His lab notebook lay open in front of him.

"What are you doing?"

"Calibrating."

"The lab timers?"

"These little things can be off by as much as plus-or-minus three minutes over half an hour. But some are very accurate, Doctor Mallow. Very accurate."

On my walk home, the wind picked up out of the north, the first serious norther of the season. Fine beach sand, leaves and empty potato chip bags swirled on the sidewalk. I stepped through our front door into the dark, smoky smell of burning flour. Mr. Kreuger was stirring a roux. "It's étouffée tonight," he announced. Brenda was at the kitchen counter working on two sazeracs, shaving thin curlicues of peel from a Myer lemon off our tree. I wrapped my arms around her waist from the back.

"Bad day?" she asked. I nodded. "Our shipment of books arrived from Bologna. With the few books we've restored, the library's really going to happen, Peter." She handed me an old-fashioned glass redolent with a dark mix of bourbon, sugar, and bitters.

"Jorge and I are going to Washington on Sunday."

"Way to go. You talked them into it."

"Behind Sokolof's back."

A loose shutter swung against the house with a dull thud and a chill cut through me.

"I'm going to light the heater in the hall," I said. After I got the heater going, I fished the sliver of lemon peel out of my drink. With the peel's bitter-sweetness rolling around in my mouth, I backed up to the old Dearborn and waited for Brenda to join me. "The real problem is Sokolof. He called today. We're meeting this weekend."

"Here's your chance to deal with him, Peter."

"He threatened me again."

I threw my free arm around her shoulders and felt the lean muscle, the firm bone underneath. The clean lines of her face seemed so fragile, as fragile and as easily fractured as the rest of our lives in this crazy world of academia. She turned toward me, put her arm across my warm back, and tugged at me.

What ran though my mind was what Brenda said as we crested the causeway last weekend. *Kick some ass, Peter. Kick some ass.* I swirled my glass and watched a tiny whirlpool form at the bottom. Brenda sauntered back to the kitchen with her drink in hand. Once she was gone, I pulled my bill-fold out and searched for that Mr. Zig-Zag paper I'd stashed. It was deep down, wrinkled and stuck together from the coastal humidity, but I could still read the number.

Jorge and I were in the lab Saturday morning, sorting out a slew of atypi-cal proteins he'd isolated from his knockout number 011. The lab phone rang and Lilly took it.

"For you, Doctor Mah-wo. No name."

"Yes. Yes," I said, my heart thrumming at the sound of Sokolof's voice. "Where?… Sure, I know it. I'll be there."

I told Jorge to put his assays aside and come to my office in 10 min-utes. There was a call I needed to make, then we'd go over our presentation for Monday.

When Jorge came into the office, we were on different wavelengths. He plunked himself on the stool, looked bored and didn't say much. Meanwhile, my mind was running amok over Sokolof's call. "Don't forget to speak up this time, Jorge," I told him. "Defend your statistics to these characters."

"Yeah, the jerks," he said with disdain. "Don't worry, I'll make good use of the time. Our appointment's for only 15 minutes, right? Look, we've practiced enough. I have work to do."

And so we concluded a conversation that wasn't. Neither Jorge nor I were really in the room, so how could it be a conversation?

I pushed the pickup hard to Houston. Over the phone, Sokolof had said he was there for the weekend, and we were to meet at 8 p.m at the Benihana across the street from his hotel. He'd be eating dinner, but I wasn't invit-ed. Our talk would be short.

The bar at Benihana was jammed, but you couldn't miss Sokolof. He was stretched out on this contraption called the "Famous Japanese Massage

Chair," looking very mellow. The chair's recording was conning Sokolof with a corny, World-War-II Japanese accent: "Velly relaxing! Velly healthy! Try again!" Sokolof shot me a bland look, then stuck a dollar into the slot.

"I'll be with you in a moment, professor. Just a bit more relaxation."

The rollers inside the chair cranked and Sokolof's wiry body jounced wildly. His pant legs rode up over a breathtaking pair of brand-new Lucchesi boots of horned-back lizard, an endangered species. I tore my eyes from the intricately-tooled boot tops to search the scene at the bar.

It was a Houston-style Benihana, packed with urban cowboys, slick Houston lawyers, weekend do-it-yourselfers in blue jumpsuits, and couples elegantly dressed for a Saturday night performance at Jones Hall. In the adjoining room, the chefs, with knives flashing, joked over sizzling grills.

Sokolof got his dollar's worth and took his sweet time getting out of the cheesy massage chair. He motioned to the only spot open, a tiny table covered with dirty glasses.

"This will do. It shouldn't take long."

As we sat across from each other, I glanced down at my own sorry boots, battered and moldy Justins, my dancin' boots.

"You know why I'm here, don't you, Mallow?"

"Buying new boots?"

"How observant. I see that you and Mr. Acosta are on our agenda for next week, penciled in, of course. I don't know how you managed it, but I have my suspicions. You intend to present new evidence, correct?"

"It's a matter of public record, Jack, all the way back to the earliest drownings in cars. More than 40 years ago, the first vehicular immersions were in Fords. Legal action was taken, and Ford fought it. It was an obvious, crude cover-up, Jack."

Our eyes locked. I tried to read what he knew about the history of immersions, or our paper slated to come out in *JAMA*, but Jack's eyes told me that it didn't matter. He wasn't about to change his mind, or his techniques. He looked toward the bar and gestured to a waitress, then settled back into his chair like a man on a mission.

"That's 40 years of criminal activity, Sokolof, and it leads right to you."

Jack gave the table a shove. The glasses rattled.

"Do you really believe our Safety Board will be surprised by your little history lesson? We are men of business, not long-haired academics. We understand each other."

"Uh uh, Jack. When the corporate ship goes down, Ford won't be in the lifeboat. I *will* get this to the press. You won't stop me this time."

"Don't be ridiculous, Mallow."

"Look. Give it a little lip service on Monday. That's all I ask. I'll keep the history of immersions buried, and you and your board will look like heroes when you fix the problem."

For an instant, he looked as if he were considering it, but then the old Jack was back. "Mallow, do you realize the difficulties of moving to a new city?" he said. "Suppose your name were posted on a website of abortion doctors? There are so many crazy, violent people, ready to do anything for a cause. And your girlfriend, your boys, what about their futures?"

I watched his cold eyes through those tiny, European glasses. My mind jumped back to Trey Findley trapped in his car, trying to beat his way out, his fists turning to hamburger. I had no recourse.

I stood up and leaned over him. He put a blank, bored look on his face.

"You're wearing pretty boots, Jack, but you're no cowboy, and you surely can't two-step." He looked puzzled and edged his chair away from the table. I adjusted my weight, softened my knees, readied myself to show him my smoothest half-turn toward the door.

"You're in Texas, tonight, Jack, and you're in for a Texas-size lesson."

His eyes went narrow and darted back and forth. Bulky shadows loomed alongside. He heard the creak and smelled the horse-piss scent of leather. I saw the face of a child who knows the bullies are back.

With my heart pounding, I spun on my worn-down Justins and strode out, leaving Sokolof surrounded by eagles, angry crimson eagles mounted on stout limbs of flesh.

Through an unsettled sky, we fled our tepid island on Sunday evening, en route to our drab national capital, where autumn was winding down into winter. Outside the jet's window, an anemic moon shone as pale as the turkey sandwiches sitting untouched on our plastic trays. We'd been tossed by turbulence for most of the flight, so I was relieved when the moon began to sweep from window to window as proof that our aircraft was circling the airport and would soon drop through the solid gray of an East Coast cloud cover to touch down on the icy black tarmac.

Jorge, fresh and ready in the seat next to me, wore the outfit Elena helped him buy for our first trip—gray slacks and navy blue blazer with an English sailing insignia on the pocket. His look was shabbier now, and the line of his jacket, all saggy and full of bulges, seemed out of synch with his lean torso.

In our hotel room that night, the instant I closed my eyes to sleep, my mind flashed back to Billy Ray and the look on Sokolof's face at Benihana. When I had called Billy Ray's cell earlier, I told him I wanted Sokolof scared, not harmed.

"He'll get the idea, Doc," he had replied.

"No weapons, and no Wayne, not with that guy's record."

"Sure, Doc."

"Think of this guy as Mr. Ford," I'd suggested in search of an analogy, "and this confrontation is Ford versus Harley."

Just before leaving Galveston Island, I had called Billy Ray again to ask how "Ford versus Harley" had gone.

"It was a rout, Doc," he'd laughed. "A great night for Harley Davidson. First, I sent my biggest boy into the ladies room. That raised just enough ruckus to escort Mr. Ford out the door. Man, we had us a *pack* of boys riding to the Island, must've been 50 bikes. Even picked us up a *police escort* to take us over the causeway."

"Police?"

"Mr. Ford was well hid in the middle of the pack, seated backward and all. Then we took him down the beach road for some speed trials and a good talkin' to. He got the message, Doc. Believe me. Wayne was awesome."

"Wayne? Not Wayne!"

"I couldn't leave Wayne out! He lends a lot of weight to something like this."

How close had I come to being an accomplice to murder? I asked myself as I lay in bed, listening to the swoosh of the Hyatt's air conditioning. I'd given the go-ahead to ex-con Wayne, the bludgeoner of men.

Near daybreak, I fell into a light trance. When I opened my eyes, Jorge stood over me, awake, fully dressed and tight-lipped. I tried to fix coffee in the room, but my eyes were burning and desiccated from the dry hotel air and I couldn't focus on the flimsy coffeepot. Outside the hotel window, a thin streak of bloodshot horizon hovered along the lower edge of the overcast. Jorge paced, his tie pulled too tight, his cockeyed jacket buttoned all the way up. I wondered what Sokolof would look like this morning.

The elevator was packed with well-suited men and women. It reeked of cologne. We spilled out into the third-floor foyer outside the Hyatt's meeting rooms where a crowd of suits congregated around tall silvery urns, piling little plates with bagels, coffee cake and croissants to steel themselves for their various workaday discussions of time lines and profit margins, solid investments and workable goals.

The Automotive Safety Board members weren't in the crowd. I walked to the end of the table, then a few feet down the hall to peek into their executive boardroom. Two waiters crisply dressed in black and white were setting out glasses and bottles of spring water. I returned to the foyer to put together a cup of coffee.

"Want something, Jorge?" His hands were thrust down in his jacket pockets. "There's Sprite." He pulled one hand loose from a pocket to check his watch. "Chill out. We're prepared. We've done everything possible." I felt the knot in my belly tighten. "You'll be fine." I clamped down on my folder filled with Szabo's papers and '60s lawsuits. My folder of surprises. Jorge was staring down the hall. I tried to concentrate on drizzling half-and-half into my coffee, carefully titrating its blackness to a more mellow brown. When I looked up, Jorge was gone.

The elevator opened and the chairman and two other board members came out. Still no Sokolof. They strode over to a coffee urn. I stepped down the hall to have another look in their meeting room, thinking Sokolof had slipped by me. The door was open a slit. I saw a splotch of blue inside. It wasn't a waiter.

I walked in, but it wasn't Sokolof, it was Jorge, and he was standing on *top* of their conference table. I quietly shut the door behind me.

"Jorge?..."

Jorge was on tiptoes, reaching overhead. He had his right hand jammed into the air conditioning vent, spreading its metallic fins. In his left hand, he held one of our cheap plastic lab timers.

"Doctor Mallow!"

"What have you got there?" I stepped closer. When I saw a microfuge tube attached to the timer, *BIO-BOMB!* sprang to mind.

"It's nothing, Doctor Mallow. Honest! Just a herpes virus. It'll give 'em a cold, flu-like symptoms and some blisters."

"Jesus, give me that! What's wrong with you?"

"Don't worry, the virus won't get out of this room. They're the only ones who'll be infected. It's a harmless herpes virus." He made a motion as if to slip the thing between the spread fins of the vent.

"Get your ass down here!" I hissed.

Jorge gingerly hopped off the table with the thing still cradled in his hand, just as a waiter pushed the door open and stepped into the room.

"What's going on here? This is a corporate meeting room!"

"I was just... checking," Jorge stuttered, "to see if the meeting had... started." He took a cloth napkin off the table and began polishing the middle of the tabletop where he'd been standing. The waiter watched, puzzled. The disfigured vent went unnoticed.

"You gentlemen must leave. They're due to start."

"Sorry, sir," I said, "but we're on their agenda. Honestly." I glared at Jorge. "Come on," I growled, grabbing his elbow.

In the hallway, I snatched the timer from Jorge. Secured to the timer was a single microfuge tube containing a couple hundred microliters of a cloudy, yellow liquid. The tube was double-sealed with layers of bulging parafilm. At the tip of the timer's circular mechanical dial was a fragment of razor blade meticulously super-glued so that when the dial wound down, the blade would puncture the parafilm. The timer was set to go off in just over half an hour. "Don't jiggle it!" Jorge gasped. "It's under pressure. The tube's charged with nitrogen." I snapped the microfuge tube off the timer.

"Let me have the tube, Doctor Mallow. I have a container for it." He rummaged around in his jacket pocket. It sounded like he had a pocketful of junk clicking around in there. He pulled out a glass vial with an airtight screw-cap. When I handed him the microfuge tube, he gently slid it into the vial and screwed down the cap. I held out my hand. Jorge hesitated.

"Give it. Now." He handed over the vial and I slipped it into my jacket.

We returned to the coffee table to wait for our appointment.

"I don't believe this, Jorge. I thought you were a responsible adult, and you pull a 10-year-old's stunt. Do you realize the seriousness of what you tried to do?" He checked his watch and feigned interest in a can of Sprite to avoid my stare. Expensive suits were filing down the hall to the boardroom.

"It was a prank, Doctor Mallow." He calmly poured Sprite over ice and took a long drink. "The virus would never get out of their room. That's the way I designed it."

I gently fingered the glass vial secured in my jacket pocket. The secretary ushered us into the executive boardroom. It was exactly 8:35 a.m.

As we took our chairs, I studied Sokolof. He was immaculately dressed, but he had a faint, brownish discoloration around his right eye and several oval black-and-blues that looked like thumb-prints on his cheeks. When he opened his briefcase, I noticed thin, semicircular abrasions gracing his wrists, like marks left by handcuffs.

Sokolof's eyes, normally squinty, were now all whites, with the pupils constricted to a dot. They were adrenaline eyes, the eyes of a man living under a very believable death threat.

"As I understand it, Professor," the chairman of the board began in his cheery fat man's voice, "you wish to present new data on this safety problem, the one about submerged vehicles."

Before beginning, I glanced at Jorge. His eyes were off in space, cocky looking. I cut to the chase. "We now have hard evidence that your industry was informed of this problem many years ago by a scientist named Zoltan Szabo," I began. The chairman arched his eyebrows. "Furthermore, illegal actions were taken in an attempt to bury this issue." The chairman's jowls dropped to his neck.

As if on cue, Sokolof interrupted. "I'd like you to hear my opinion on this, gentlemen. I've concluded, I'm afraid, that this is a very real concern for our industry."

Yamata joined in. "I've also examined the problem, at Jack's request. Several possible engineering solutions come immediately to mind, and...."

"Jack!" the chairman blurted. "What's going on here?"

Sokolof pushed his chair back and stood up. He stepped away from the table and paced the plush carpet, his hands clasped behind him, a study in corporate concern. "Vehicular immersion. It's a solvable problem and we *must* provide a solution." Smooth and slick as ever, Jack took charge. The only incongruity I noticed was the trace of gray sand in the creases of his fancy lizard boots.

Mouths gaped around the table and heads jerked.

"We can make this a win-win situation," Yamata chimed in. "I've consulted our finest Nissan engineers. We need not admit to a design flaw, and...."

Sokolof and Yamata were with the game plan, but as they volleyed back and forth, Jorge's look of confidence faded, and he began twisting and fidgeting in his chair. "Say something," I whispered. His breathing was shallow and sweat beaded along his temples. "Now's your chance, Jorge."

"I don't feel good. Are we finished?"

The bewildered chairman called for order. "Yes, yes, very interesting discussion. Obviously, we'll need additional time to consider our next step."

"I suggest you don't take too long, Mr. Chairman," I said. "This problem will soon be brought to the attention of the medical community and the general public in the *Journal of the American Medical Association*." Yamata nodded his head in recognition of Steve Leitmann's plan. "You'll be hearing much more about this."

Without warning, Jorge jumped out of his chair and turned like a caged animal toward the door.

"I'm sick," he hissed. "Come on, let's get out of here!"

"Hold on!" But Jorge fled out the door with his jacket flapping.

"If you need to leave, professor," the chairman said, "we'll gladly continue on our own." To his secretary he added, with a sigh, "Cancel the rest of this morning's appointments, would you?" I settled back to listen to the chairman drone on, assuring me that the board was seriously concerned and would "stay in touch." The atmosphere in the room seemed to grow thick and heavy with the fat man's breath. Eager to see Jorge, I eventually excused myself and headed for the door. The chairman was still addressing the group.

"Gentlemen, we are way behind schedule for the morning, but...."

Jorge was already upstairs in the room, flat out on his bed, breathing heavily into a brown paper bag.

"What the hell happened in there?"

"One of... my attacks." Jorge's voice was muffled by the paper bag. "Used to... happen in high school." He kept manically checking his watch, as if he were timing his anxiety attack. Then he panted even faster and shot me a look of abject terror. "My God!"

"I don't believe this shit!" I yelled into his face. "All you cared about was your obnoxious prank. You never intended to convince anybody, did you?"

"I had to get out. I had to puke."

I paced by the bed, trying to get myself under control. "I should turn your sorry ass in for this. It doesn't matter if it's a harmless herpes virus. What you planned was assault and battery!"

"They deserve it," he said softly. He held the paper bag away and sat up. "What about all the people who'll drown in their cars this year? And next year, and the year after that? Nothing's too bad for those shitheads."

"Wrong, Jorge, wrong. Thank God I stopped it."

We argued until he was breathing easily without the bag. I decided to drop the whole thing, get out of the room, and go somewhere to kill the rest of the afternoon before our flight home later that evening.

"How about some art?" I said. "The National Gallery's always good."

"Fine."

Silence in the elevator. A young guy in a red jacket held the hotel door for us and we walked out of the Hyatt, climbed into a cab, and headed down Wisconsin Avenue.

The works of Edvard Munch hung in the East Wing of the National Gallery. Jorge, who'd been raised on the high desert of west Texas, couldn't see much in the cold, dark paintings of a long-dead Norwegian. For me, Munch's paintings dredged up memories of New England ski trips and winter camping in the Presidential Range of New Hampshire, where snow lay thick above the tree line, and northern lights flickered overhead.

Jorge moped along as if he'd breathed the last of his energy into the brown paper bag. He drank compulsively at every water fountain. He was back and forth to the men's room. I had hoped that the museum might be a good place to quietly discuss Jorge's stupid stunt, and his anger. Eventually, the hush of the museum started to work.

"This Munch guy was crazy," Jorge said. "The sky's all lit up in these paintings."

"That's the northern lights. You never see them in Texas."

Jorge was drawn and gray, as if he'd aged prematurely, like the homeless we'd seen on the D.C. streets. His voice quavered.

"I never should have done it."

"Such a thing can never be justified, Jorge, no matter how harmless."

"I… I'm afraid now."

"Well, I've got it," I said, feeling in my coat pocket for the glass vial.

Jorge's hands were trembling at the thought of what might have been. "I never should have…." he said, and he ran off to the men's room.

I smiled to myself. Maybe Jorge was beginning to realize that he was part of the world, no matter how imperfect it might seem to him. That thought was giving me some solace when I came across Munich's masterpiece *The Scream* and, like Jorge, became mesmerized by its fiery winter sky. As I studied the painting, from the corner of my eye, I saw Jorge pass like a shadow along the line of canvasses by Edvard Munch, and disappear.

When I returned to our room, Jorge's things were exactly as he left them. Time was short, so I packed both our bags. Then I noticed that the message light on the phone was lit.

It was Sokolof.

"Professor Mallow, I wanted you and everyone involved to know that I will be totally dedicating myself to this project. I have convinced the other members of our board of its importance. So, please inform *everyone involved*. Please inform them all."

It was well past midnight when I crossed the causeway onto the Island and drove by Jorge's apartment. His truck was parked in front, but Jorge was nowhere to be found.

I got some sleep and this morning, I went back to the apartment. Jorge's truck was gone. I called the landlord to open his door so I could check the place out in daylight. At first glance, things looked the same. The neglected computer sat moldering on the table, the kitchen was in disarray, the bathroom looked medieval. Then I noticed the dresser drawers had been pulled out and emptied, and a fresh note replaced the notices taped to the wall.

DR. M,

I AM SORRY. I AM GOING HOME.
TAKE ANTIVIRALS IN CASE
THE TUBE LEAKED. GOOD LUCK
WITH THE RESEARCH.

PLEASE FORGIVE ME.

J

"He owes me rent," the landlord said. "He live far from here?"

"By now, he's probably halfway across Texas."

Wednesday, November 18

I handed Lilly the glass vial. The cap was still tight. Inside, the microfuge tube and its bulging parafilm cover appeared intact.

"Genotype this, would you, Lilly?"

"Need I handle it in the Level 4?"

"Yes, and take extra care. The virus might be mixed with liposomes." I didn't explain further. I wanted her to treat it as an unknown.

"So it's a herpes?" I asked, when she was back with the DNA analysis.

"Not even close. It's knockout, Jorge's knockout, the KO-008."

"What the hell?" I muttered. "The 008?"

"You were right about the media, Doctor Mah-wo. Liposomes, two microns. But this tube of virus was outside Level 4. That could be dangerous, couldn't it?"

"If someone inhaled it, sure. The virus would go deep into the lung."

Only now it dawned on me that, by setting the timer for half an hour, Jorge was making sure that our 15-minute meeting would be over and we'd be out of the conference room when the bio-bomb went off. I decided, on the spot, to take acyclovir, an antiviral, as Jorge had suggested. The seal on the microfuge tube couldn't have leaked, but better to play it safe.

"Jorge has left?" Lilly asked. "Before finishing his fellowship?"

"I'm afraid so. I talked to his mother, and best I can tell from our conversation in Spanish, nobody has a clue where Jorge's gone."

"Too bad. Such a smart boy, and dedicated. But so crazy."

"Who knows, Lilly? Maybe he'll be back."

"Lucky thing tube was sealed."

"Yes," I agreed.

And lucky I grabbed the damn bio-bomb before it went into the air vent.

❋ ❋ ❋

An unexpected breakthrough came at the end of the day. Lilly was entering data into her notebook at my desk. I sat at the laser-capture 'scope, scouring freshly-stained microscopic sections of infected duck heart.

"I've never understood how this virus injures the heart when it's still in the colon," I said, talking to myself. "It's got to travel. It's got to get to the heart cell before it throws the *SWCH*."

I cranked the slide slowly along. The section showed the same familiar picture that every duck's heart shows at the beginning of the lethal heart-phase of *Bangladesh*. "Lymphocytes," I whispered. "That's all I see. A sea of lymphocytes. Plump, activated lymphocytes insinuating themselves between the heart cells of the duck. A sea...."

"... of lymphocytes," Lilly murmured, mimicking me as she bent over her notebook.

I shifted my weight on the stool and looked up. "Have we ever measured the viral load in lymphocytes, Lilly?"

We sterilized equipment, raced up to the Level 4, suited up, and began decapitating ducks. By midnight, Lilly had the data on the lab bench in front of us.

"Such high titers of virus, Doctor Mah-wo. Extraordinary!"

Now we understood. We had the answer, or at least one answer. The virus sequestered itself in the protected intra-cellular environment of its host's lymphocytes, hitching a ride to the heart in a common white blood cell, a cell with unlimited access to every tissue.

"Lymphocytes," I said. "I'll bet these babies have the *SWCH* on full."

Friday, November 27

On Thanksgiving Day and all through the night, a powerful norther pounded the Island with the crash of thunder and scattershot blasts of rain and marble-sized hail. Well before daybreak this morning, I snapped up my rain suit and walked to the research institute. It was a holiday weekend, and I was dragged out from antiviral drug, but Lilly and I were committed to assembling the pieces of the *Bangladesh* puzzle, and nothing would break our stride—not my negotiations for a new job, not acyclovir fatigue, and certainly not a little lousy Texas weather.

By mid-afternoon, the norther relented and we had a high yield of squeaky-clean *Bangladesh* from the lymphocytes. I decided to leave the routine assays to Lilly and drive to the mainland to see my old pal, Ron Rocker. Since he went on permanent sick leave, I'd made it a point to visit Ron every Friday. With each visit, he seemed to grow weaker.

On the other side of the causeway, I turned the Datsun onto the narrow coastal road to San Leon. After the hurricane, Ron and his wife set up a small used trailer on Galveston Bay, at the confluence of Clear Creek and the turbid effluent of the Sterling Chemical plant. They've got a nice view of the bay, except that every 15 minutes, day and night, an 18-wheeler tank-truck loaded with molten sulfur rumbles along the bay road within a few feet of their trailer.

Ron's wife, Clarice, came to the door dressed in a worn purple chenille housecoat pockmarked by a thousand cigarette burns. She'd taken leave from her job with the University Housekeeping Service to be with Ron, but she was so worked up over Ron's illness that her smoking doubled after he quit.

"Come in, Doctor," Clarice said. "He's in here. Right in here. Y'all doing all right?"

I pushed newspapers and laundry off an easy chair and sat down. Ron slouched on the caved-in, threadbare spot on the couch where he'd been sitting for weeks. Covered by a worn, malodorous blanket, he was alternating between a thin smile and a grimace.

"How's it going, Doc?"

"I'm fine, Ron."

Ron looked a lot duskier than he had last Friday. I asked if they had any beer in the fridge. Clarice jumped up and found two beers. They were Lone Stars. We drank them anyway.

"How's the job hunt going, Doc?"

"I might get that position in Boston. A directorship. I'm waiting for an official offer."

"Go for it, Doc. Remember our pact. 'No crybaby shit.'" Ron's breathing was shallow and rapid.

"I brought you something, Ron. It's from Brenda." I reached into the plastic bag I'd carried with me and pulled out an 8 X 10, black-and-white photograph that Brenda had meticulously selenium-toned, matted and framed.

"The M&M!"

"Brenda loves that old metalwork on the front."

"Right there's where you had all them bikes stolen." Turning to his wife, he said, "Baby cakes, put it somewhere nice."

Clarice carefully edged the framed print onto a crowded shelf until the M&M was embedded in the middle of a ceramic hodgepodge of knick-knacks and souvenir salt and pepper shakers. "Look's real pretty up there," she said.

"Can I bring you anything from town, Ron?" I asked. "Maybe a po'boy from the M&M?"

"No, nothing, Doc," he said. The jutting bones of Ron's pelvis under the thin blanket should've told me Ron's diet was mostly morphine. "They're bringing oxygen tomorrow."

I envisioned the green tanks, the tangles of tubing. An ominous sign. When the man with the oxygen shows up, you can hear the death knell begin to sound.

"You get outdoors, Ron?" I asked.

"Baby cakes wheels me across the road. It's nice, looking out over the water."

I drank my beer and most of Ron's while Clarice smoked up the room and bitched about the evils of alcohol, as if it mattered a damn when you had wide-spread metastases. She tried turning the conversation to Jesus, but it didn't take off. She and Ron were worn out, it was obvious. I waited for the next 18-wheeler to grind by outside the trailer, then said goodbye, said I'd be back next week, and got up to leave. When Ron shuffled around on the couch to give me his hand, his coverlet fell away from a cluster of bed sores that sank to the bone like fetid, volcanic craters.

I stepped out of the trailer, drew a deep breath, and crunched over the coarse gravel, past Ron's rusted wheelchair, to my pickup. The sun had sunk halfway into the bay and, for a moment, I thought of watching the rest of the sunset, but I needed to move on before I got caught behind a sulfur truck on the twisting two-lane.

As soon as I hit the Island, I headed for the M&M. I needed a beer. Moose was still open and he bought me a sandwich. I swilled his last two Coronas.

"How's your friend with the cancer?"

"Not good, Moose."

"Tell him I'll buy him one next time he stops in."

"I don't know. I don't know. Let's just pray for a few more Fridays for Ron, huh?"

"Amen to that," Moose said softly.

I drove home in the stark light of a full moon that looked as though it were cast of concrete. I was awake long after Brenda had gone to bed. I had plenty of energy. I could've gone back to the lab to set up a gel or start some bloody work in the Level 4. One group of ducks was due to be dispatched. Instead, I stood the night watch with Mr. Kreuger and let the work, and the blood, wait until morning.

Tuesday, December 1

They want me in Boston. I interviewed twice at the New England Institute of Virology and Genetic Bio-Diversity, and yesterday I received their formal offer to be director-in-chief of the world-class institute that, since 1887, has been dedicated to the study of obscure, oddball, and deadly bugs, exactly the ones I love to work with. They promised me a huge lab, guaranteed three postdoctoral positions, and would match whatever NIH-grant funds I brought into the institute. And their new Level 4 facility was nearly finished, complete with avian housing facilities suitable for ducks.

I rushed into the lab to tell Lilly. She hesitated. She was sure to get her McKinney fellowship. She might even be offered a junior faculty position in Galveston. Nevertheless, she agreed to move to Boston. Our research with *Bangladesh* would go on.

Brenda read the letter that night. She was exhausted from a three-day lecture series by a visiting professor, a neuroscientist whose textbook Brenda had been poring over for weeks, a text titled *The Role of the Amygdala in Stress, Grieving and Depression*. Perfect for Brenda.

"Boston again." She held the letter in her hand.

"Come with me, baby," I said.

"New England didn't work for Tom and me."

"I need you."

"I need you back."

"There'll be jobs, Brenda. Gotta be."

"Sweetheart, our visiting lecturer happens to be from Boston University. It's unbelievably interesting, the amygdala. The seat of the grief response, you know."

"You're saying yes?"

"I'd go, job or no job, Peter. I love you too much to let you go alone. I'd die, missing you. What about the boys?"

"I think it's best they stay. Their friends... their school. Maybe later...."

"Get them for the summer, sweetheart. Please?"

I expected it to be my hardest speech ever, to tell Chad and Travis about Boston. After dinner, Brenda and I led them to the upstairs porch. "It's a great opportunity in Boston," I said. "Brenda and I have decided to go. You two should stay with your mom on the Island, maybe come up summers." I paused and looked over the tops of the palms, toward the Gulf.

"Director of The New England Institute!" Travis, the budding naturalist, exclaimed. "That's where they discovered the first inverted retrovirus."

"That's disputed, son," I said, sniffling, and blotting up a schmaltzy tear with my handkerchief. "The French still claim they had it first."

Chad's sole comment was, "Summers off the island will mess up my band!"

"Not really, Chad," Brenda countered. "We're planning a summer place on Cape Cod. The Cape simply *overflows* with teenage girls."

"What about Mr. Kreuger?" Travis wondered. "Can he come for the summer, too?"

"We can ask him."

"Sweet!"

The old house goes up for sale after New Year's. Lilly and I will pack the lab, and we move in early spring. Brenda will pursue a fresh, new career direction. She's even vowed to pull her dissertation off the shelf for an hour each morning and edit it from an amygdala point of view.

Mr. Kreuger was excited for us, too, though he made me promise that, when I sold, he'd go with the old house, like a fixture.

Monday, December 7

It's been only three weeks since the D.C. excursion, but Lilly and I have amassed all the facts we need to explain how *Bangladesh* causes myocarditis.

"What a masterful virus!" I exclaimed as we reviewed our red-hot data in the first cool days of December. "It's adopted the perfect disguise. By lurking in the lymphocyte, it circulates unimpeded through all tissues, then directs its attack from the high ground, throws the *SWCH*, and floods the heart cell with lethal *BADMORPH*."

Only *PAKG*, Jorge's gene, continued to puzzle us.

We had probed the darkest secrets of *Bangladesh horrificans*, and now it was time to write its story. Lilly and I began to draft a paper. In a way, I missed Jorge as we worked to weave together the vestments that cloaked the *Bangladesh* virus, piece in the grander parts of its biologic fabric, and expose its seamier, deadly tricks. A few ugly, unruly threads still stuck out from the complex patchwork, however. Most importantly, how did the lymphocyte *recognize* the heart cell so it could zero in for the kill? We knew the *PAKG* sequence was full of adhesive domains, but to what? It made no sense, until Lilly stayed up all night matching the viral *PAKG* sequence to hundreds of available genomic data banks.

"Receptors, Doctor Mah-wo. It's receptors." Lilly sat in front of her computer, her eyes bleary, her slacks wrinkled, her silk blouse disheveled. "The *PAKG* protein of *Bangladesh* attaches to receptors on duck heart."

"Receptors! No wonder you kept finding those adhesive domains, Lilly. This explains why the heart was never involved in the victims of the Bangladesh epidemic. There's a human heart receptor, but the virus doesn't match it."

"Yes, but...."

"Great!" I exclaimed, ignoring the concern in Lilly's voice. "This'll clinch my next grant proposal. We'll characterize these receptors, their tertiary structures, their adhesive domains...."

"Please listen! I found one sequence that *matches for human heart receptor*," Lilly said forcefully. "Not duck, but human."

"Where'd you find it?"

"KO-008, Jorge's most virulent virus."

We dropped the draft of our paper to scrutinize Jorge's lab notebooks. The first two he filled early in his fellowship were stored in my office. Lilly found his most recent, unfinished notebook stashed in a lab drawer under a pile of old glassware.

We were impressed by Jorge's precise, thoughtful entries in the earlier notebooks. The detail in his experimental descriptions was exquisite. His expertise at genetic manipulation was honed to a fine edge by his work on *PAKG*. The intensity of his science grew and focused during the summer. In the most recent notebook, however, his notes grew sparse as Hurricane Eduardo approached at the beginning of September. For nearly three weeks, Jorge made no entries at all. Elena! I thought. That's when Dr. J. figured out what was going on between Elena and Jorge. And then, after Eduardo, when Elena... pregnant by Jorge...committed suicide....

As abruptly as they'd stopped, the notes on Jorge's knockout manipulations came back in a flurry. His preoccupation with the virulent 008 knockout was evident:

SEPT. 28: ... ON 12TH TRIAL, CANARYPOX GENE TRANSFER WORKED PERFECTLY IN **PAKG-KO-008**.

Few labs use canarypox transfer. It's technically difficult, but the most effective means of inserting genetic material into a virus. With canarypox transfer, once Jorge had the proper sequences to match the human heart receptor, he was set to go.

OCTOBER 2 GEL CONFIRMS CORRECT **PAKG** SUCCESSFULLY SPLICED INTO 008. NEW OBJECTIVE: REFINE DELIVERY SYSTEM.

Receptors are notorious for relying on their tertiary, or 3-D structure, for their biologic function. The chances of Jorge randomly picking a *PAKG* protein that would work with the human receptor were a million to one. Did he know something we didn't? Lilly decided to test it. She loaded the sequence data and lugged a box full of jump drives and CD-ROMs to the

Bioinformatics Computer Center, where they have the Bio-StarFighter computers, the ones with high resolution holographic monitors. Six hours later, Lilly called back to the lab.

"Come... right away!" she exclaimed, unable to catch a breath. "You must see this on the center's computer."

I raced across campus to find Lilly at a Bio-StarFighter. Electronic media were strewn all over the floor. Multi-colored three-dimensional graphic displays of chemical structures danced on the screen. I grabbed a pair of special glasses to watch the show.

"Here's the human heart receptor," Lilly began. With a few keystrokes, an irregular, multi-colored spheroid began to twist brilliantly on the screen. "In human, the adhesive domain contains three beta-strands flanked by a bundle of helices." It looked like the moon's surface, all fissures, pockmarks and craters. "Right here," Lilly continued, "at these proline side chains, are binding sequences that form a distinct pocket."

"Like a landing site."

Lilly slowed the spinning receptor, and it took on the appearance of an ancient, well-traveled mother ship awaiting her fleet's arrival.

"Now I bring in *PAKG* proteins," she said. Our dozens of known *PAKG* proteins whirled onto the screen like misshapen, hapless asteroids spinning through space. "Since I loaded human receptor, most of our *PAKG* proteins shouldn't fit the pocket." She manipulated the viral proteins, with no success at engagement. "Except this one. It fits perfect."

Lilly guided a single *PAKG* protein to a gentle touchdown on the mother ship. It sunk into the human receptor like a hardball into a catcher's mitt.

"That's the one he spliced into the 008 virus?"

"It's a perfect replacement for the duck sequence, Doctor Mah-wo." Lilly grunted softly as she tried to jockey the protein back out, with no success. "It's latched on. Irreversible binding. It will work on human heart."

I rushed back to the lab and took Jorge's final notebook to my office.

According to his last experiments, Jorge mixed the virus with small-particle liposomes to ensure that it would easily reach all the way down into the lung's distant air spaces. It was an obvious method, taken directly from our old lab notebooks on the U.S. Army project on Select Agents and

Biological Warfare. Jorge assumed that immobilizing the virus in liposomes assured it would never spread further than his targets at the Hyatt.

OCT. 16:   LIPOSOME DELIVERY WILL CONFINE EXPOSURE
TO ROOM WHERE UNIT IS DISCHARGED.

If he had asked me, I would have told him he was mistaken. Once you stick human sequences into a gene, especially a virulence gene like *PAKG*, strange things can happen. The virus adapts, alters the expression of other genes, changes its lifestyle to conform to the new host. Jorge's genetic manipulation would need to be tested in mammals. Jorge knew that. But this is what he wrote on the day I told him about our second meeting in D.C.:

NOV. 13:   MEETING ARRANGED BY DR. M.
ONLY ONE DAY TO RE-CHECK DELIVERY
METHOD, THEN ULTIMATE EXPERIMENT
WILL BE PERFORMED,
AND <u>EVIL WILL PAY THE PRICE</u>.

I was stunned by this, but I shouldn't have been. I should have known. Jorge felt so much disappointment and anger, not to mention the devastation he refused to admit to himself over Elena, and the pent-up grief. I tried to stay close, but I should've tried harder. At the very least, I should have known what he was doing with my virus. I broke into a cold sweat every time I thought how fortunate I was to surprise him at the Hyatt and get his bio-bomb away from him.

On the day before we left for our showdown in D.C., Jorge filled page after page with entries in his fine, mechanical hand. He recalculated the accuracy of his "delivery units," the nitrogen charge in pounds-per-square inch of pressure, the sensitivity of the delicate triggering mechanism, the particle size of aerosol formed when the parafilm ruptured and liposomes loaded with viral particles spilled out.

Jorge's bio-bomb was such a simple, elegant mechanism. But something came out in Jorge's last note about its final assembly, written just before we boarded the plane.

NOV. 15: ... THREE TIMERS ACCURATE TO $\pm$ 1 MINUTE CHOSEN.
THREE DELIVERY UNITS WILL PROVIDE ADEQUATE BACKUP.

Three units? Three bio-bombs?

Jorge backed up his experiment! He had *three* bio-bombs, and I intercepted only one. Had he already loaded two of them into the vent when I caught him? Jorge bolted from the meeting, but... *Was I still in the room?*

Friday, December 11

For days on end, salt storms howled hot and sticky off the Gulf, stunting the coastal vegetation until the indestructible oleander was the only green standing in a brown landscape. When the storms abated, the oblique December sunshine lay gently in the palm fronds and our island was, at last, abandoned by the tourists. "We need to get outdoors!" Brenda exclaimed.

Deeply in love, with Christmas just ahead and the restaurants to ourselves, we should have reveled in the quiet of a tropical autumn.

Instead, the phone calls started.

"I am Dr. Rita Sanduja here, calling from Washington, Walter Reed Pathology." She had the rough-edged accent of someone new to this country, maybe a first-year resident. "I'm calling in regard to three cases from our intensive care unit, all in these two days, an extraordinary incidence, really, and I'm right now autopsying a *fourth*."

"Please describe your findings for me, Doctor Sanduja."

"Enlarged hearts, over 500 grams. All chambers massively dilated, myocardial muscle pale, ventricular walls markedly thinned."

"Have you heard of other cases?"

"My colleague at George Washington Medical Center had two. I believe the findings suggest an outbreak of viral myocarditis, Doctor Mallow, with a fulminate course of heart failure. The microscopic finding of a lymphocytic infiltrate in the heart suggests...."

"A heavy lymphocytic infiltrate?"

"Yes. Quite striking. Could this be a new bird virus? I've seen your recent papers on the organism from the Dhaka epidemic and...."

"No, no. There's no evidence for that."

"But isn't it possible that the virus has adapted and now it's...?"

The calls kept coming, over 50 in less than a week. The virus got outside the room and went for the human heart with a vengeance. Jorge had been mistaken about the liposomes. The virus spread from the board members into the city and beyond. The calls proved it. They came from

California, Oregon, and Virginia, where Yamata lives. Then the Oschner Clinic in New Orleans, Sokolof's town.

Tuesday, December 15

My first symptoms came with the calls. I ached with fever, and my eyes were on fire. Chills shook me till my teeth rattled. When the cough started, I grabbed Brenda's cell phone, dragged myself into the abandoned carriage house, and collapsed on the floor. I told Brenda I had a bad flu, and that she should stay out of the carriage house until I felt better. She was worried, but I had to be alone. This was the infectious phase, when any droplets I hacked up would be packed with virus. Jorge had been so wrong.

The fever must've lasted three days; in the state I was in, I lost count. When the cough subsided, I phoned Marv and had him bring me the toughest antivirals known—AZT, interferon, ritonavir—anything to slow the virus.

The acute phase ended. Then my herpes flared. I should have expected that. Once *Bangladesh horrificans* commandeered my lymphocytes and weakened my defenses, every virus I'd collected during a lifetime was free to have its way with me. Despite the antivirals, my resident *Herpes genitalis* virus mercilessly blistered my private parts, my nostrils, and the inner lining of my eyelids. Large confluent blisters filled my mouth and spread as bloody sores onto my lips.

I increased the doses of antivirals. Just as abruptly as they'd appeared, the early symptoms subsided, and I was back to normal. I rushed into the lab, called Marv from the office and tried to explain what had happened, that I had some strange new virus. He thought I was delusional from my fever.

I contacted two of my virologist friends at the NIH, but when I tried to explain that a duck virus was causing an outbreak, they thought I was losing my mind. I called Laura Sacchi. She recognized I was sick, but I couldn't tell her it was Jorge's virus. Without hard data about the virus, she said, the CDC couldn't care less. She tried to be understanding, but you could hear disbelief in her voice. She assured me it was probably a bad case of the flu, and I'd feel better soon.

Then the killer frontal headaches began. I struggled to stay in the lab with Lilly. She was back at work on *Bangladesh*, but I couldn't tell her the truth. She looked at me crazy when I told her to make an anti-sense to block the human heart receptor she'd uncovered. I thought that might work. We needed to try, but Lilly kept asking questions, and the gels... I couldn't read them with those dull fists thumping on the inner table of my skull.

The phone kept ringing. The virus spread. Europe, Russia, Japan.

Friday, December 18

The symptoms abated, but not for long. My abdomen became hot, red, and stiff as a board. My blood boiled. Then my guts turned inside out. The GI phase. It was just like *Bangladesh horrificans* in the ducks.

I lay flat out on the bathroom floor in the carriage house for two days, holding my feverish head in my hands. It was the darkest of moments. I knew I was suffering virus-induced depression, the melancholy of grave illness, but despite this understanding, for the first time in my life I wished were dead.

I lost consciousness for an unknown number of hours, and then, the torture of the GI phase ended. Soaked in a cold sweat, I felt as if I'd been drawn and quartered, or stretched on the rack. I was exhausted, drained, but glad to be alive. I stumbled up, rehydrated myself with Gatorade, washed down every surface of the carriage house apartment with bleach, and made my way back to the laboratory.

Lilly was confused. She saw I was obsessed, crazed, but how could I explain? I crashed around, ruined dozens of gels before my mind cleared and I realized the truth. I had seen the black heart of this virus. I knew better than anyone where I was headed. I felt better now, but just ahead I envisioned my own death, the myocarditis phase—the weakness, swelling and decline I knew would come.

Saturday, December 26

I had picked out Christmas presents before the first symptoms hit. For Chad, I found a '60s Hagstrom bass in a pawn shop, its neck as solid and straight as the day it was carved. For Travis, a new skateboard, the Eric Kosten Pro-Skater model. Brenda's present was something special.

"I'm holding out on yours," I said, "until New Year's Eve, when we're dancing at Bayou Bob's." I told her this, hoping against hope it would be true, but suspecting the worst, the myocarditis phase yet to come.

"You're looking better," she said. "That's all that matters, Peter."

A hard freeze hit late on Christmas night, and Galveston Island was wrapped in a sheet of ice and a blanket of fog. Then, this morning, word came of Ron's death. I needed to attend his interment, but Brenda was feeling ill. She had locked herself in the bathroom. Still weak myself, I struggled alone through the sleet to help carry Ron over the slate walks of Mid-Island Cemetery where, in the stillness of a darkened vault, his wife Clarice threw herself wailing onto his casket. Big strong men in fine suits and long dark overcoats pried her off and slid the casket onto its icy stone shelf.

I couldn't find my voice, so I clasped my hands in silent prayer for a man who led his life his own way, and all of it special. I prayed for a man wedded to his bloody work, a friend with whom I'd made a pact while he waited to tie on flying shoes. Then I went to Clarice. It was another time I was glad I'd tucked a clean handkerchief in my pocket.

Back at the house, I warmed my hands by the heater and called for Brenda. She came out of the bathroom, looking grim.

"I'm your sweetheart, right?" I said. "Your lover? Your one and only?" Brenda gave me a weak nod.

"Then marry me." Brenda didn't look a bit surprised, but her wan face lit up with a big grin. "Baby, I want this more than anything," I said. "We'll find a Justice of the Peace later this afternoon. We can take Chad and Travis along."

That's when I pulled out the ring I'd been holding back. Brenda looked surprised. It wasn't a large diamond, but it was pure, it was true. "I couldn't love you more, you know."

"Oh, sweetheart," she sighed, trembling in my arms. "Of course I'll marry you. I've never wanted anything as much, even feeling the way I do. Let's do it... maybe tomorrow afternoon."

"Not today?"

"We'll see, Peter. This morning sickness has been simply horrid."

Monday, December 28

Today I went to the lab early and stayed until mid-afternoon, when Brenda starts feeling better. She's real happy about the baby, when she's not in the bathroom sick to her stomach. It's going to be a girl, she says. She "just knows." It's "a woman thing." We've agreed on the name. Our daughter will be Helen, and she'll be beautiful.

In the lab, I've started Lilly on constructing an anti-sense to the human heart receptor. Now that my head has cleared, I'm convinced it's the best approach to Jorge's virus, and a first step toward a vaccine. My heart is weakening, and I can't do much in the lab, but I force myself. I need to steer Lilly in the right direction. She's got to stick to 008. Deep down inside, she must know something about Jorge's virus, just not the why or how.

As for me, there's only one hope—Marv Stepinski's experimental catheter. I went to him yesterday and told him I thought I had fatal myocarditis. When he put his stethoscope to my chest, what I saw on his face was the look of a physician who knows he will fail. My heart was quivering like a bag of worms.

"There's the usual drugs we can try, Peter," he told me, unable to look me in the eyes.

"They won't work on this, Marv. There's only your catheter."

It was incredibly unethical, but he wheeled me into his cath lab last night at midnight, prepped me himself, injected antivirals straight down my coronary arteries, and hit the switch on his experimental catheter. It burned like a hot knife in my chest, but it's my last hope for the days ahead.

Tuesday, December 29

Laura Sacchi called the lab from the CDC today. I transferred the call to my office.

"Glad to hear you sounding so much better, Pete," she said. "Back to normal?"

"Almost."

"I knew you'd be okay. Listen, Pete, it's scary, but I think you might be right about an outbreak. Something bad's happening. The preliminary reports we're getting are very disturbing, though it's not clear whether this is some sort of toxic exposure, or infectious, or what."

"It's infectious, Laura. I'm sure."

"Well, a minority of us here would agree, but whatever it is—virus, prion, toxin—it's now been reported from 43 countries. Every part of the globe has cases, though the western world seems hardest hit."

"Where are most of the U.S. cases?"

"Our East coast. The area around D.C., actually. Nearly 1000. Globally, over 20,000 as of today. But the most troublesome thing, Pete, is the computer projection we've generated. Even with a low infectivity ratio, this thing is so global and moving so fast that it's beginning to look *catastrophic!*"

What could I tell her? She hardly listened the first time I tried to explain. And it's not like I want to protect Jorge. He can go to hell as far as I'm concerned, and probably will.

I *should* tell Laura all about Jorge's 008, but would it get us a cure one bit faster? A scientific ethics investigation would do nothing but shut down my lab and ruin Lilly's chances to find a vaccine, while millions died in the pandemic. What law did Jorge break, anyway? He screwed up some genes. I can hear the sharpie lawyers arguing the case now: "Ladies and gentlemen of the jury, my client is guilty of nothing more than a youthful mistake, a harmless prank gone awry!"

"Pete, listen," Laura said, her voice wavering and thin. "We'll need the help of every scientist on this. The death toll will be unthinkable. And the way victims die... it's gruesome."

Laura described her "catastrophic" future all too clearly. The slow, horrible deaths. Babies, teens, the healthy, the infirm—slipping into heart failure, gasping for air as they drown in their own bodily fluids. KO-008 will change the world. Airports will be empty, food and water more precious than gold, all of humanity hunkered down while starvation, death, and wars rage over the globe. It's blacker than the blackest plague. Who will be taken? Who will be spared? My boys? Brenda? Our new baby?

"The computer algorithms," Laura went on, "are estimating 50 million dead in the first year, and that's the low number. This could be the worst thing mankind has seen, far worse than the Great Influenza of 1918."

"Have they got a name yet?" I asked.

"They're calling it FMS for 'Fulminant Myocarditis Syndrome.' Human samples are beginning to roll into CDC for analysis. All our divisions are being put on it."

"Laura, remember something for me. As things develop, as the science progresses on this thing, please do whatever you can, devote whatever resources you have, to help my lab."

"You know I'll do that. We'll beat this thing, Pete."

"And I don't mean just me. I mean Lilly, too."

"What happened to your goofy student with the vehicular immersion project?"

"He left the lab, Laura."

"He was pretty bright, I thought. You could use him. He's gone for good?"

"Not a chance of seeing him again. Of that I'm sure, too."

Wednesday, December 30

Jorge is dead, a suicide. His mother called the lab to let Lilly and me know that he left a note to us, saying simply, "I'm sorry." He was found hanging from a beam at the family hunting lodge in the Guadalupe Mountains, where he's been hiding out since he left the Island.

Jorge must've finally admitted to himself how evil his plan, how idiotic his mistake. Now that the "Fulminant Myocarditis Syndrome" is out in the press, and CDC is mandating travel precautions and monitoring cases, it would be hard to not know about the pandemic.

It's too bad about Jorge, but I can't forgive him, not ever. Sure, I understand that smart people do stupid things, some, like Sokolof, because they make big bucks for it, and others, like Jorge, out of some twisted sense of honor. But for me, greed, madness, grief, vengeance—one reason's as bad as the next. It's sad, really. Jorge was so blinded by his anger that he couldn't see we had them outsmarted, we had them whipped. And he was so bright that he could've joined Lilly in the lab and helped fix his mistake, when I'm not around any more.

It'll be up to Lilly to find a cure, a vaccine. I've already asked Marv to help get her promoted to an assistant professor so she can write grants. The money will roll in, she'll do the work, and if the experiments go well, two or three years from now, they'll give her a Nobel Prize for discovering the cure to Jorge's 008.

That's science for you. Crazy.

Thursday, December 31

Until today, I held out hope. But Marv's catheter did nothing. I'm getting weaker. Each breath is a struggle. How long will I last? Maybe the antivirals bought me a few more weeks, maybe a few days.

What bothers me most is that I'll never finish my life's work. All those beautiful viruses. Never in two lifetimes could I conquer them the way I wanted, experiment by experiment. Still, that sudden thrill of discovery, that jolt of understanding is nothing compared to what holding a beautiful new daughter on my lap would be. That's where I'll really miss out—bouncing sweet Helen on my knee on Christmas morning. Seeing the lights of the tree in her eyes.

Another norther is on its way but you'd never know it from high above the street on our second floor porch. Here, it's another breezy, balmy, Galveston evening. Not a bad way to end, sitting quietly with Brenda in the fading tropical light, listening together to the clatter of the palms.

"Can I get you something, Peter?"

"No, nothing."

"The man with the oxygen is coming tomorrow."

I'll close the notebook for good tonight, then I'll make it to the lab one last time, and let the notebook tell Lilly the whole sad story. She'll have the heart to do what's needed, when my heart fails me.

7